A SHAREVERSE

STARSHIP
BLUNDER

Jason Abofsky
Ross Baxter
Sill Bihagia
Edward Cooke
Susan Eschbach
H. Hackman
Mac King
Melisa Peterson Lewis
Beth Martin
Chris Morton
Ariele Sieling
Edward Swing

Edited by Beth Martin

**BETH MARTIN
BOOKS**
BethMartinBooks.com

CONTENTS

PREFACE

I used to say I was too long-winded to finish a story in anything shorter than a novel. But then, I tried writing a short story, and then I put together another and another. Like many other writers, I accrued a collection of polished short stories that I hid away. Writers tend to hoard our little troves of narrative treasure, unsure of what to actually *do* with them.

My writing friends considered the short story conundrum, searching for an outlet for our shorter works. We could put together a collection of disparate tales but preferred to create something a bit more cohesive. After some thought, fellow indie author Edward Swing proposed the idea of several writers crafting stories in a shared universe.

The existence of this book should show you how captivated I was by the idea. I immediately set to work. Within days, I put together a description of an ill-fated space vessel called *Starship Blunder* and the world it lived in. Then, I began detailing characters who I thought might work on the comical ship. I conjured up a handful of images, plopped them all into a website, and presented my idea to the world.

All of my careful planning and thoughtful world-building paid off as writers around the globe found *Starship Blunder* both humorous and inspiring. Many writers I know, and several I haven't had the pleasure of meeting yet, submitted the stories which you'll read in the following pages. I had so much fun poring over the entries, chuckling at everyone's wacky humor, and selecting the best stories to appear in the anthology.

Although I created some of the characters, other writers took them to new heights. Xylo's incompetence as a starship mechanic proved to be excellent comic relief over and over again. Despite her scary style and unwelcoming attitude, Luna Knight found herself in several romantic entanglements. Chef Bluebottle oscillated between culinary brilliance and gastric disaster. The real star of the *Starship Blunder* crew, Sarah Hawkins, went above and beyond on every adventure. She out-performed her title of Starship Pilot with varying degrees of poise and grace.

This project has been a wonderful reprieve from writing longer-form fiction. I'm so pleased to present the first Shareverse Anthology, and I look forward to writing engaging stories in other original universes.

I hope you have as much fun reading these stories as I did.

Now, go grab a handful of antacids and an extra salt-shaker, buckle up, and get ready for a tumultuous ride, because galactic misadventure awaits! And perhaps steer clear of the bologna sandwiches.

All the best,
Beth Martin

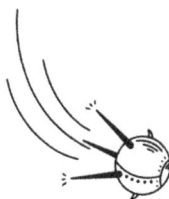

THE GREAT NEPTUNE STORM

Beth Martin

Pilot Sarah Hawkins couldn't believe the current *Starship Blunder* team had failed.

Again.

She grabbed the comm and pressed the button before shouting, "This is *Starship Blunder* approaching for landing from the northwest, E.T.A. about ten minutes, over."

"Thank the Higher Power that mission is over!" the alien Xylo proclaimed. "I never want to deal with the Droconos planet ever again." The blue spots on his shimmering silver-blue skin glowed, showing his excitement.

Her body, in contrast, hummed in frustration. "We went to Droconos on a peacekeeping mission, but that cool little gadget you made to pump water for the village blew up their well! How are they supposed to get water now? You are the *worst* mechanic!"

Sarah adjusted the sleeves of her bright purple flight suit, the color of which beautifully complemented her deep brown skin. Of the hundred or so crew members and residents on the ship, she was the only one who wore the *Starship Blunder* uniform. Everyone else dressed as they pleased. Xylo typically donned a set of gray coveralls, which currently were smudged in soot from the explosion he'd caused in the village.

"How was I supposed to know minerals would contaminate the water?" Xylo asked. "It short-circuited my invention."

A static-filled message began over the communication device, but it was hard to discern its content, and Sarah was too busy telling off Xylo. "Well-water always has lots of minerals—especially on a planet with metallic soil!"

Xylo shrugged his narrow shoulders. "Whatever. I'm going to buckle in for the approach. It looks pretty tumultuous out there."

Sarah directed her attention to the bridge windows and saw what Xylo was referring to. A colossal storm surrounded the floating city of Terminus, their final destination on their home planet of Neptune. A large torus-shaped structure enclosed the entirety of the city, with large bay doors on one edge for spacecraft to dock. However, the gray swirling clouds currently made the doors impossible to see.

"Shit," Sarah said as she buckled herself into the pilot seat. "This hunk of junk can't maneuver fast enough to avoid the storm, so we're going in." She grabbed the comm and pressed a button before announcing, "Everyone, brace yourselves! We're coming in for a bumpy landing." She then switched the comm to the radio to speak to Terminus Space Control. "This is *Starship Blunder*. We're unable to avoid the storm and will be coming in for an emergency landing."

Clutching the steering yoke with both fists, Sarah turned the starship hard left as the strong winds blew the vessel to the right. Usually, she'd point the nose of the craft up to help them decelerate, but the storm had slowed them down more than they needed. Counterintuitively, Sarah increased the thrusters.

The other crewmates on the bridge buckled up–then screamed in terror as Sarah engaged the engines, hurtling toward the dock at a harsh angle. "Brace for impact!" she yelled a split-second before the landing wheels smacked against the Terminus landing pad. The craft wobbled a bit to the left and right before slowing down to a stop at the inside edge of the pad. Rain pelted the bay around them as Sarah guided the ship through the dock and stopped at a gate. "Woohoo!" she shouted. "We made it!"

A single figure raced from the Terminus Space Control Office to the *Starship Blunder* hatch and knocked loudly.

"Xylo, get the door!" Sarah ordered.

The alien huffed but got up and strolled his tall, lean figure to the hatch, where he easily hefted the heavy door open. "What are *you* doing here?" he said with a sneer at the soaked Commander, who pushed his way into the craft before slamming the hatch closed behind him and locking it.

"Commander Rex Sterling—" Sarah began, surprised to see the leader of the prestigious *Starship Prime* onboard her ship.

"What the hell did you think you were doing, crash landing like that!" he reprimanded. Where's your commander?"

Xylo shrugged. "I think he's in his quarters sleeping off a hangover."

Commander Sterling's eyes widened a moment, and Sarah had no doubt he'd report their newest captain to the Conglomeracy and get yet another poor sod assigned to their ship fired.

"Control told you to turn around. The storm is too dangerous!" Rex shouted. His normally perfectly coiffed brown hair hung limp, water dripping from it down his chiseled jaw. At least his navy blue flight suit with tasteful gold trim was waterproof and still looked pristine.

Xylo appeared to ignore the raging Commander and went to his locker, where he began gathering his personal items. "*Starship Blunder* always crash lands," the alien muttered.

"The... the comm... must be broken," Sarah stammered.

Rex surveyed the interior of the bridge. "Everything in this pile of bolts appears to be broken."

"Looks fine to me," Xylo said with a shrug, his arms now full of clothing, books, a rubber ducky, and other random gear. "I better be going—"

"You can't," Rex stated, stepping swiftly to block Xylo's pursuit to the hatch. "Terminus has declared a Code Blue. Everything's on lockdown until the storm blows over."

"Then why did you board our vessel, Commander?" Sarah asked.

Rex shook his head. "*Starship Prime* landed just moments before your approach. We were able to evacuate everyone from the ship in time, but as commander, I waited until everyone got off safely before I disembarked. Control locked all the gates before I could enter, so I got trapped out there. Pilot Hawkins, I request your permission to stay aboard your starship until the storm dissipates."

Sarah found it amusing that Rex quickly went from scolding her for her impressive landing to requesting refuge aboard the *Blunder*. Of course, she would never turn away a being in need. "Of course, Commander Sterling, you have my blessing to shelter with us for the duration of the storm."

A sudden crack of thunder made Commander Sterling jump—a bolt of lightning flashed through the space dock. The *Blunder* crewmates aboard the bridge were familiar with such disturbances and unfazed by the extreme weather phenomenon. However, the immense energy of the lightning made the lights on the ship glow brighter for a second and then flash before turning off entirely.

"Damn surge must have blown another fuse," Xylo remarked. He shuffled over to his locker and haphazardly threw his items back inside with a sigh. "I've got replacement fuses somewhere on this ship. But first, I gotta figure out which one went out." The blue dots on his head, neck, and arms glowed dimly, hinting at the alien's frustration with the current situation. On the bright side, his luminescence did make it a touch easier to see on the bridge.

"I can check the left-wing circuit breaker if you want to start with the mid-deck panel, Xylo," Sarah suggested. "Commander, there's a circuit breaker in the daycare for the residence quarters. Could you see if one of the fuses in there stopped functioning?" Typical starcrafts have all their circuit breakers and fuses in one central location, but *Starship Blunder* had been pieced together using parts of several other decommissioned ships, giving it a patchwork appearance and causing numerous quirks other crafts didn't have to deal with.

Instead of jumping into action, Rex paused for a moment before asking, "Is there a blow dryer or something I could use to dry my hair first?"

Xylo shut his locker door and shook his head, the glow from his spots shining a bit brighter. "I'll go get Commander Sterling a towel."

☆ ☆ ☆

In the daycare sector, Miss Luna Knight pulled a box full of toys from a low shelf and placed it on the lightly padded floor of the main room. "All right, children, instead of using flashlights, let's embrace the darkness and play with some bats!" With a smile, Miss Luna removed the top bat puppet from the box and slid her right hand inside. In a scratchy voice, she added, "I love the dark and only come out at night," while bobbing the puppet like it was the one talking.

Miss Luna dressed unlike any other daycare teacher. She wore a black dress that buttoned up the front, paired with black leggings and boots. Aside from her face, the only skin visible on her body was her arms, which were covered in colorful tattoos. With smooth black hair, pale skin, deep brown eyes, and black lipstick, she embraced her gothic style despite how poorly it meshed with her occupation.

"I don't like bats," a little boy with long curly hair stated while the other six children dove to the box and grabbed puppets.

Miss Luna removed another puppet and tentatively held it out to the child. "I bet you'll like bats after learning about them. Lots of bats eat fruit. Do you like fruit?"

The child nodded yes, then reached out and took the puppet offered by his teacher.

Footsteps and an intense beam of light approached from the hallway, then came to the half-height door that served as the entrance to the daycare.

"Eeeeeee!" Miss Luna screeched in a tone befitting of a bat. She squinted and held up her hands, including the one with the bat puppet, trying to block the glow from a super-charged flashlight.

Commander Rex Sterling turned down the brightness of the torch while the children got up and started running in circles, waving their toys through the air and screaming in their high-pitched voices.

"This is the daycare?" Rex asked, clearly unimpressed as he surveyed the unruly children and their goth teacher. "Don't you have backup lights here?"

Miss Luna stood to her full height, which was about a foot shorter than the Commander. "Yes, you've found the daycare. We do have emergency lights, but I prefer the dark. I'm Miss Luna, the teacher."

"I need to check the circuit panel for this portion of the starship," he said, getting straight to the point.

"It's over there," she responded with a gesture down the hall, "past the restrooms."

"Thank you." He turned on his heels and quickly strode away to get to work, his flashlight back on high-beam mode.

Miss Luna observed the unruly children momentarily before declaring, "All right, my camp of bats, let's go to the cave for some rest! Naptime!" The screeching children followed her into another dark room and settled down on the waiting sleeping mats.

☆ ☆ ☆

The emergency lights in the dining hall shone an eerie green instead of the typical emergency red. Chef Bluebottle had replaced the annoying red lights the previous time the ship's power had unintentionally shut down, which couldn't have been more than a week ago.

Located mid-ship, the room only had windows on the ceiling. Panes of thick acrylic gave a view of the gloomy weather outside. The storm continued to rage as raindrops slapped against the windows.

Bluebottle sat alone at one of the dining tables, playing a game using a well-worn deck of playing cards. Once, the old man had served as lead chef of a renowned restaurant in the largest city on Mars. Now, he cobbled together whatever dishes he could, using the limited ingredients available to the typically forgotten starship.

Bluebottle recognized the sound of an over-confident swagger from the footsteps echoing down the hall, then scoffed when he saw Commander Rex Sterling approaching. Bluebottle knew his type well. *What's that asshole doing on this hunk of junk?* he wondered.

"Good day, Chef," Rex greeted. Bluebottle's profession was obvious since he always wore his chef hat, even while playing card games during a power outage.

"Wish I could say the same," Bluebottle retorted, turning over a new card. He glanced over the playing field—still no pairs—and placed another card, forming a grid.

"I am glad to see this section has working emergency lights, although the color is not regulation," Rex mused. "I'll have to notify Xylo and see that he replaces them with the appropriate shade of red."

"Ain't anything wrong with the lights," Bluebottle grumbled.

"My apologies, I haven't introduced myself. My name is Rex Sterling, and I'm the commander of the *Starship Prime*." He held out a hand to Bluebottle.

The chef shook his head, grumbling. "I know who you are." He placed another card on the table. *Still no pairs.*

Rex lowered his hand when it became clear the surly chef had no intention of participating in social graces. "Is there a control panel in this area of the ship? I'm assisting Pilot Hawkins in tracking down the cause of the power outage."

"I already checked it. It's fine," the chef replied.

Rex crossed his arms, making Bluebottle suspect the commander was losing patience with him. *Good*, he thought.

"I hate to impose," Rex began. Bluebottle stopped playing his game, set the deck back on the table, and glared at the tall, handsome commander. "But I haven't eaten today and am famished. I missed the *Prime's* lunch hour since I've been sheltering on this ship. Can I have something to eat while I take a quick break?"

"Hmmm. I can make you a sandwich."

"I know the options will be much more limited without power—" Rex continued.

"I can make you a sandwich," Bluebottle repeated, interrupting the Commander.

"Yes, a sandwich would be great, thank you." Rex tentatively sat at the same table as the Chef's card game while Bluebottle excused himself and entered the mess.

The kitchen proper was pristinely clean—a testament to how little cooking activity took place in the space. Bluebottle opened a refrigerator cabinet and extricated two square slices of bread, a circle slice of bologna, and a square of cheese product. He stacked them on a plate and brought the meal out for the visiting Commander.

"Here," he said as he plopped the plate on the table near Rex before resuming his game at his seat.

"Thanks," Rex said, then proceeded to eat his sandwich while watching Chef Bluebottle with curiosity. Halfway through his sandwich, he asked, "How do you play that game?"

"Look for pairs," Bluebottle muttered.

"What happens when you find one?" Rex continued.

Bluebottle rolled his eyes. "You find another one." To himself, he thought, *For being a starship commander, this Rex Sterling isn't too bright.*

☆ ☆ ☆

Crackling electricity arced from the wires into the space around Xylo. The alien withdrew his tools quickly and hissed. His spots shone bright blue, reflecting his surprise at finding a live wire in the medical bay of all places.

He followed the wire with his screwdriver up to the ceiling, this time making sure not to physically touch it, across the sick bay where beds were waiting for patients, down another wall, then behind the watercooler.

That's not right, the alien thought. *Why is there a loose wire next to the water cooler, and what's that thing inside the water tank?*

He reached into a pocket and withdrew some gloves, put them on his hands, then grabbed the loose wire and stuck it against a screw protruding from the back of the water cooler. The metal spiral inside the water tank began to glow red, and a moment later, little bubbles formed around it.

"Is that supposed to be a..." he trailed off as he grabbed the finger of his right glove with his teeth and pulled his hand out. Then, he pressed the lever on the cooler with his thumb and held his fingers in the water stream for a second before dropping his glove from his mouth and declaring, "I knew it. It's warm! Bluebottle!"

Xylo marched into the dining hall to find Chef Bluebottle seated at a table playing a card game and Commander Rex Sterling loudly masticating a sorry-looking sandwich. "What the heck, Bluebottle?! I told you not to rig random heating elements in the water coolers when you need hot water. You've caused a massive short circuit that blew the power for the whole ship!"

The chef shrugged, "My kettle broke."

Xylo held up his hands in frustration. "You're supposed to *tell* me when something breaks! I can fix your damn kettle, but you have to tell me it's broken first!"

"Why would I tell you?" Bluebottle retorted. "You can't fix anything. You haven't fixed the power outage."

"I was about to!" the alien spat. "But I needed to inform you that *you caused this* first!" He hissed at the chef, who had already returned to his card game. He turned and began stomping away, but paused after a second to add, "And why are these emergency lights green? They're supposed to be *red*!"

Rex shuffled from his seat and stood abruptly. "Mechanic Xylo, I would be happy to assist in repairing any electrical wiring that requires attention. I had an internship with an electrician when I was a young man—"

"I don't need any help!" Xylo shouted back, cutting off the *Prime* Commander.

☆ ☆ ☆

By the time Commander Rex Sterling returned to the bridge from the dining hall, the power had returned and all the lights were back on. The confident man breathed a sigh of relief. He'd known boarding *Starship Blunder* would be an interesting experience, and he couldn't wait to return to his starship and the elite crew of competent workers.

Sarah was already checking on all the gauges and controls in the bridge but stopped when Rex arrived. "Leaving already, Commander Sterling?" she asked with a smile. "I hope you've enjoyed your time on the *Blunder*."

"Yes, I'm leaving," Rex confirmed, "and to be frank, I hope I never have to step foot on your cursed ship again."

Sarah looked out the window. "Storm seems to have cleared. Have a safe stay in Terminus, and good luck on your next mission."

He smiled and said, "Likewise," but paused before departing. "Actually... I knew that sheltering on your ship would be unpleasant—which it was—but I'm surprised by the crew. Miss Luna did a good job keeping the little ones calm in the darkness of the blackout, Chef Bluebottle made me a surprisingly filling meal, and Mechanic Xylo did get the power operational after a while. Even you, Pilot Hawkins, showed some real skill landing this older starship despite the inclement weather."

She smiled even broader and said, "Thanks, Commander Sterling. Your compliments mean a lot." She walked over to the hatch and opened it for the commander. Before he left, she added, "Oh, and if you ate one of Chef Bluebottle's famous bologna sandwiches, you might want to stay close to a restroom—just in case."

Rex chuckled and gave a half smile. "I'll keep that in mind," he said before disembarking from the starship. Sarah closed the door and let out a sigh of relief. A blue glow from behind the lockers caught her attention, and she added, "He's gone now, Xylo."

The tall alien stepped out from his hiding place. "I thought for sure he was going to ream us out. Did you know that Bluebottle set up the water cooler in the medical bay to make hot water? That's what blew the circuits and caused the power outage."

"Oh," she said, looking away briefly. "Actually... I did that. I wanted some tea, and the kettle in the dining hall wasn't working. I thought I grounded it properly. My bad."

"Seriously?!" Xylo said, throwing his hands in the air before looking down, shaking his head, and finally exiting the bridge. "I'll go fix the freaking kettle."

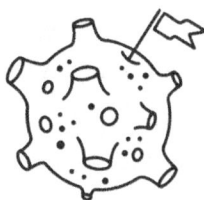

THE SOO-SACAN CAPER

Edward Swing

"I *hate* this ship!"

Vance Pittman examined the latest rift in the *Blunder's* outer hull. The long gouge stretched over a meter long but hadn't penetrated deeply enough to threaten the inner hull or any of the starship's systems. "We don't need to rush, so let's do a good job this time," he transmitted to the three service robots floating near him in the vacuum of space.

Each of the robots—Dash, Stick, and Slap—flashed lights in response and awaited his orders. Around the *Blunder*, a few asteroids tumbled through space, but none approached the vessel. The ship had deactivated its engines so Vance and a few other hapless crew members could repair the craft again.

"You'd think they'd avoid flying through asteroid fields when the shielding was offline," Vance grumbled. "Stick, spray durapoxy around that tear, then clear out of the way. Slap, ready the new plate," he ordered.

The lights on Stick's main body flashed red, and the robot remained motionless.

"What's wrong now?" Vance fired the jets on his space suit and drifted toward the robot. Little more than a tank of adhesive on a hover-chassis with sprayers and small manipulator arms, Stick had a light illuminated near its hose, which helped Vance spot the rupture.

"Did you tear your tube on the way out of the airlock, or did a tiny space rock hit you?" Vance sighed, aware that Stick lacked both the diagnostics and voice to reply.

"Dash, I need a new flexible, two-centimeter-diameter tube, one meter in length," he called to the smallest of the robots. "Fetch one from storage. And remember to go through the airlock this time."

Dash's thrusters ignited, and the small robot jetted toward the nearby airlock. After manipulating the hatch controls to open it, the speedy robot darted through, and the hatch closed again.

While he waited for Dash to return, Vance removed the torn tube and flung it into the void of space. Then he gazed at the outer hull of the starship.

Despite the ship's shielding, dents and scrapes from countless collisions with space debris covered the surface. Vance could see over a dozen patch-plates without turning his head; he'd placed many of them himself.

"They need to replace the hull," he complained. Then he gazed at the mishmash of features protruding from the hull—a spare engine from *Drellon 2*, a non-functioning phase array the captain had won from the Hagrinites in a bet, two quozivon cannons that wouldn't stay aligned, and other "enhancements"—and resigned himself to the asininity of his circumstances. The patchwork of the *Blunder* made the blasted starship too irregular to allow the use of new, nicely machined pieces for repair.

After fifteen minutes, Dash returned with the wrong replacement hose. Rolling his eyes, Vance repeated his instructions and described the needed part in even more detail. Once the small robot had repeated its task and brought the correct part, he twisted it into place between Stick's adhesive tanks and its spray nozzle.

"Okay, Stick, spray durapoxy around that rift. Slap, ready that plate."

This time, both robots flashed green lights. Stick covered the damaged plate with the durapoxy, and Slap swung the patch plate into place with its four large arms. Vance could imagine the clang he would have heard if he weren't floating in airless space.

He inspected Slap's placement. "It'll do," he admitted. "Now, let's go back inside. You three need to recharge before the next work shift."

☆ ☆ ☆

Vance's mood didn't improve, so he joined his friend Zabella Soldado and his alien roommate Agulatai in the mess hall. Chef Bluebottle had cobbled together something vaguely resembling spaghetti; Vance had learned long ago not to question what the chef added to the sauce.

"Did you have any problems with the patchwork?" Zabella asked.

Vance let his gaze linger on her features before replying. Her purple hair, trimmed in a bob, contrasted with her dark eyes and olive-tinted complexion. *I could lose myself in those eyes*, he thought.

Then he snapped back to the conversation. "Nothing serious. Stick tore a tube somehow, but we patched four damaged plates. Did anything interesting happen in the medical bay today?"

"No, just a sprained ankle and some bruises when the ship lurched. And Vijaskix caught her wing in the door again," she replied.

"Will it grow back?" Agulatai asked.

The nurse patted the worm-like alien on the chitinous shell covering Agulatai's foremost segments. "Don't worry.

She'll be helping you clean the corridors again in a week. I'll keep her company until then."

"At least you two have pleasant work environments," Vance complained. "And people who'll talk to you."

"Aww, poor baby," Zabella teased. "Tired of Slap's fascinating repartee?"

"None of them talk," Agulatai remarked. He fumbled with the forks he held with each of his four hands, then gave up and shoveled most of his food into his mouth.

Agulatai didn't understand sarcasm—or how to politely eat spaghetti. Vance demonstrated, twirling a glob of noodles on his fork. "I'm tired of both the drudgery and dealing with problems caused by the incompetents around here. But unlike both of you, I can't quit."

"Not as exciting as your former career as a master thief, I suppose," Zabella teased. "How many more years do you have on your contract?"

"A little over four. But it beats prison. Barely." He shoved the wad of noodles into his mouth. After swallowing, he added, "If I could figure a way off this ship, I'd take it."

"You'd leave the *Blunder*?" Agulatai asked.

"In a heartbeat," Vance snapped.

"But this ship has many wonders left to explore," the worm-like alien countered. "I was so grateful to join the *Starship Blunder* crew when she visited my home planet, Insia."

"We needed better janitors," Zabella quipped.

Agulatai didn't react to her remark. "You should cherish your time aboard the *Blunder*, Vance."

"Besides, why would anyone call a ship *Blunder*?" Vance groused. "Aren't ships supposed to have bold titles like Valiant or be named after someone famous?"

"Insians have birth names but must earn our adult names," Agulatai replied. "Perhaps *Blunder* is this ship's birth name, and when it achieves enough renown, it will gain an adult name too."

Zabella shook her head. "I heard the captain lost a bet."

"Whatever. I just want off this ship," Vance said.

Zabella leaned forward and placed her hand on his arm, sending pleasant chills racing through his body. "Maybe you'll enjoy the upcoming shore leave. I overheard we're scheduled for a three-day stopover on Soo-saca."

"Shore leave?" Vance repeated. "Maybe, but—"

"I have finished my food," Agulatai interrupted. "Vance, have you finished? Or you, Zabella?"

"I'm done with my salad," Zabella replied.

"I'm full too." Vance slid his tray toward his roommate. "You can have the rest."

"You should not waste food." The alien dumped the remnants of Vance's meal into his mouth, then gathered up all three trays. "I must return to work. The ship needs more cleaning."

Vance held up a hand. "Agulatai, before you head out for your janitorial shift, can you stop by our quarters? I left my space suit on my bed. Stick splattered a bit of durapoxy on it. Can you clean and stow it? "

"Yes, Vance. Thank you." Agulatai slithered through the doorway.

Zabella leaned back in her chair. "You really should stop dumping extra work on him."

"He *likes* cleaning, remember? He thinks it's an important job."

Zabella rolled her eyes but didn't reply.

"So, tell me about the planet we're visiting. Do you know anything about it?"

She shook her head. "Only that the natives are friendly–mostly pacifists, and they enjoy visitors."

"Sounds too perfect." Vance crossed his arms. "I'm sure something will go wrong."

☆ ☆ ☆

Two days later, the *Blunder* descended onto the surface of Soo-saca. It landed with a loud thump that hinted at only minor hull damage. After the captain had announced they'd opened the hatches, Vance hurried outside with the rest of the crew. He joined a gathering with Zabella, Agulatai, and a few other crewmembers on the landing pad and gawked at the spires of the spaceport along with the tall, curved buildings of the cityscape to their north. A few other ships, including bulky cargo ships and gleaming passenger shuttles, rested on nearby pads.

"Here come the natives," Zabella remarked.

A long train of carts wheeled toward them, separating and spreading out to approach the different groups around the *Blunder*. One parked in front of Vance and his group, and two natives hopped out.

The Soo-sacans only stood about a meter high, with pink fur covering their bodies. Each looked like a traditional snowman, with three rounded segments to their body. A pair of spindly limbs connected to the middle section ended in small hands. And rather than walking, the legless Soo-sacans bounced.

"Welcome to Soo-saca," one said. "We hope you enjoy your visit to our world, and we have prepared electronic pads for you. I can recommend natural wonders, our cultural center, parks, or shopping districts. We will drive you to wherever destination you desire. We only ask that you respect our laws."

Zabella accepted the pad offered by the small Soo-sacan and spent a few minutes browsing it. "Let's visit their cultural center first," she suggested. "I'd love to find out more about these people. There is a small museum and shrine. We can shop or visit parks tomorrow."

Vance didn't care about the comical inhabitants or their culture, but he wanted to spend time with Zabella—while also staying away from the ship. So, he joined her and a half-dozen other crewmembers on the small cart and rode toward the city. Along the way, one native recited facts about the city and world that Vance entirely ignored.

They arrived at a lavish plaza surrounded by ornate buildings mixed with a few eateries. Natives were hopping around the square or resting on soft-seated benches. Several garden plots featured orange-leaved plants with bright green blossoms arranged around plastic statues.

Zabella consulted the brochure on her pad and then led their group into a museum. Vance meandered through displays of historical relics from Soo-saca's past but failed to find anything that interested him in rooms of artwork. Once Zabella had finished exploring the Soo-sacan cultural exhibits, the group gathered again in the plaza.

"Let's grab lunch," Vance suggested, pointing to one eatery.

"But we don't know what they serve," Zabella protested.

"I don't care. Anything is better than ship food," he replied.

Their group separated, filling half the tables in the small café. He and Zabella dined on a gelatinous meat dish cut into cubes and adorned with lime-colored fruit.

"You're right—it's not ship food," she remarked. "It has a strange taste and texture... but I like it."

"What's next?" Vance asked between bites. He slid the last of his food toward Agulatai, who shoveled it into his gullet.

"There's a shrine to something called the Sinikor," she replied, pointing to a small building nearby. Several groups of the bouncing natives had already lined up to enter.

Vance and Agulatai accompanied Zabella into the small building that housed the shrine. Inside, a single exhibit dominated the interior—a dead Soo-sacan on an ornate chair, preserved for eternity. Embedded in the corpse's chest, a blue stone glowed with a pulsing light.

Four Soo-sacan guards stood around the exhibit, and a flimsy fiber-plastic barrier surrounded it. A few blue signs around the room read, "Do Not Touch" or "Stay Away from the Sinikor," followed by several other words in the native script. Vance ignored the illegible signs, but the glowing Sinikor intrigued him.

"Why is it so special?" he asked one guard.

"Protect... world... Sinikor," the guard replied in a broken jumble of the spacer common language garbled together with words in the Soo-sacan's native tongue.

Vance shrugged but continued to stare at the fascinating blue stone.

☆ ☆ ☆

That evening, Vance browsed the electronic pad about the Sinikor and local laws while enjoying a drink in the *Blunder's* lounge. Other crewmembers chatted and socialized around him, and he spotted a few Soo-sacans taking a guided tour of the ship.

"Something fills your mind," Agulatai remarked as he slithered into the chair opposite Vance.

"Yeah, the Sinikor," he admitted. "The Soo-sacans believe it came from another world, and the pad warns of dire tragedies that will strike anyone who possesses it. But they think this stone is special." He set the pad on the table.

"Do you believe in the Sinikor's dire tragedies?" Agulatai asked.

"They're either superstitious nonsense or exaggerated stories spread to keep away thieves," Vance replied with a dismissive wave. "I've heard similar hogwash on other worlds."

"Did you find anything else of interest on our visit today?"

"Not much, aside from Zabella," Vance answered with a grin.

Agulatai helped himself to the entire bowl of bar snacks Vance had been nibbling on. "I heard Markos Beyne punched several Soo-sacans during an altercation. They're detaining him on the planet for the moment."

"Markos always had a temper. Did they imprison him?"

His roommate flicked his four arms outward, an Insian gesture that meant the same thing as a head shake. "No, the Soo-sacans don't imprison wrong-doers. I heard they lodged him in a small apartment, where he'll be doing service work until the *Blunder* leaves the planet."

Vance tapped on the pad and reviewed the Soo-sacans' justice and penal system. "Hmm. He's lucky they only required him to work for two days. For dire-enough crimes, the Soo-sacans have even demanded that visitors remain on Soo-saca long enough to complete their sentence."

Then, an idea began to form in Vance's mind.

If I commit a bad-enough crime, perhaps the Soo-sacans will demand I stay here! I'm already doing service work on the Blunder, *but it's not like being indebted to the Soo-sacans will threaten my well-being or sanity.*

"Agulatai, my friend, I need another drink and some quiet time. Do you mind leaving me alone for a while?"

"I will fetch you a fresh beverage," the wormlike alien replied.

Once Agulatai slithered toward the bar, Vance continued his planning. *The Soo-sacans guard that precious Sinikor like it's a national treasure. But I'll need help pulling this off.*

He watched Agulatai fumble with drinks at the bar and shook his head, then scanned the other crewmembers loitering nearby. He didn't want to involve anyone else, but his gaze lingered on two other men in the hull maintenance team who were having an arm-wrestling match at a nearby table.

I don't need anyone else! I know the perfect helpers!

☆ ☆ ☆

The next day, Vance eschewed Zabella's company and returned to the cultural center with other shipmates from the *Blunder*. Rather than accompany them into the various museums around the square, he sat in the café for several hours, observing both the shrine and the guards around it.

After the group had finished their museum tour and went to eat lunch, Vance rejoined them. He suggested they visit the Sinikor, and a few agreed. But while the others ogled the preserved corpse and the glowing blue gemstone in its chest, he examined everything else.

The doors have both physical and electronic locks. I'd wager they have a security system too. No major problem for me.

Then he strolled around the interior of the shrine, spying on the four guards inside and noting the positions of the cameras and other sensors he could identify.

Each guard carries something dangling from their belt, probably a weapon. Zabella said these people were pacifists, so those weapons probably couldn't kill me. Let's test their readiness.

He sauntered toward the Sinikor and leaned over the protective barrier around the mummified Soo-sacan, pretending to get a closer look. Immediately, two guards bounded toward him with impressive leaps.

"Stop! Don't touch that!" one guard cried. "Stay behind the barrier!" He pulled the weapon, which looked like a glowing baton, from his belt.

"Easy! I just wanted a closer look," Vance confessed. He backed up and forced a repentant expression onto his face. Then he realized the Soo-sacans probably didn't recognize it.

No proximity alarm, so they have lax security. I don't think I've ever seen such an easy target.

He endured teasing from other crewmembers for a few minutes, then returned outside. For another hour, he strolled around the plaza, memorizing the surrounding layout and plotting his nocturnal approach to the shrine. With his preparations complete, Vance decided to enjoy the last few hours of sunlight and visited the upscale shopping district nearby.

☆ ☆ ☆

Vance examined the pad again. "We made it to the plaza. Now follow me and stay quiet." He crept across the open square, then ducked into a small walkway between build-ings near the shrine.

Dash, Stick, and Slap glided behind him, their hov-er-engines whirring with a faint hum.

Once hidden in the alley, he studied the shrine again. Two guards stood outside, but the Soo-sacans hadn't added any additional night security. Pole lights illuminated the plaza, so Vance stowed his unneeded night goggles in his pack.

After rehearsing the plan one more time in his mind, Vance turned toward the three robots. "Slap, ready that plate, and when I give the word, smack against that build-ing at least five times. Stick, I want you to spray the ground at the mouth of this alley with the quick-bond once I leave the alley again. Dash, follow me."

As the largest robot pulled a two-meter-square sheet of aluminum from its carrying bed, Vance darted out of the alley with Dash floating behind him. He dove into a clump of orange bushes and called, "Now, Slap!"

Following the commands he'd given it, Slap whacked the aluminum sheet against the nearby building. The dis-cordant din echoed through the courtyard.

The Soo-sacan guards hopped toward the alley entrance, clearly unaware of Vance's presence. They bounced into the pool of fast-acting adhesive Stick had spread across the plaza grounds. It immobilized them after a few feeble hops; one fell over, and his hands stuck to the ground.

With a smirk, Vance strutted toward the shrine, slinging his small pack off his back. When he reached the entrance, he placed the electronic lockpick against the door and activated it. The device's localized electromagnetic pulses disrupted the door's electronic security systems. Then, he unlocked the mechanical latch with a metal pick.

As he swaggered inside, a lone guard gaped at him before drawing her glowing baton.

"Dash, grab that gem!" he yelled as the guard sprang toward him.

He stepped toward her and extended his hand. The guard swung her weapon, barely grazing Vance's arm before he shoved her squarely on her chest. His forearm tingled where she hit it, but the force of his blow knocked her backward.

Meanwhile, Dash yanked at the Simikor with its two small arms. The glowing blue gem popped free of the preserved corpse, which tottered over.

The guard's eyes gaped wide. "You can't take that!" she cried.

"I can and I will," Vance taunted. "Remember the name Vance Pittman!"

Then, he plucked the Sinikor from Dash's grasp. But the moment he touched the blue gem, it vanished from his fingertips. A tickling tingle raced up his arm, filled his chest, and then concentrated into a point on his breastbone.

"Where's the gem?" he yelled. But the guard said nothing.

He opened his shirt and peered down. The Sinikor had reformed in the center of his chest, continuing to glow with its eerie blue light. He tried to pull it free, but it wouldn't budge.

"Get this off of me!" he demanded. "Arrest me! I give up!"

But she kept her distance, even leaning away from him.

Frustrated, Vance tried to pry the Sinikor from his chest with his lockpicks but only succeeded in scratching his skin. "Take me to your hospital! Or prison!" he pleaded. "Get this stone off me!"

"We can't," the guard replied in a solemn voice. "It has joined you now."

Vance rushed outside to the guards stuck in the glue. "Stick, apply the solvent," he ordered. As the robot obeyed, he turned to the guards. "Tell me how to remove this!"

But both guards shied away from him.

"Aren't you supposed to protect this stone?" Vance asked. "I stole it! Now you have to take it back!"

Finally, one guard answered, "We don't protect the stone from visitors. We protect foolish visitors from the stone."

Flabbergasted, Vance fled toward the only place that might help his plight: the medical bay on the *Blunder*.

☆ ☆ ☆

At any other time, Vance would have welcomed Zabella leaning over him and stroking his bare chest, but the medical bay hardly matched his ideal romantic destination. The Sinikor still glowed, now nestled among a bizarre collection of medical probes attached to him.

"We can't remove it," she announced. "According to Doctor Ossler, it fused with your nervous system. The Sinikor also has a psychic aura we can't identify yet, though he suspects it manipulates probability."

"Wonderful," Vance grimaced. "So I'm stuck with a gemstone nightlight."

"It's not actually stone, but some sort of organic material we can't identify." Zabella sat in the chair beside his bed and flashed him a wry grin. "So you couldn't resist another challenge. You had to steal it."

He shook his head. "I... wanted the Soo-sacans to catch me," Vance admitted.

"Why?"

"I thought that If I stole it, then let them catch me, they'd demand I stay on their planet. I'd finally escape this blasted ship!"

"But they might demand you stay on Soo-saca for years."

"I planned to slip away on the next human ship that visited here," Vance replied. "They don't have tight security. I knew I'd be able to escape at any time."

She yanked the medical probes off his chest with only a fraction of her usual tenderness. When he gaped at her, she reprimanded, "That's for trying to leave without telling me."

"Sorry."

"Anyway, Kojak wants to talk to you. Apparently a group of Soo-sacans have assembled outside the ship."

Vance sat up. "Maybe they've come to take me away."

"Maybe." Zabella patted his shoulder. "Doctor Ossler has approved your discharge, so you can leave any time."

"What about this?" he asked, pointing to the Sinikor.

She shrugged. "We can't do anything about it, and we don't know its properties. If you remain on the *Blunder*, we'll have to keep you under periodic observation."

☆ ☆ ☆

Vance, escorted by Sheriff Kojak in his floating hovercart, approached the group of Soo-sacans. The security chief's oversized cowboy hat concealed most of his features, but the smaller man had donned his dress uniform for the occasion, complete with a gold star on his vest. A few other crewmembers from the *Blunder* watched the spectacle from the shade of the ship.

Among the crowd of Soo-Sacans, Vance recognized the two guards he'd encountered the previous night. As the Soo-sacan entourage approached, one wearing a sash and a decorative cap bounced forward ahead of the others and then stopped three meters from them.

"I am Governor Smohn," the leader announced. "Are you the new bearer of the Sinikor?"

Rather than replying, Vance unbuttoned his shirt to reveal the glowing blue gem. The Soo-sacans in the crowd hopped backward. Even the governor leaned away, though he didn't retreat.

"I am prepared to accept my punishment," Vance announced. "You can lead me away to my fate."

"Punishment?" the governor gaped. "Why would we punish you? You have dared to brave the misfortune the Sinikor carries. When you leave Soo-saca, you will be removing it from our world. We salute your bravery."

"More like stupidity," Chief Kojak remarked.

Vance gaped. "You're... not going to make me work for you?"

"No. We celebrate your departure. Thank you, Vance Pittman."

Vance's jaw dropped.

"Don't worry about having enough work," Kojak added. "For recklessly using the robots and disobeying local

customs, I'm adding three months to your penal contract."
He whirled toward the *Blunder's* boarding ramp.

"No!" Vance wailed. "You're supposed to get me off this
ship." He didn't move as the Soo-sacans returned to their
carts and drove away.

Only then did he turn back toward the waiting *Blunder*
and shook both fists at the uncaring vessel. "I *hate* this
ship!"

THE GREEN GLOB

Melisa Peterson Lewis

The alarm sounded, but the last thing the crew expected to hear on an intergalactic mission was disco tunes from centuries ago. An atmospheric disturbance was causing their landing on a relatively unexplored planet outside the Egadolis system to be rougher than usual.

Commander Thatcher MacRae buckled himself into his chair and gripped the armrests. His auburn hair, sprayed with enough product to be flammable, bobbed with the ship's chaotic flying. "Turn it off, Xylo! That's an order."

"I'm attempting to silence the alarm at this very moment, Commander." Xylo's slender blue fingers darted over his control panel. The ship vibrated and jolted through a swampy cloud mass, limiting visibility. Xylo, the crew's tall, slender technician with shimmering luminescent skin, tried to maintain his composure. His massive, wide eyes blinked.

Pilot Sarah Hawkins, a middle-aged black woman with nicely curled hair and enough grit to outshine most pilots in her ranking, groaned as she held onto the controls to keep the ship steady. A bead of sweat rolled down her cheek. "Who changed the alert tone?" she screamed.

"The former three-beep tone was insufficient in getting the crew's attention," Xylo responded. "I modified it with an audio selection provided by Chef Bluebottle. Is it not—ouch!" Xylo banged his head on an overhead compartment while fumbling to shut the alarm off. "Is it not superior to the previous version?"

The disco tunes blared, making the flashing lights on the bridge seem more like a late-night party than a life-threatening situation.

A few seconds later, the ship broke through the dusty clouds and began skimming the tops of trees. Crewmembers screamed as the chubby, fingerlike leaves brushed against the belly of the ship, making tiny thuds barely audible over the alarm.

"Sarah?" Thatcher pleaded in the sternest voice he could muster. "Can you land us in one piece?" He regretted accepting this mission, but what choice had there been? The powers that be handed out assignments at the end of the month, and this was what had been left after the more prestigious starships had gobbled up all the good ones. One day, the Conglomeracy would recognize the *Starship Blunder* as a team player, a worthy member to lean on and have drinks with. Instead, the *Blunder* crew were the leftover choice, the crumb sweepers. All the dirty jobs no one wanted landed on their shoulders, including this one, which might be their last if Sarah couldn't land the dang ship.

She groaned again while her hands held the steering yoke, and her teeth clenched hard enough to crack. "I need a clearing!"

"Turn this alarm off." Thatcher twisted his head to find Xylo's spotted, luminescent skin flashing. That couldn't be a good sign. Previously, he'd only seen a soft glow from the creature when in distress—never flashing.

Xylo stepped back, closed his eyes, and struck a series of buttons on the control panel. The sound grew louder—so loud that Thatcher had to cover his ears. "Off! Off!"

The ship bumped and veered hard to the left, sending Xylo flying with a high-pitched shriek.

"Eeeeeeeeeeeeeeeeeep!" His body slapped against Sarah, causing her to let go of the controls for a moment, which sent the ship diving down into the trees.

The red lights in the cabin intensified as the ship's computer system spoke: "Impact imminent. Impact imminent. Maintain your seated position." The robotic voice continued to repeat the warning as branches and leaves flashed by the front window. "Impact imminent."

"Oh, dear god!" Sarah regained control and pulled them up. The ship rose quickly, causing everyone on board's stomach to flip. "There! There's our opening!"

Thatcher saw what she was referring to. A beachy shore met against turquoise waters, but the sandy area was limited. They'd have to crash.

The ship passed the shore, and just as it went over the water, Sarah swung them around so they spun like a thrown disk. They rotated several times before the starship plopped onto the ground, creating a sandy tornado in the process. Thatcher's body jerked against his restraints as the ship came to an abrupt halt. Thankfully, the disco tunes finally stopped.

Silently, Thatcher patted himself to ensure he was intact. His hand brushed over his hair. Still good. He turned to Sarah, "That was mighty tricky flying, Pilot! Good work."

Sarah raised a finger, turned her head, and threw up in the trash drawer before responding. "Thank you, sir."

Xylo peeled himself off the floor and rubbed his head. His blue skin was dark and no longer glowing. "Permission to rest, Commander?"

"Granted?" Thatcher replied, though he didn't think now was a good time for a nap. They had to explore, and he had to verify that the members of his ship were okay.

With a *thump*, Xylo returned to the floor with his tongue dangling from his thin lips.

Sarah stepped over the alien. "I'll run a damage report."

Xylo whispered, "I'm damaged."

"Very good," Thatcher agreed with Sarah. "I'll check on our crew and prepare for exploration." They were to gather plant-life samples from a checklist provided by Neptune's lead scientists. The island produced fauna with possible cures for various illnesses. The mission sounded critical when he thought of it that way... yet the truth was, the Conglomeracy could have sent an unmanned ship to gather clippings. He wanted to ask the admiral why they hadn't considered that option, but after their last disastrous mission, he'd determined it'd be better to keep his mouth shut.

Last mission was a success, he reminded himself. It wasn't every day you found a group of friendly cannibals representing themselves as universe-loving hippies. Friends don't eat each other, Thatcher had tried to explain. The *Starship Blunder* and her crew escaped with their lives and were able to mark that planet as hostile, saving future voyagers from the same near-fatal error of accepting a dinner invitation from the natives.

Commander Thatcher attempted to stand, but his seatbelt held him down. The frayed edges snagged against his white pants, leaving a green stain across his lap. He made a mental note to ask Xylo to replace the belt when he woke up from his nap.

The hallway of the ship was empty, but the mumbles and groans of fellow passengers echoed out from different rooms. Thatcher paused at Chef Bluebottle's residence and rang the chef's doorbell. The convoy needed provisions before their mission, and he wanted Bluebottle to check that the next meal hadn't splattered all over the floor.

When no one answered, Thatcher knocked on the door. "Blue, you there?" The chef was an older man with weathered skin, the only hair on his head white eyebrows. He always insisted on wearing a chef's cap. Bluebottle didn't need to wear the cap, but the old timer was set in his ways, so Thatcher let it be.

The door slid open and Bluebottle, standing just under five feet tall, waved a ladle at Thatcher. "Well, that was some landing. You nearly cost us *weeks* of rations. The freezer latch isn't working, so I held it shut with duct tape. When that peeled off, I had to use something else."

Behind Bluebottle was a table turned so the top side was against the freezer door, with a set of chains holding it in placc.

"I see. So, can you prepare a meal for the convoy in an hour?"

A long, steady whistle escaped Bluebottle's lips.

Thatcher wasn't sure what that meant. "Is... that an affirmative?"

Bluebottle crossed his arms and shook the ladle once again. "Whose going with you?"

It wasn't unlike Bluebottle to ask questions, and Thatcher knew he'd figure out the answer anyway. "I've picked five cadets, including Pilot Hawkins, if the ship doesn't require her attention. Why do you need to know?"

"Can I come? I heard this planet has a variety of good plants. Food, you know, the green stuff that's hard to come by at home." Bluebottle was referring to their home planet of Neptune, which imported most of their green stuff, as he called it, from Earth. Neptune's few farms were only able to grow plants using a potent fertilizer that, unfortunately, made things taste like rocks.

"You're not prepared for a mission outside the ship," Thatcher explained.

"How hard can it be? Put on one of those suits, walk around, chop off a few things, document it, return to the ship."

Thatcher scoffed. "It's much more complicated than that, I assure you."

Bluebottle leaned against the doorframe. "Oh, yeah. Tell me about it."

As Thatcher's mind went blank, he realized the mission truly was that simple. The hardest part was landing the ship, which was behind them now.

"I'll think about it. Can you prepare the food?"

"Thinking about it means no, doesn't it?"

"I said I'll think about it, okay?" Thatcher turned away from the café area before Bluebottle could ask him more questions. Even if the mission was as simple as the chef insisted, he still didn't believe Bluebottle was up for the task. The old man would find some way to muck everything up.

Thatcher continued down the hall, checking in on each individual in his convoy crew. In the process, he'd discovered more than one had gotten injured during the landing. Two of them had sprained wrists from trying to catch themselves; one was now vomiting violently from motion sickness, and the other may have received a concussion and was going to see the medic.

Thatcher hadn't been prepared for so much bad news. It left a single other convoy member, Sarah, and himself. He needed at least two more people if they were going to complete the mission. As he returned to the bridge, he wondered who he could trust to add to his team.

On his way there, he ran into Miss Luna Knight, the ship's schoolteacher. The interesting young woman mostly kept to herself. She only smiled when working with the kids, and every parent on the ship, including him, feared her. The all-black sleeveless jumpsuit she wore revealed her tattoos that covered her arms and led up her neck.

"Commander Thatcher," she said, brushing her raven-colored hair off her forehead.

He jumped, cleared his throat, and then gathered himself enough to respond. "Miss Knight. I didn't expect to run into you outside of the daycare room."

"Call me Luna."

"Luna."

"School is closed while we're planetside."

He looked puzzled. "Why?"

"Need I remind you of the cannibal friends we made on our last trip? I don't think it's a good idea to have the kids wandering the ship when we're on an alien planet that hasn't been marked safe." Her dark eyes dug in, clearly daring him to argue with her.

A sudden burst of disco music almost dropped them both to their knees.

Luna grabbed her ears, shouting, "Why is that happening?"

The music cut off just as Thatcher began to yell back, so he wound up much louder than necessary. "Xylo uploaded some terrible noise Bluebottle gave him."

Behind Thatcher, someone cleared their throat. He turned to see who it was and spotted Bluebottle standing there with his arms folded and his ladle pointed at them.

"That's the best disco-tech music from Earth's best era. You two need more education on American culture. Did you know—"

"Yes, thank you, Blue," Thatcher cut him off.

"I wasn't done yet." Bluebottle waved the ladle close to Thatcher's face.

"Luna was about to ask me something. I think." Thatcher turned his attention back to Luna, whose glare at that moment made him shiver. He hoped whatever her request was, it didn't involve him spending real time with her.

"I was trying to tell you something," she said. "I'm available if you need me anywhere. With school closed, I have time to—"

Thatcher grinned. "Not necessary. I'm sure you need to plan or clean your room or something."

She waved her hand absently. "Fine. Whatever. I'm an educator. While often undervalued, I have many talents. Let me know if you change your mind." Luna stepped back into her classroom and closed the sliding door, leaving Thatcher and Bluebottle staring after her.

Close call avoided, Thatcher sidestepped Bluebottle and quickly walked to the bridge. That was when he found Xylo was up and about, doing diagnostics.

"Damage report," Thatcher requested as he returned to his seat, which reminded him that he still had a green stripe across his lap from the seat belt. "Can you please replace this when there's a moment?" He pointed to the strap, and Xylo nodded in agreement.

Sarah's complexion had returned to normal after her vomiting session earlier, and she reported, "Damage to the undercarriage will need to be examined by the mechanics from outside, but all other systems are in check. The convoy can exit the ship on schedule."

"Very good." *No, wait*, Thatcher thought, remembering things weren't good. "We are down several convoy members. Who do we have in reserve?"

"Me." Xylo raised his long, thin arm, and some of his luminescent dots glowed excitedly.

"That'll work, provided the *Blunder* can depart when needed and all systems are functioning." Thatcher counted off in his head.

A burst of disco music filled the ship once again. Xylo punched the controls, and the sound slowed until it stopped. "Almost repaired, Commander."

The makeshift convoy team took the next hour reviewing the plants they needed to hunt for. It would have been better if they had divided into two teams, but Thatcher didn't want anyone to split up after their last mission. The lifeforms on this planet weren't documented, but that didn't mean they didn't exist.

"Mostly fauna," Sarah responded as if she could read his mind. "And a few simple life forms too small for us to see without a microscopic device."

Thatcher turned to his intercom system and called Bluebottle. After several beeps, the chef picked up.

"Yes?" Bluebottle responded.

"Are previsions prepared?"

"Yes. And?"

"And?" Thatcher asked, confused.

"Anything else you want to talk about?"

They still needed one more member for the convoy. But with all the other eligible participants taking care of repairs and injuries, Thatcher had little choice. "You can be assigned, but you must stay with the group. You must wear the protective clothing we provide."

"Aye, Commander. Looking forward to the mission."

"And you can't bring foreign matter onto this ship without running it by me first."

"Oh." The intercom was silent for a moment. "Very well," Bluebottle grunted before cutting communications.

Thatcher turned to Sarah. "I was going to tell him when to meet us at the decontamination cell. Let's have the convoy convene in thirty minutes."

"Very well."

Thirty minutes later, Thatcher stood in the decontamination room, which resembled a sterile silver closet with a hatch leading to the outside. He had on his white suit and a glass mask that covered his face to filter the air. Beside him, Sarah helped stuff Bluebottle into a suit of his own. As they did, the two argued about Bluebottle's chef cap, which stood a foot off his head.

"There is something called wind here, Blue," she tried to explain. "You'll likely lose your hat."

"Nonsense. I've not taken this thing off in forty years." He smacked her hand away from his head.

Thatcher imagined a pale ring of hairless scalp under the hat.

Xylo entered the room, ducking to avoid the ceiling. He held out a silver bottle and leaned toward Bluebottle. "The contents of these provisions smell off."

"Off how?" Bluebottle became defensive anytime someone questioned his cooking. However, his culinary creations were often brown, no matter what ingredients he used, so the off-smell Xylo mentioned only had three varieties: cheese, bean, or tuna fish. Despite the smell, however, nothing ever tasted like those things.

Sarah interrupted before Bluebottle could get into it. "Aren't we supposed to have one more convoy member?"

As is in response, Luna walked into the room, suited up as if they'd been expecting her. "I'm here."

"No. No," Thatcher said. "At least one of our members wasn't injured during the landing. We're waiting on her now."

Luna tapped her face mask, and the ventilation system kicked on with a gentle hum. "She's trapped in her room. Tech is getting her out, but it could take a while. Turns out several doors have jammed on the lower level. So, you got me."

Sarah handed Luna a tablet. "You can help by reading off our tasks and recording notes."

"I can do that." Luna took the device and began flipping through it.

The room was tight with five people standing around, elbows knocking together. The door behind them shut, and over the next few moments, the pressure in the room adjusted to the same levels as outside. Light beams scanned from top to bottom for a few minutes to complete the decontamination process. Finally, a green light gave them the okay to leave the tight space and venture outside the ship.

Thatcher surveyed the others as they exited onto the platform and worked their way down the steps. He and Sarah had been outside the ship on missions like this before, and Xylo had also done several. For Luna and Bluebottle, however, this was their first time participating in a convoy. Both were gazing out at the landscape with curiosity.

The sand underfoot was a brownish orange, and the grains were as fine as Earth's granulated sugar. Water lapped up the shore toward them in a gentle rhythmic pattern. The water was clearer than what they'd seen on most planets, indicating that no settlers with heavy machinery had polluted the life here. The sky was blue, vastly different from the black sky on Neptune.

Thatcher adjusted his face mask to a darker tint so the double suns above them wouldn't cause a glare. Behind the group stood a forest of tall trees with smooth gray bark and plump, round leaves like sausages. The rocky ground at the forest's edge gave way to dark green moss.

"First item?" Thatcher questioned.

"We're looking for the Dremarium plant," Luna said. "Here's a picture." She showed them the tablet. It was a tall, slender green stalk topped with a white barbed flower. "Notes suggest the scent is very sweet, so we might smell it before seeing it. Sounds gross."

"Can we eat it?" Bluebottle asked.

Luna scanned the tablet. "Not advised."

"Dang it."

The crew moved forward across the sand and onto the spongy moss. Each step gave them a little spring, which Xylo seemed to enjoy, hopping from one foot to the other.

"Let's fan out but keep each other in view." Thatcher directed everyone.

They formed a side-by-side line with about ten feet between them and began moving forward. During their trek, Luna recited facts about the first plant from the tablet.

"Whoa, this flower can be an aphrodisiac. It has medical properties that could help with fertility issues too. That plays nicely together." She muffled her giggle.

Xylo frowned. "What is that word, aphrodisiac?"

"You know how little Xylos are made?" Bluebottle replied.

"Yes. It's when two of our species agree to mix genetics and create a hybrid clone of themselves. The first step is to—"

"Let's just say it puts you in a happy mood," Luna interrupted before she had to learn what Xylo's species did to procreate. "A mood that you may want to share with others. Okay?"

Xylo considered this momentarily, and his mouth parted, but he held his question until several minutes later when the group had made it farther into the forest. "What does a happy mood have to do with making more of my kind?"

"Um..." Luna stumbled over what to say next.

"Never mind that," Sarah jumped in. "Do you smell that?"

Everyone tilted their heads up and, through their ventilated masks, began to sniff. The air had taken on the scent of a cake baking in the oven. Of course, not one of Bluebottle's cakes, but one from another time, lodged deep within their memories.

Luna pointed. "There. White flower on a tall stalk."

Tall was the keyword. The stalk was six inches thick, and the flower they needed to sample was a full fifteen feet off the ground. Thatcher walked around the plant, noting similar vegetation behind them, but all were even taller than the one in front of him. The surrounding trees were too smooth to climb, so he figured they would have to cut down the stalk in order to reach the samples they needed. It wasn't their standard practice to destroy the vegetation, but he saw no other way.

Xylo withdrew a handheld laser, but Luna stopped him.

"Wait, what if we can bend the stalk down and snip what we need?" she asked.

Thatcher cocked one of his brows and considered Luna's statement. "Why don't we lasso the stalk and pull it toward us? Then we don't need to cut it."

"That's basically what I said."

Being the more prepared one, Sarah took a climbing rope from her pouch and threw it around the stalk. Together with Xylo, she attempted to pull so the stalk would bend, but it wouldn't. Thatcher grabbed the rope behind Xylo, and then Bluebottle joined at the end. Their efforts paid off, and the flower drew close enough for Luna to take a clipping.

"Hold it," she instructed. "I want to get more than one in case something is damaged."

Bluebottle groaned. "Hurry, my foot is slipping."

Luna put the specimen in a tube and placed it in a pouch clinging to her hip, then leaned in for one more sample. "Hold it. Hold it. Done!"

Everyone but Bluebottle let go of the rope, which sent the stalk upward fast and the chef catapulting off the ground. His feet smacked into Xylo as he went, knocking off Xylo's mask. Thatcher and Sarah watched as Bluebottle flew through the air and thrust into a patch of blue fuzzy bushes several feet away.

Xylo unintentionally took a breath of the atmosphere's air as he tried to fix his mask. His body dropped to the ground, his eyes closed, and his mouth twitched.

Sarah knelt to adjust Xylo's mask so it correctly covered his face. He responded with a drooling, sloppy smile. "The air here is high in nitrous oxide," she said. "I'm not sure how it will affect his species."

Xylo raised his hand and gave them a thumbs-up. "Whoa. Whoa. Yeah, Mom. I'll go to school soon."

"Nitrous oxide?" Thatcher asked. "He's essentially inhaled laughing gas? Shouldn't be anything to worry about. It'll wear off soon with his mask back on."

"Commander," Sarah said. "The mask isn't reattaching properly. We need to return him to the ship."

Thatcher rubbed the back of his neck. *So far this mission, Xylo's gotten high and Bluebottle's hidden in a bush,* he thought. They needed to finish up and leave the planet before nightfall, or they'd have to wait forty hours until the suns rose again and they had another chance.

"Someone go check on Bluebottle," Thatcher instructed. They could hear him swearing and whacking at the bush in the distance. After securing her tablet, Luna ran over, and Thatcher turned his attention to Xylo, whose blue spots had began to glow.

Sarah helped her alien comrade to his feet. He wobbled a bit but straightened up. Clearly, they couldn't trust Xylo to get back to the ship alone. The rest would have to carry on without Xylo or Sarah.

"Once he's in the decontamination room, the effects should wear off," Thatcher said, trying to reassure both Sarah and himself. "If he can, have him get the ship ready for departure. I don't want to waste any precious time when we return." He hoped the smaller, less skilled remains of the convoy team could hurry through the rest of their tasks.

"Will do, Commander." Sarah linked her arm around Xylo's and began to walk away.

Xylo ran his fingers through the air as if trying to catch something. "The atmosphere is furry. Can you feel that,

Sarah? I think I've found the happy mood we were talking about. This is a happy mood, isn't it?"

She tugged him forward. "It's something, come on."

Once Sarah was out of sight, Thatcher focused on regaining control of the mission. He went over to find Bluebottle and Luna to see about moving them along quickly.

Luna's black hair draped over her shoulder like a curtain, hiding Bluebottle from view. When Thatcher came upon them, he discovered a green slimy substance was covering Bluebottle's suit. His mask seemed to be in place, though, which was good.

"Oh, my goddess, what *is* that stuff?" Luna stepped away, unwilling to touch him.

"Smells awful," Bluebottle said. "Feels warm. Kind of squishy under my armpits."

"Gross." Luna stepped back so Bluebottle could stand.

The green globs on Bluebottle's body began to move, causing Bluebottle to go stiff with fear. Each wet puddle slid across his suit, forming a single larger blob on his shoulder. Thatcher's eyes widened.

"Is it alive?" Thatcher asked Luna. "Take an image and upload it to our database."

She did as told while the glob grew as big as a grapefruit on Bluebottle's shoulder. Still unsure what was happening, the chef held still.

"Nothing is coming up. How does it feel?" she asked.

"Um, like a million crawly things are wandering over my uniform. Can you help me remove this stuff so we can get out of here?" Bluebottle reached up to touch the blob, but in doing so, the blob began to create a second cluster on his gloved hand. He shook it, trying to get it off, but it had no effect.

"Super gross." Luna scowled.

"What do I do?" Bluebottle asked in a panic, jumping up and down before running in circles. "Get it off! Get it off!"

"Try to roll on the ground," Thatcher suggested.

Bluebottle threw himself on the ground, rolling around in an attempt to wipe away the goo, which only caused chunks of moss to stick to the glob.

"We can't let you on the ship with that suit on," Thatcher said.

Without further instruction, Bluebottle began to unzip his suit and climb out. The glob and the clumped-up white suit that had once protected Bluebottle fell to the ground, including his gloves and boots, which remained attached to the suit.

He stood wearing white socks, blue boxer briefs, and a chef's hat. The mask remained in place–luckily, the glob was no longer on him.

"Get me out of here!"

Thatcher instructed Bluebottle to remove the hat, but Bluebottle refused.

"Wait, there's another specimen we need over there," Luna pointed to a patch of pink hairs growing on a rock. "It's a type of moss that can cure stomach ulcers and more! Let me grab some really quick." She sprinted away from them.

With another sample down, Thatcher retained hope that they could complete the mission before dusk.

"I'm going back unless you want me to walk around in my underpants." Bluebottle began shuffling toward the ship.

"Wait," Commander Thatcher instructed. He didn't want to lose yet another convoy member. "The temperature here is mild, the moss will cushion your feet from injury, and we're already down two members. Without your help, we'll have to stay here another day in order to complete the mission."

"How long is a day on this planet?"

"Eighty hours."

Bluebottle shrugged. "Let's go get those cuttings. The next one was marked edible; I'm bringing a bunch back!"

"Fine," Thatcher agreed.

The three of them stomped through the forest, collecting samples from all the plants on their list. Luna, an educator fascinated by science, was in fauna heaven. She beamed with every specimen collected and read the full descriptions aloud as they walked. Bluebottle, now terrified of touching anything else green and globby, pointed at every plant, asking if he could eat it. He finally celebrated when Luna noted a set of red-capped mushrooms marked as edible. She took a spore test and several images to verify its safety before letting him pick any.

With the okay to do so, Bluebottle scooped up as many as he could carry.

Once back at the ship, they stood in the decontamination room while the laser lights scanned them. An alarm beeped a moment later—the door to the ship refused to open.

Bluebottle sniffed back a tear. "Is it the mushrooms?"

"I'm afraid so," Thatcher confirmed. "Toss them out, and we'll try to decontaminate again."

He threw the precious lot back outside and mumbled that his budget never let him buy anything fun.

The lasers scanned them again, and the alarm beeped once before quickly turning off. Then, their ears were accosted with disco music once again. Thatcher banged on the door until Xylo opened it.

"Sorry. Won't happen again, Commander."

The three removed their masks and then stepped through the door.

Luna handed Thatcher the tablet and bag full of samples. "Good time, old man. Thanks for letting me partner with you."

"Old man?" Thatcher interjected, but Luna had already left, Bluebottle following after her. Xylo remained, and Thatcher felt the need to clarify. "Humans live well beyond a hundred years now. I'm not an old man. I'm still *quite* in my prime."

"Yes, Commander. Well, my species lives to be four hundred and twenty years of age. Therefore, I am nearing middle age too."

Thatcher, stunned by Xylo's statement, took a step back. "You're almost two hundred?"

"Yes, sir. And I, just as much as you, feel quite... how do you humans say it... like a spring duck."

"Chicken. A spring chicken. Also, that term hasn't been in use for centuries." Thatcher exhaled and left the area to drop off the report for the scientists to take over. All the while, he considered the crow's feet pulling at the corners of his eyes. *Xylo looks great for being two hundred years old,* he thought. *Maybe his species doesn't get wrinkles or gray hair. Wouldn't that be nice?*

When he passed the café to check in, he was astonished to see everyone in the room had green globs growing up their legs.

"Oh, for the love of all mighty. How did this get past decontamination?" Thatcher ran into the room, promptly slipping on the green substance that had multiplied on the floor. The warmth of the glob grew steadily up his fallen body, causing him to shudder and scream.

"It's bad, Commander." Bluebottle came out of the kitchen, completely covered in several inches of the green mass. "It must be multiplying in here for some reason. I can't get it to stop!"

Thatcher noticed the substance only adhered to his clothing and did not creep onto his hands or neck. *It must have stuck to Bluebottle's chef's cap when he removed his clothing outside.*

"Everyone, get undressed and get to the door." Thatcher stood, unzipped the white suit he was still wearing, and scrambled out. Those in the room began to do the same. Soon, a pile of clothing was in the center of the room, with a group of naked crew members making their way to the door.

"No one leaves with anything on!" Thatcher yelled.

Undergarments were cast off and thrown into the heap in the middle of the café. Thatcher, though wanting to avert his eyes, inspected everyone before they could leave. When Bluebottle attempted to pass him, Thatcher put his arm across the door's opening.

"The hat," Thatcher instructed.

"Oh, Commander, you know I never take it off."

"Then you're going to stay here with the green glob. Forever."

Both Thatcher and Bluebottle eyed the pile of clothing and the sloppy mass that was pulsing and growing.

Bluebottle reached up and tugged the hat off, revealing a bald head with a tattoo covering his scalp. "What the heck is that?" Thatcher muttered.

"I'll never tell a soul." Bluebottle thrust his cap onto the pile and pushed past Thatcher.

With a better look as he passed, Thatcher could see there were numbers and what seemed to be a map drawn in black ink. Some of it had faded, but it was otherwise crisp.

There was no time to think about the strange life Bluebottle lived outside the walls of this starship. Thatcher, wearing nothing, slammed the door shut to trap the green glob inside the café.

He turned to find Luna holding out a towel for him.

"Cold in here?"

"Funny." He whipped it away from her. "Get Xylo to test different temperatures in that room to kill the glob."

"I'm not your crew."

"You were a few minutes ago," he said.

"That was then. Now I'm off the clock. Bye."

He wrapped the towel around his waist a split-second before Sarah appeared from around the corner; concern warped her face. "I saw a group of naked people running down the hallway. I thought it might have been nitrous oxide leaking into the ship."

"Sarah, could you request Xylo heat this room to kill off whatever that is, and then dispose of it through the trash chute?"

"Yes, sir. Also, Commander? We need to depart sooner than anticipated. The water we're next to has a tide and is rising quickly. If we don't take off soon, we'll be stuck in the sand underwater until the tide lowers again."

"I never get a break. Very well. I'll meet you at the bridge in ten minutes."

"*Now*, sir. We need to leave now."

"Now?"

The ship rocked, making Thatcher lose his balance and drop the towel. He quickly scooped it back up and held it around his waist.

Sarah continued, "I'm a good pilot, but the engines cannot get wet. The waves are already making the sand underfoot unsteady. We have to take off immediately, Commander."

Together, they ran to the bridge, where Thatcher took a seat in his chair once again. The cold metal against his bare backside made him squirm, but he bit his tongue.

"Alert passengers to get in departure seating immediately." Thatcher scanned the room, making sure everyone was in their seats. "Xylo, work on heating the café to destroy the glob."

"Right, sir."

"Sarah, countdown to when you're ready." Thatcher buckled his fraying seatbelt around the towel. The announcement to ready for launch echoed throughout the ship, and the revving engines vibrated the bridge.

A smell wafted through the vents, catching Thatcher's gag reflex.

"What is that?"

"The green glob proved quite resilient, so I heated the café to above three hundred and seventy-five degrees," Xylo replied. "Anything left in there will get destroyed. However, the glob is releasing gas."

"Is it nitrous oxide?" Thatcher asked with a giggle, then cleared his throat.

"Confirmed. It is nitrous oxide." Xylo ran his fingers over the lighted keys in front of him. "Let me turn the vent on to release the gas away from the ship."

The ship lurched as Sarah brought it off the ground. It wobbled, making its way along the sand, and after hovering across several yards, it began to accend.

Sarah burst into tears. "My tongue feels like a marshmallow, sir."

Amidst hysterical laughter, Thatcher ordered, "Xylo, get that vent working pronto!"

As the nearly naked Commander rolled his head back, trying to stifle his chuckles, the crew began to join him. Together, their roar and fits of laughter echoed through the halls. The outside view of the shore began to shrink as Sarah piloted them away from the planet and into the tempestuous clouds that had caused the rough entry.

"Hang on," she shouted over everyone's giggles.

The ship jerked when the *Starship Blunder* hit the clouds, and the disco alarm went off with red warning lights flashing once again.

The crew had completed another successful mission and were finally headed home.

BOOMERANG BLACK

Sill Bihagia

Kal always had a keen nose, but he wasn't sure what he smelled as he entered the *Blunder's* galley for the first time. Acrid, earthy, but with enough savory notes to indicate that the intention was to create something edible. The strident white lights glared over his new crewmates' heads, a motley collection of over a hundred spacefarers of various species, sitting or mingling beside dented metallic tables. None seemed to notice or recognize Kal hovering by the door. Some groups sat clustered with easy camaraderie, while other faces only showed resignation as they waited for the captain to commence the pre-meal meeting.

The ship was busy and cramped compared to the private starships he'd traveled on previously. Kal was accustomed to first-class cabins, lush houses, and five-star hotels in inner Sol or major ports in nearby systems. He was used to his family's quiet mansion on Neptune, where he was constantly under surveillance, unlike now.

This might not be so bad.

Sarah Hawkins arrived, the pilot he'd first met only an hour ago. She took long strides to the front of the galley, gesturing for him to follow. She looked over the crew with pride and confidence, her face etched with smile lines. Kal could only conclude that her fast-roving eyes collected quite a few details he'd missed. He decided he liked Sarah; even her call for order embodied a contagious enthusiasm.

Kal kept as far to the edge of the room as he could, near the counter where Chef Bluebottle had laid out a tray of pasta—or was it worms? Worm-based Pasta?—which he identified as the source of that smell.

"Good evening, crew. The captain is recovering well after the electrocution wounds from his overenthusiastic margarita mixer. Aside from that little accident, it is a good evening!" Sarah's voice boomed, momentarily drowning out a shuddering groan from an unhappy warp engine.

The crowd didn't seem to bat an eye.

"I'll be acting as interim captain while he recovers," Sarah continued in a cheery voice. "We picked up a fresh crew member in Neptune today, who I am very excited to introduce! Please welcome Kal Batra." She gestured toward him.

The crowd clapped with polite regard. Kal managed to stand straight and wave rather than fidget with the collar of his uniform that didn't seem to fit quite right. He noticed Sarah was the only other person wearing the ugly purple uniform and made a mental note to change clothes as soon as possible. He felt his bronze skin flush as he avoided looking into any particular face in the crowd. Batra. That name ripped a hole in the air, destroying the fragile veneer of anonymity he preferred to hide behind. Batra, the beacon of a name his mother had insisted he take pride in; the name fifteen generations of noble Neptune citizens—back to the planet's founders—shared, all of whom his father had made him memorize.

"As many of you must know," Sarah continued. "Kal is the son of Senator Arana Batra—"

Kal's parentage was his greatest accomplishment in his twenty-one years, in fact. He tuned out the rest of the glowing introduction, and he could tell he wasn't the only one.

One crew member, a large-eyed Zentaran with shimmering blue skin and mismatched goggles, added a powder to a flask and stirred it with a screwdriver. Beside him, a pale-skinned human in black sat hunched in her seat. She kept stealing glances at her handheld, clutched in tattooed arms just under the table.

This was his welcome aboard the *Starship Blunder*. He couldn't be more relieved.

Sarah's smile widened as she clapped Kal on the back, which almost sent him sprawling into the tray of wormy pasta or what he hoped was vegetable mash now laid out beside it in a chafing dish. "So good to have you aboard, Kal."

Kal stood up straight. "Thank you, Ms. Hawkins."

Sarah's booming voice lowered to a conspiratorial stage whisper as she said, "So, Kal, tell us. What inspired you to sign on? Your mother said she thought this would be a meaningful experience for you as you prepared to follow her into government. Can you tell us more about that?"

Kal's cheeks burned hot. A glance around the room revealed the crew's expectant stares. Even that tattooed woman looked up from her handheld long enough to raise an eyebrow. There was no point in trying to save face.

"It's, uh… community service," he mumbled. "But I'm glad to be here."

The galley fell silent. Sarah's smile wavered, then crashed completely, and Kal couldn't help but feel for her as she endeavored to not just plaster on a fake one but rebuild something genuine. Maybe joining the *Blunder* had been a mistake. He'd let enough good people down.

"Well, we're delighted to have you too." Her tone sounded genuine.

Full of shame, Kal slunk into the seat next to the tattooed woman, one of the few crew members who appeared to be about his age. When she glanced up, he offered a friendly smile, but she shifted her gaze almost instantly back down to her holographic book, which was complete with a computer-generated spooky forest.

"Nice to meet you. What's your name?" Kal asked, holding out his hand anyway.

"Luna," she said, looking up for only a moment to glare at his hand.

Sarah rapped a spoon against a metal pot, silencing the crowd again. "All right, crew, listen up. Our next stop will be in the Kepler system, planet Terengal. Besides the usual peacekeeping, we'll also be taking on a new type of mission, one that has the potential to be quite lucrative."

The crew gave her skeptical glances, but she stood undeterred by the weight of them. Chef Bluebottle grunted from behind the counter while continuing to stir a large bubbling pot with his thick arms.

"This mission involves locating a missing person and escorting them safely to the Neptune Embassy," Sarah continued. "We'll be looking for a musician and social media influencer by the name of Boomerang Black. Apparently... well, let's just say his most recent song, which incorporated some of Terengal's local motifs and gestures, earned him quite the backlash. We'll be touching down near the place he was last seen on the planet. Since he took the song down a week ago, he hasn't posted or responded to messages from friends, despite posting about every twelve hours for the bulk of his career."

Kal didn't want to correct Sarah Hawkins, but as an ardent fan of Boom's music, he knew this was a conservative estimate of the celebrity's posting habits. At least a couple times a year, Boom would do a 24-hour live-stream, improvising new mixes all the while.

"That last song was *so* tone-deaf," said a woman in the crowd.

The blue-skinned engineer set down the notebook he'd been scribbling in. "A musician who can't discern musical tones? How did he get famous?"

"Metaphorically tone-deaf, Xylo," Sarah explained.

Kal couldn't help but come to the artist's defense. "Boom layers some of the best bangers in the universe!" He hadn't heard Boom was missing until now—it had been a rough couple of weeks.

Luna's head snapped up to Kal, though it drifted back down to her handheld when Kal tried to meet her gaze.

"Bangers? The metaphorically tone-deaf musician makes sausages? Are these metaphorical sausages?" Xylo asked.

Chef Bluebottle let out a disgruntled snort.

Sarah grimaced. "No, Xylo, there are no sausages. As for the troubles, it seems Boom made a sideways peace sign, which, combined with his micro-expressions, translated to a rather... colorful insult in Terengali." On the display above the kitchen counter, she played Boom's last video.

Kal had never been to any planet in Kepler, but Terengali, the predominant language in that system, was not an easy one for humans to learn. True, humans have both the correct number of fingers for the gestures and the critical muscle groups in their faces to produce the language, and they even have the vocal range to achieve all the tones. But few humans could incorporate the complexity of all three components at once. Boom was one of the few humans even to try, and Kal had to give him props for that.

The song Sarah Hawkins played represented Boom at his best: heavy bass and familiar motifs from Inner Sol that evoked the warmth of their sun and the taste of Earth's air. The haunting vocals of the amphibious Terengali language were layered on top, making Kal miss a place he'd never visited.

"He *didn't*," Xylo said, flushing when Boom threw what must have been the offending gesture. "Please don't make me translate this with children around, Boss."

"You speak Terengali?" Kal asked, and it seemed he wasn't the only one around who was surprised.

"I spent a year at a community college in Terengal, so I picked it up."

Luna looked up at him, muttered something under her breath, then returned to her device.

Sarah gestured for silence. "Buckle up, because it gets worse. Boomerang Black, bless his oblivious heart, attempted to live-stream a public apology, memorizing a speech in Terengali for the occasion. According to the police report, the crowd accepted the apology graciously—until, during the group hug that was supposed to conclude the video, he accidentally used an archaic gesture that translates roughly to 'Females, release your unfertilized eggs on my hot driveway.' "

Xylo burst out laughing. "Everyone knows proper etiquette dictates the male offer his spermatophore first. The ignorance!"

"Are we qualified for a missing person mission?" a sandy-skinned woman grumbled from the table beside him.

The crew exchanged bewildered looks and titters. Sarah seemed to absorb all the grumbles with an understanding nod.

"Look," she said, "I know we can pull this off. And when we do, we'll earn the funds needed to fix climate control on the bridge and finally get produce back in our diets. No more replicated vegetable mash for at least a month."

The grumbling stilled. Even Chef Bluebottle seemed to perk up a bit.

"This is a volunteer mission, so we still need most of you to assist with the refugee camp north of the capital," Sarah continued. "For those who accept, we'll track Boomerang's movements, question the locals with tact, and find him before he... uh... incites any more trouble for himself."

"Xylo, can you teach us a couple Terengali phrases?" Sarah said. "*Hello* and *thank you*, perhaps. We'll use the translation app for everything else."

Xylo stood, his face distorting into a series of twitches before he flicked and waved his wrists. The effect was somewhere between a flapping butterfly and stretching a stiff muscle after a long night's sleep. "That's hello."

"Perfect. Let's all give that a try," Sarah said.

Hands fluttered and faces crinkled across the room. Xylo twitched his face again. At first, Kal thought the alien was repeating his demonstration of 'hello,' but quickly realized the facial movements were from irritation instead.

"For most of you, that was indecipherable gibberish. Dai, you managed to say 'cactus water.' Boss, I'm not sure which was more insulting, what you said about my sister or your rigid opinion on interior design." He scratched his head. "I guess it's *how* you said it that rankles the most."

Sarah gave an apologetic nod. Luna, who had been fiddling with her handheld device, raised her hand. A generic humanoid hologram projected in front of her, face blank. "Hello," Luna whispered into the device. The hologram gave a perfect rendition of Xylo's movements, the ripple of face twitches and all.

Sarah's grin widened. "Excellent! Luna, that app is far more detailed than the government software. I'd appreciate it if you'd share it with the crew. And thank you very much for volunteering on your day off!" She smiled with confidence before addressing the entire room, saying, "So, who is willing to help find Boomerang Black and make this mission a success?"

Kal shot his hand up to volunteer. Luna raised her hand with a grimace and then crossed her arms over her chest when Sarah turned away.

"You don't want to go?" Kal whispered.

"No. I just started a good book, but I'll get over it," she whispered back.

"But doesn't this sound much more exciting than holing up in your cabin with your handheld?"

Her chilled glare melted to something sinister. "Staying in my cabin would carry a lower risk of additional community service, wouldn't it? I suppose you should know that's why I'm here too—kept kneecapping guys who asked me questions. I thought for sure the stabbing would land me back in prison, but..." She sighed. "Guess they're desperate for help around here."

From her deadpan delivery, it took Kal far too long to realize it was a joke.

Sarah gestured toward Xylo. "All right, crew. Time for Xylo here to unveil his secret weapon for finding our lost

Boomerang Black." Sarah nodded her head toward Kal. "Or should I just call him Boom?"

"Yeah, Boom," Kal said, returning her smile.

"Great. Take it away, Xylo."

Xylo puffed out his chest a little, his mismatched goggles gleaming under the harsh lights. "Thank you, Boss. I'm excited to explain the new tech for this mission. Thanks to some innovative research from Dr..." He paused, consulting his handheld. "... Dr. Helikpeno of Neptune Institute of Bio-Sonics, we have a promising strategy."

Xylo took a few proud steps forward to the front of the galley, cradling a small, open flask in his blue hand. Chef Bluebottle, somehow still fully engrossed in stirring his enormous pot of mystery stew on the other side of the counter, didn't look up as Xylo set down the flask beside the green, vegetable-like dish.

"This," Xylo continued, his voice trembling with excitement, "is an Echoic Aptamer Based Assay, or EABA for short. I built out the nanotech using a sample of Boomerang Black's... uh..." he cleared his throat, "genetic signature."

A collective eyebrow rose from the crew as Xylo held up his flask once more. Kal wondered just what exactly was in that murky brown liquid, but someone else beat him to the question.

"Yes, uh, well," Xylo stammered, "it seems Boom sells a signature perfume with his own pheromones. Every bottle of Pre-Post Drip contains a guaranteed minimum of one drop of his fresh sweat. I was able to sequence his DNA from that." Xylo shrugged, set the flask back down, and then shoved his hands in his pocket. "Apparently, Pre-Post Drip is quite the rage amongst his fans."

Luna, for the first time, looked intrigued, turning to Kal. "You buy any?"

"No," Kal whispered, a bit defensive. "It smells like rotten oranges."

"You know that without buying any?"

Kal shifted in his seat.

"Anyway," Xylo continued, gesturing to the screens above his head, "this EABA will replicate until it comes in contact with more of Boom's DNA. Once it finds enough to give us an error probability under .0001, EABA stops its self-replication cycle and produces a nanoparticle instead. Our sensors at the bridge will detect the signal and allow us to calculate Boom's location."

The main screen showed a video of gleeful scientists pouring EABA into aerosol containers and spraying them over smiling faces in a crowded shopping mall. "EABA is non-toxic, precise, and biodegradable—eventually. Even a breath of air out of Boom's lungs should be enough for EABA to find him. This hasn't been easy to build, but I'm so excited to give this a try!"

Xylo finished with a flourishing gesture to the flask, but his whole body froze when he saw it was no longer sitting on the counter. Chef Bluebottle, at that very moment, was pouring the contents of the flask into the vat of bubbling stew.

Xylo's jaw dropped as the room went silent. "Chef, no!"

"Synthesized Worcestershire sauce is all we got right now," Chef Bluebottle fumed, proceeding to sprinkle a mysterious green powder from a dirty glass shaker into the stew next.

The crowd rumbled. Sarah sighed, her shoulders slumping. The chef looked between Xylo's flask and his sauces. Clearly not up to date with a current retinal-implant prescription, Bluebottle squinted at the bottle from arm's length for a few moments before realizing what he had done. The galley picked up a new odor similar to that of a middle school locker room. It smelled exactly like the bottle of Pre-Post-Drip in Kal's bathroom trash, the bottle he'd only bought to support the cause.

"You said this stuff was non-toxic, right?" said Chef Bluebottle.

☆ ☆ ☆

Luckily, it was. Kal and the rest of the crew were still alive a few hours later when they touched down at Terengal, feeling fine. Although it was approaching the start of his sleep cycle, he felt invigorated as he stepped into the morning breeze to find a vibrant marketplace.

Red-brick construction blended into rusty hillsides among fountains and canals, with flowers blooming along the streets. A kaleidoscope of vendors hawked their wares from the docks and boats in the shallow canals. Doiwze, another native species of the Kepler system, shimmered their iridescent beetle wings next to glowing cacti. Humans and humanoids buzzed with a cacophony of alien languages alongside the many Terengans, who were tall, salamander-like creatures with colorful, sweeping tails.

Terengans never seemed to venture more than a few meters from the water. Some waded through the shallow reflecting pools along the street, their long, flexible limbs leaving ripples in the still water and distorting images of the turquoise sky. Others stayed in their boats piled high with goods, buying and selling everything from seafood to nanoelectronics. Kal listened, transfixed as a cyan Terengan woman hummed tones every few phrases of gestures, the overlapping notes around the market creating a raucous melody.

"Such a beautiful day," Sarah said beside him. Kal and the rest of the eight volunteers turned to listen. "I'll be confirming with the police that all our information on the case is up to date. The rest of you will split up to check the locations in Boom's last video. Pilo, you take the library

with Aramina. Lim and"—she consulted her handheld—
"The-Feeling-Of-Finding-A-Perfect-Curved-Log-For-
Your-Behind-By-A-River-At—" She paused. "Can I call
you River?"

The shimmering four-armed humanoid raised two
sets of eyebrows. "If you don't mind being rude to my
ancestors."

Sarah grimaced, then looked back at her handheld.
"—By-A-River-At-Twilight-When-You-Take-A-Sip-Of-
Cold-Water-After-A-Long-Hike-With-A-Good-Friend."
Sarah drew in a long breath. "You and Lim talk to the staff
at the local toy store." She flicked at her handheld again,
squinting. "I think the police gave us too many locations.
The part of the video where a giraffe ejects a rainbow from
its mouth must be computer-generated content."

"Oh, that's Philip," said Xylo, pushing his hands into
his overalls. "Local legend, great guy. I'd love to talk to
him again."

"Fine," said Sarah. "Tara, go with Xylo. Kal and Luna,
you check the park where Boom rolled all those bat-
tery-operated toy cars into the river."

"He did that to symbolize the negative impact of trace-
metal pollution," Kal clarified, wanting to highlight the
genius of the artist.

Luna didn't react.

Sarah continued on, saying, "There will be some park rangers who should have overlapped with him during the filming and, one would assume, subsequent clean-up efforts."

Luna nodded, not looking at Kal at all while she pulled up the navigation on her handheld.

The noises of the city thinned as Kal and Luna wound through the hilled streets to the park. Everywhere Kal looked, shallow ponds in yards, alleys, and even balconies reflected the cloudless day. Houses thinned and grew larger with each new block. Luna's tattoos seemed to soak up the light, shifting color in the heat. Kal watched a winged horse on her upper arm as its wings' green color morphed to a fiery pink.

"That's some incredible work. Where'd you get that done?" Kal gestured to the tattoo.

"Prison," she muttered.

Kal wasn't the only one to have taken an interest. One brave, blue-skinned Terengan child broke off from a gaggle of kids to run alongside them on shuffling feet, pointing at Luna's inked arms with wide, curious eyes. Luna smiled back at the child, then stopped to kneel at her level while bringing up the translation app. "Can you repeat that, please, friend?" Luna said into the device.

The child beamed, her long tail flushing yellow as she gestured. "Why doesn't it have a horn?"

Luna smiled as bright as the Kepler sun. "Well, this is a Pegasus, not a unicorn. Do you like unicorns better? Even though they can't fly?"

The two kept talking, mirroring joyful expressions as Luna explained the meaning of each symbol on her arm, cooing at every random thing that came out of the kid's mouth. A few minutes later, she caught Kal's gaze long enough for him to gesture with his chin up the street. Luna's smile froze but warmed again when she turned to say goodbye to the girl.

They continued to the park, Luna seeming content to walk in silence.

"Why do you like kids so much?" Kal asked.

She wrinkled her nose at the question—as if he'd asked her if she liked oxygen. "There's no bullcrap with kids. They see the world as it is with a clear conscience. Besides, four-year-olds can learn it's possible to solve their disagreements with words. Most grownups forget that lesson."

"What do you think we're using to rescue Boom if not our words?"

Luna sighed. "Why do you think most of the crew is at a refugee camp? When grownups get big feelings, they do something stupid like kill each other, hoping those feelings ease up. Never mind that it never works. The centuries-old civil war in South Terengal is one of many examples of that." Her brown eyes glittered.

"Not all of us are like that." Kal wiped sweat from his brow.

Luna squinted at him. "What crime did your mom cover up for you? It must be pretty bad if you're being punished instead of simply paying a fine."

Kal's stomach fell under her scrutiny. "It's not that bad."

Luna snorted, a sound devoid of humor. "Tax evasion? Dealing synth to minors?"

Kal choked. "What? No."

Her dark eyes gleamed with predatory menace. "Spying? Intergalactic smuggling? Assassinating a political rival?"

"Seriously, nothing that bad."

Luna raised an eyebrow, then leveled a smug stare until he broke.

"Fine, I... shoplifted a bag of Gummy Worm Sparkle," Kal confessed to the ground.

Luna's smirk faded. "Gummy... what?"

"Gummy Worm Sparkle," Kal mumbled, kicking at a pebble on the road. "They're at just about any corner store in the... less-affluent neighborhoods. My favorite. But my parents—"

A single laugh escaped her lips. Kal stopped talking.

Luna feasted her gaze on him, picking him apart. "You stole candy because you thought Mommy would disapprove? How old are you?"

Kal flushed scarlet. "It's hard to explain. I made a promise. My parents insist on full transparency for everyone who works for the family campaign. Every credit I spend that is not legally mandated to remain private is public record, and my father's assistant monitors it all."

"So? Why would they care about a bag of candy?"

Everyone wanted Kal to suffer for his misdeeds. But after studying Luna's wide brown eyes, Kal found much less vitriol than he expected. None, in fact. It seemed like she genuinely wanted an answer.

He drew in a long breath. "When I was nine, there was an... incident at SNAP, the Sentient Nematode Awareness Parade."

Luna nodded.

"I was caught on camera biting the head off a bunch of those worms while I waved from a float." Kal continued. "Rivals spun that into a political statement against the Ayzierian religion—you know, the primary religion of the greater nematode community..." Kal waited for a gap in her laughter. "Anyway, to prove how sorry I was to my parents for how much trouble that caused them, I promised I'd never touch the stuff again."

"You were a kid! It's not like you knew what you were doing!"

"I did, though. I looked into the camera and winked after every decapitation."

Instead of giving him a look of judgment or disgust, Luna threw her head back with a roar. Kal could only stare, dumbfounded, as the sound of her laughter echoed through the trees in the park.

"Still, why resort to petty theft?" she said, squinting her eyes. "If you can face off a jeering crowd at nine, why not stand up to your mom?"

My mother understands me well enough for her insults to draw blood, he thought. "When I stole the Gummy Sparkle, I might have been... Okay, I *was* drunk. Still, I should have known better. My mother insisted the judge punish me to the full extent of the law, and when the law didn't punish me beyond a fine, she insisted the judge hold me to a higher standard so I'd learn my lesson." Kal let out a long sigh.

"Have you learned anything yet?"

By that point, Kal had reached the river in the video, which had featured an army of drone-controlled mini-vehicles traffic-jammed their way into a watery grave over haunting whistles and heart-beat tempo drums.

"I dunno," Kal said, shifting. "But we have more important things to worry about now."

It was a dead-end. Although the park rangers had insisted Boom clean up his mess, no ranger had seen him helping with any of the efforts, just his staff.

The police had found Boom's empty transport parked several blocks away. To try to salvage something from the day, Kal insisted on taking the long way back. Though if there was a clue on the suburban street and empty parking lot, he couldn't discern what.

Kal couldn't escape that sense of overwhelming defeat on the walk back to the ship. It was an unsettling sensation in his gut that, over the years, had come to be his most loyal friend. Looking over at Luna as they reached the market-place, he saw her hand on her stomach, her steps slowing.

That's when he remembered the stew. As that sensation moved low into his belly, he suspected there was a different explanation than anxiety.

"You feeling alright?" he called to Luna over the noise of the crowd.

She pointed to the huddled and yelling crowd. "I think that's Xylo!"

The crowd of uneasy Terengans nearby were pitching their tones high, their gestures wide and fast enough that even Kal didn't need the app to sense danger. Xylo stood between a burly Terengan with a police sash and an angry mob. A muscular violet Terengan growled at the forefront, whipping her tail. Kal fumbled with his handheld to get the translator up. The violet Terengan woman swiped at Xylo with her tail, pulling him down hard to the ground. Xylo sprawled, goggles askew, as the crowd pressed in.

Kal ran, edging through the bodies to kneel beside Xylo.

"Stay down, kneel, close your eyes," Kal hissed to Xylo. He had learned that much about Terengal diplomacy while preparing for a tense trade treaty several years prior. To de-escalate and apologize, one must lower oneself and close their eyes. It was one of the few things he remembered about the Terengans that seemed to make some sense.

Xylo closed his eyes, rubbing his head. "I need to explain to them!"

"They're too angry to listen. Just stay down," Kal said through gritted teeth, putting his arm over Xylo's shoulders.

The Terengans, their faces contorted in rage, jabbed accusing fingers, waving hands and humming. Once Kal was sure Xylo would remain where he was, he pulled up the translation app, avoiding eye contact all the while.

The slender, violet-skinned Terengan sliced her long tail close to Kal's face with a hiss, and her throat pouch pulsed in fury next to his face. She gestured her arms like skipping pebbles across a stream. "He tried to poison me!" she accused through the app. The bulky Terengan cop barked for her to stay back and let him handle this, his croak booming like a sonic cannon, sending tremors through the ground. Kal hadn't known a Terengan could make a sound that loud.

"He didn't mean it. May we offer you water?" Kal said through the app, digging an unopened bottle out of his pack. He gestured for Xylo to take it.

The violet Terengan blinked, humming low.

Xylo, his goggles dangling by a single strap, grabbed the water and held it up, shivering.

"Pour it on her hand or her arm so she can drink," Kal said.

"Not in this case," Xylo nodded, blinking. The muscled Terengan woman lifted a foot, glaring until Xylo poured the water over it. She seemed to calm down, which surprised Kal—his training for the trade summit had not mentioned anything about feet.

Kal's app buzzed with a cacophony of overlapping phrases from the crowd. Xylo dug in his bag for a second bottle of water, then gestured something that translated to 'I'm very sorry.' The violet Terengan unfurled a series of fluttering hand movements, like ringing a row of bells, indicating her acceptance. With a rumbling croak, the cop dispersed the crowd, including the violet accuser a moment later.

A wave of relief washed over Kal. He looked back to Luna, who was wandering away, one hand still on her stomach.

Kal returned his attention to Xylo. "What happened?"

"I was just trying to ask her about Boom. She was in the video's background behind Philip," Xylo said, hunched with his arms curled around his chest.

Kal took a moment to remember Philip was the sentient giraffe. "And she got that angry just over that?"

"Well, I also threw up on her feet," Xylo said, his already huge eyes widening when he saw Kal's face. "Whatever you do, do not laugh, and keep your arms at your sides."

"Okay." Kal wasn't in the mood to laugh anyway. He wished he still had that bottle of water, beginning to feel dizzy under the Kepler sun.

"How'd you know about the water, Kal?"

"I guess the stuff I picked up half-listening at international war councils is good enough for accidental vomit," Kal said, rather surprised by that. But he also felt some tension roiling in his gut, that lingering anxiety he never could shake.

Nope, that's stew again, he thought. A cold sweat prickled his skin as he looked for the nearest restroom. He followed Xylo as the pair navigated down an ally to the public market restroom. Xylo paused outside the simple outhouse, gasping for breath. Luna was already there, leaning slumped in a chair.

"Are you *sure* that EABA stuff is non-toxic?" Kal bit through his teeth. This was not normal. Judging by how he currently felt, a multitude of angry nanobots were working to embed themselves in his intestines.

Xylo fidgeted with his pockets. "Technically, anything is toxic in high-enough doses."

"Xylo," Luna snarled.

Xylo threw up his arms. "Between the heat of the stew and human stomach acid, I expected the EABA to denature."

Kal made a noise that was something between a laugh and a groan, offering Luna a hand up. To his shock, she accepted it and leaned on him as they walked.

"You said you can turn off the replication cycle, right?" Kal asked.

Xylo cocked his head. "Sure, but it might not do any good now. Is there any biomass left in your digestive tract?

They both stared, dumbfounded and exhausted.

"I suppose I can fire up the computer and check."

☆ ☆ ☆

The harsh fluorescent lights of the bridge felt like a physical assault after the darkness of sleep. Kal winced as he rubbed his temples, taking a long draught of water. In the galley for breakfast, the rest of the crew hadn't looked much better, faces drawn and eyes heavy. Even the normally jovial Sarah Hawkins had a distinct lack of pep in her step that day.

After most of the Blunder's crew had left for the refugee camp, Kal and the others working to rescue Boom met at the bridge to take advantage of the computing powers there, despite the climate control having been out since the installation of the last warp drive. The room felt like a sauna under the Kepler sun. Rivulets of sweat traced paths down Kal's back. Before this mission, he'd thought climate control was as integral as oxygen to a starship, that nothing short of annihilation would disrupt the layered backup circuitry. The *Blunder* was truly a marvel.

"That's unexpected." Xylo tapped away at his handheld, setting it up to project to the main screen.

With bleary eyes, Kal watched a series of flashing lights on the display jiggle around as Xylo mumbled through a statistics report. After a few flicks of Xylo's fingers, the plot rearranged to a shifting heat map.

"Where's the signal coming from?" asked Sarah.

"Everywhere. All over the city, with highest concentrations south and east," Xylo said with a gesture to the map. "But for concentrations like that, I don't understand why we aren't getting a stronger signal."

Sarah leaned forward, brow furrowed. "That should put it four meters below the surface... Underground? How is that possible?"

Xylo froze.

Kal groaned. "The sewers. It's in the sewers."

Sarah gave Kal an assessing glance.

"Do we *need* to go down there?" Kal's stomach was not ready for that just yet, lurching at the thought.

Xylo shook his head. "Presumably, the musician's DNA entered the sewer system in a similar manner to the EABA." Xylo leaned back in his chair, eyes tight with concentration.

"Oh," Kal said, realizing he had deposited some of that EABA himself.

With a start and a few more hand flutters, Xylo overlaid the EABA-density map over what appeared to be a map of the local sewers.

"It's too dispersed. In order to triangulate where Boomerang Black last..." He trailed off. "I need to calculate how fast the water is moving in the main sewage canals."

Kal's face flushed. "So we do need to go down there?"

"What we need down there are trackers," Sarah said, sharing a look with Xylo as he drummed his fingers on the table.

"Low tech, small, easy to fabricate," Xylo confirmed.

Kal bit his lip, sinking into himself a bit, wishing he had something useful to contribute.

Xylo got up to pace the room, hands in his overall pockets. "We'll need to affix them to something that floats, biodegradable. We'll toss them under the manhole covers from different points in the city or flush them down public toilets."

"Popcorn?" Sarah suggested with a smile.

"Perfect. Popcorn and a little waterproof adhesive." Xylo drew his hands down his shiny blue face. "We should account for variability. The sewers might flow at different speeds at different hours of the day."

"Good point. We'll need to drop our trackers en masse as close as possible to the time you first deposited the EABA," Sarah said, taking sewer-popcorn triangulation in stride, apparently.

Kal looked at his handheld. "That gives us eight hours."

"Let's be ready to move in five. Releasing the trackers might take a good part of the day."

"Yes, Boss," Xylo said, bringing up the interface to the fabricator on the main screen.

Kal leaned over to Sarah. "What should we tell people who ask why we're throwing popcorn in sewers? Police in particular."

Sarah bit her lip. "Act casual. Be polite and vague, and if necessary, direct them to me. The longer Boomerang Black is missing, the less likely we'll find him alive and well."

Kal nodded.

"I'll make two thousand trackers, just in case." Xylo gestured to the map, pointing out the first few of what must be close to a thousand sewer lines. "The more we can map, the better. And we should double up wherever we can, releasing upstream and downstream on the same line to ensure we miss nothing."

"Two thousand. Won't we need the full crew to drop that many?" Kal said, squinting between the map and Sarah. "Are you sure this plan will work?"

The twinkle in Sarah's eyes seemed to suggest anything was possible.

☆ ☆ ☆

Kal had expected the preschool to smell like potty training and spilled sippy cups, but he found it clean, organized, fresh-smelling, and bright. Kal leaned over the half-door leading to the daycare, where the least colorful feature in the room was Luna herself. She wore her usual black dress and sat at the center of a circle of toddlers with a large picture book in hand. She must have seen him by now, but she kept reading. Kal got lost in her cadence as she agreed, in her squeaky mouse voice, to gnaw through a rope net to free a tiger.

"May I help you?" she asked a moment later in a tone so feral that Kal at first thought the question came from the tiger in the story. She was looking at him, though, black-painted lips pursed.

Kal's eyes gleamed, holding up several bags of popcorn and a sheet of adhesive trackers. "It's for the mission. Do you think your toddler battalion can help me apply two thousand stickers to some popcorn?"

"Cheesy popcorn?! Best day ever!" one kid screamed over the onslaught of high-pitched cheers.

Luna blinked at him before returning his smile and walking over.

"Sounds like a great way to develop hand-eye coordination." She scanned the children. "Let's all sit down at our tables, friends! Snack-time first. Sticker when you all are full."

☆ ☆ ☆

When it was time to toss popcorn down sewer cleanouts, Sarah Hawkins paired Kal with The-Feeling-Of-Finding-A-Perfect-Curved-Log-For-Your-Behind-By-A-River-At-Twilight-When-You-Take-A-Sip-Of-Cold-Water-After-A-Long-Hike-With-A-Good-Friend, who turned out to be a friendly guy.

Kal learned that in his partner's language, his name only had three syllables. Since Kal could not pronounce those syllables, he recorded the name on his handheld, ready to use the next time he needed to get his partner's attention. Kal also learned the 'good-friend' part of that name was important to denote realistic expectations for a child. All that brilliance with a *best* friend would be too much to grow into, like naming your kid after a god.

Although Kal coaxed several smiles out of his new partner, his colleague stuck to short, courteous replies and only asked a few simple questions about Kal as they walked their route. Tired of carrying the entire conversation, Kal let the silent stretches grow, the words between them draining away, much like the brown water in so many of those sewer lines.

He missed Luna.

Hours later, Kal wondered if his partner had an opinion on Pegasi vs. Unicorns but refrained from asking. Of course he agreed with Luna: Pegasi were, obviously and axiomatically, more awesome.

His thoughts cleared with the buzz of his handheld.

<<Found him. Great job, team! Refugee group can return to the *Blunder*. Mission team, meet here.>>

The message from Sarah Hawkins included coordinates east of the city.

☆ ☆ ☆

Kal and his long-named partner took public transport as far as it would go toward the Terengal monastery, then walked the last kilometer between mossy rock gardens and a maze of ponds. On both sides of the mud-brick path, water lilies floated atop still water with gold and pink kelp fluttering just below the surface. Rusty desert stretched out beyond the edges of the oasis, harsh and windy.

The mission team, eight in all, gathered in the courtyard just outside the monastery's gate. Kal looked up to see Luna. He tried to hide his bursting enthusiasm when she walked his way, then quickly felt silly for attempting to play cool. In that moment, he decided not to dim a smile for her ever again.

She narrowed her eyes at him before he caught a ghost of a smile in return.

The monastery, a rugged monolith of ochre stone, seemed to absorb sound itself. Kal whispered, "I thought you'd be wiped after Heimlich-maneuvering a tracker from your second toddler today. You still have energy for your second job?"

"Do you have the energy for this job? This is your first *real* job—the ones where Mommy was the boss don't count," Luna said.

Kal's eyes glittered. "The work environment is a little more toxic than I'm used to," he lied. "It seems I should expect constant ridicule around here." Kal gestured his head toward the weathered stone building, his jaw tightening. "I just hope he's in there."

Xylo arrived with Sarah a few minutes later, and the group entered the gate.

Kal didn't know enough about Terengal tech to decipher how the gardens outside were so silent even when the path to the door filled him soul-deep with the sound of low chanting, too slow to be music and too rich to be much else.

Following Sarah's lead, they entered the main hall. Water trickled over the moss-carpeted floor as robed Terengans sat in silent clusters, eyes closed. No humans or other tourists were among them. None of the Terengan priests so much as looked up. Anxiety gnawed at Kal as they walked to the door at the far end of the chamber.

Beyond the creaking door lay a serene courtyard bathed in the golden light of a broad setting sun. In the center, by a reflecting pool that mirrored the fiery sky, sat a solitary human figure, back turned. Kal was enough of a fan to immediately recognize Boom's spiky black and metallic hair.

"Boomerang Black?" Sarah called out. "Is that you?"

"Yeah, that's Boom," Kal said when Boom proceeded to ignore them. The musician tensed, then took a long breath. Boom let the silence build, his back still turned with his signature keyboard in front of him. On the walls of the courtyard, Kal noted an array of mounted cameras.

After exchanging glances, the *Blunder* crew inched forward, hopping across a narrow channel of water bisecting the greenery between reflecting pools. Sarah knelt to face the musician. Kal did the same.

"Boomerang Black," Sarah said. "There's a missing-person's report filed for you. Many people are worried about you."

Boom opened his eyes with a sigh, his face serene.

"Glad to know you're okay," Kal whispered. "I'm a big fan."

Boom turned to Kal, his face lighting up. "For finding me, this next song is dedicated to you."

Kal beamed.

"We're here to escort you to the Neptune Embassy," Sarah continued.

Boom gestured in a sweeping arc, tilting his head down in Terengali gestures.

" 'No,' " Xylo translated, then turned back to Boom. "Why no?"

Boom closed his eyes and straightened his posture, shivering then flapping a hand by his ear.

" 'Just listen,' " Xylo translated.

Boom's fingers counted down to the handheld clipped atop his keyboard. Three. Two. One. The keyboard began playing a programmed melody.

Kal hadn't heard anything like the tones that filled the air, soaking through him from lungs to bones. Ethereal, slow, and haunting, the music seemed to emanate from the rusty stones beneath their feet just as much as the keyboard.

Boom, eyes closed in a state of deep meditation, swept his arms up in an arc as he stood. His body became an instrument, weaving a tapestry of gestures that flowed with an unexpected grace. Xylo translated, his tone still and reverent:

Does the first raindrop embody the monsoon or the last?
A tadpole opens her eyes to change the world.
The flicker of her tail is a change, but will that be enough?
In her pond, irradiated to the brink of death, would surviving
*   be enough?*
Would you tell the nine that float in death that their life
*   meant nothing?*

Boom pointed a dramatic hand at the sky, then mimed what Kal imagined to be a fistfight with a cactus. Boom lost the battle, collapsing on the ground.

We build foundations deep and stony to protect ourselves
*   from the indifferent earth.*
We build our walls high in our minds to protect ourselves
*   from words that never become sound.*
In each moment we stop to feel the sun, we live.
I live for each smile.

*I live for the heartbreak that reminds me I have a heart
to break.*

Boom looked around the garden, making eye contact
with everyone.

*We do not die for victory; we die in spite of it, in each triumph
we choose for ourselves.*

The music shifted. Boomerang Black's dance became
fluid and purposeful. His hands painted stories in the air,
his body a vessel for a silent symphony. The gestures in the
rap moved too fast for Xylo's translation now. Kal brought
out his handheld and earpiece and let the translator app
capture the rest.

The lyrics and music crashed through Kal in resounding
waves. The song spoke of finding peace within the storm,
of harnessing the power of silence, and of a happiness that
transcended the external world. Each moment of con-
sciousness was a gift he'd never asked for. Each second alive,
no matter how tragic, transcended the void of non-being.

Kal looked around the courtyard, so much smaller than
it was a moment ago, which made him feel closer to the
people around him. Sarah's eyes shone wet. Luna stared
wide-eyed in the shadow of Boom's graceful dance. Kal's
heart bloomed like a flower—no, in that moment, he felt

like that giraffe opening its mouth on screen to release a rainbow.

The music swelled, and his gestures became a frantic search, connecting with each person in the room as Boom assured them that their life mattered and their efforts made a difference. He held Kal's gaze until Kal truly believed him, not just pretended to. Boom followed up with a triumphant flourish as he cupped his hands to his chest, encouraging everyone around him to discover the source of happiness and the heart of the universe within themselves.

Raw emotion lingered in the air as the music faded. Kal's breath hitched in his throat. He felt vulnerable and spiritually naked. Sarah wiped away tears.

"Thank you," Sarah said, sniffling. "After so many disappointments, the problems we seem to make worse—" her voice broke on that, so Boom waited for her to recover, eyes intent. "I really needed to hear that."

Boom closed his eyes with a nod, raising a single hand, a tear tracing a glistening path down his face. With a final flourish, he collected the tear in a small vial.

Not just a vial. A cologne bottle with a colorful label.

"Enlightenment Drip," Luna whispered beside him, voice flat, reading from the branding images that were now projected around the monastery walls.

Boomerang Black grinned and swept his arm to the screen. "Enlightenment Drip is my latest pheromone perfume that is guaranteed to help you find both inner peace and a date, in that order."

★ ★ ☆

The harsh desert wind whipped through the oasis after sunset as the group shuffled back down the path toward the transport stop. Xylo, his brow furrowed, glanced at Sarah. "Think we'll get any reward out of this? We still technically tracked him down."

"He live-streamed all of that. He's not missing anymore," Kal said, running his hand through his short, dark hair. The cool chill mirrored the renewed sense of emptiness that had come back to him the moment he saw that stupid cologne bottle.

Sarah sighed. "I'll draw up the report. Perhaps the embassy will throw us a bone."

The surrounding pond came alive with frog songs and the chirping of insects.

"It isn't a bad song if you can forget he's full of crap," Luna said.

Xylo and The-Feeling-Of-Finding-A-Perfect-Curved-Log-For-Your-Behind-By-A-River-At-Twilight-When-You-Take-A-Sip-Of-Cold-Water-After-A-Long-Hike-With-A-Good-Friend laughed.

Sarah gestured back to desert twilight with a smile. "That song reminded me of how proud I am of all of you, working so well together, and how wonderful the universe really is. I'm not sure which I find more beautiful," she said, looking out across the hills.

Kal took a deep breath of fresh air too, deciding to let that be enough to feel the peace of the place. It really was a gorgeous sunset, somehow more beautiful when reflected in Sarah's eyes.

Back in the market, Kal turned to find Luna, only to spot her disappearing around a corner.

"I'll see you back at the ship, Luna!" Sarah called back, continuing to walk away with Xylo and the rest. Kal debated with himself, deciding to wait for her even though she hadn't asked anyone to stay behind. Signs winked on in the cool desert air as the city came alive for the night. A crowd of Terengans meandered past toward a booming bar down the street.

Just when Kal was starting to wonder if Luna had taken another route home—or worse yet, took a different route home just to avoid him—she emerged with a mischievous glint in her brown eyes and a small, multicolored bag clutched in her hand. He instantly recognized the packaging.

"They sell Gummy Worm Sparkle on Terengal?" Kal stared open-mouthed when Luna tossed him the bag.

Luna smirked. "You're actually a good team player. You deserve a reward."

Kal raised an eyebrow and crossed his arms. "Bullcrap."

"It's not. Between helping Xylo, saving that third choking toddler while I was busy with the second, and being the one to get Boom to talk to us, you've done amazing work on your first few days here. Too bad you won't be on *Blunder* long."

A warmth spread through Kal as he studied her face. She meant that.

"I will not be thanking you for getting that free crate of Enlightenment Drip from Boom, though," she said, crossing her arms over her chest.

"Maybe we can resell it?"

"Maybe."

Kal opened the bag as the crowd drifted by, offering her the first. "You ever try these?"

Luna picked up a sparkling gummy, which burst out phosphorescent light in her mouth, bringing the only color to her features. "Tingly, weird, and delightful," she concluded. "*Totally* worth enraging your mother."

Kal frowned. In two weeks, he'd have to face his mother again back on Neptune. He'd be able to see his friends, people who only praised him and never accused him of intergalactic smuggling. They were, after all, people who saw him as a political connection first, a friend second. Perhaps it was dangerous to see him any other way—or maybe they weren't friends at all.

He didn't realize until too late that he'd been staring at Luna.

"What?" she said.

Kal grinned. "I'm a square peg my parents have been trying to squeeze into a round hole for far too long. If it's inevitable that I'll disappoint them, perhaps I'm better off doing that away from Neptune."

She cocked her head at that. "You're thinking of signing on?"

"Yeah," Kal said with an exhale, holding up the bag of candy. "The bribes around here are too good to pass up."

MURDER IN THE DINING HALL

Mac King

orn on Pluto in the Stardate 1986, the future sheriff was named DaBears by his parents, who had met in the Earth city of Chicago. Sheriff Kojak began his professional career with the star of the fleet, the *Starship Prime*. As a new security officer, the young man had cut an impressive figure in his black pants and red shirt. DaBears looked the part of a true professional, unfortunately, his work never matched his self-vision.

During the first half of his security career, during their extensive downtime, the security members enjoyed watching old TV shows from planet Earth. They were especially drawn to shows stored under the title of Police Procedurals.

While other security members recognized the entertainment value of the shows, DaBears mistakenly interpreted the labeling of the genre to mean that the fictional police dramas were actual training videos. His favorite ways to train included watching Adam-12, Dragnet, Kojak, and even one he found a bit unorthodox called Dirty Harry.

Normally, the redshirts downed beers and horsed around while watching the shows. Not DaBears—he sat alone, attentively taking notes.

Poor performance did not stop DaBears from gaining rank in the security forces. These promotions were not due to any demonstrated leadership skills but solely due to the disproportionally high number of casualties suffered by his redshirted peers. DaBears's survival in those deadly situations was attributed by his superiors to either divine intervention or dumb luck.

During one such event, as his team confronted a hostile force on the Xinc satellite of Jupiter, DaBears tripped over a rock. His backward fall ended at the base of a five-foot ditch. Moments later, his position in the ditch protected him from the sonic grenade that eliminated all seven of his teammates.

Seeing a chance to rid themselves of their Gomer Pyle impersonator, his supervisor arranged fot a promotion for DaBears that sent him packing. It transferred him not only off the *Prime* but jettisoned him to a small outpost near the South Pole of Uranus. If the forever-ice environment was not enough of a punishment, his posting occurred at the mid-point of Uranus' forty-two-Earth-year period of total darkness.

If not for repeated watching of the "training videos" DaBears had taken with him from the *Prime*, he may have totally lost his mind. Instead, four years later, he emerged only slightly altered.

As often happened to DaBears, the stars lined up in his favor. When the Star Fleet closed the Uranus outpost, it needed a security leader for the *Blunder*. That starship's operational rating placed it in the lowest tier. Since no one else had applied for the position, DaBears won the slot.

Arriving at the gate to the *Blunder* minutes before his first mission, DaBears skillfully sidestepped the spaceport's Administrative Officer's questioning of his name.

"Hold on a minute," the puzzled administrator had commanded. "These orders are for a man named DaBears, yet your name tag and signature indicate you're Kojak." The little creature from Mars turned a darker shade of green, reminding Kojak of how his supervisor on *Prime* turned red whenever Kojak messed up.

"As I told you, because of my ability to successfully solve complex crimes during my tenure on Uranus, the Conglomeracy approved my name change in honor of one of the most brilliant detectives in law-enforcement history."

Hearing the final announcement of "Ship door closing in thirty seconds," the flustered Martian had approved the documents and shoved him in as the last member to board the *Blunder*.

"Good luck," he'd shouted after Kojak as the airlock had closed behind him. Then mumbled to himself, "You'll need it on the *Blunder*."

☆ ☆ ☆

Having reinvented himself as Sheriff Kojak, the ship's security director fully embraced the role. That included wearing a cowboy hat on his freshly shaved head and sucking on lollipops. On an average-sized human, the cowboy hat would have been impractical to wear within the tight confines of the *Blunder*, but at 5'1", the Sheriff was at no risk of bumping it into the ceiling.

Even though the *Blunder* was one of the smallest starships in the fleet, Kojak buzzed the corridors of the ship on a personal transporter that he'd repainted to reflect the black-and-white pattern he remembered from the old police videos. In another departure from standard Conglomeracy protocol, Kojak had switched the radio call signs. The first digit reflected their rank, but the remainder of the radio identifier mystified everyone but Kojak. He never explained it, but Kojak always grinned when they called, and he answered, "1 Adam 12."

☆ ☆ ☆

Starship Blunder cruised through space for another mission. Their destination was Hydra, the third moon of Pluto. Mishaps began immediately upon their ceremonial arrival. In front of the host moon's leaders, the starship's landing navigation system had misidentified the designated touchdown pad. Settling too close to the welcoming delegation, the spray from its thrusters coated the hosts in bluish-gray surface dust.

That was just the beginning of trouble. The low point of the operation occurred during the final diplomatic session between the ambassador of Hydra and Jordon Jackson, the Conglomeracy's rookie diplomat. Seated in the back of the conference room and bored by the six-hour negotiation, one of *Starship Blunder's* security team had been toying with his laser pistol. While flippantly reholstering the weapon, he discharged a single heat bolt.

Luckily, the laser was pointed at the floor and not at any of the Hydra staff seated nearby. Unluckily for the security officer, before the heat bolt impacted the floor, it went straight through his right foot, dispatching a toe into a galaxy far, far away.

The situation could have escalated into a full-blown disaster. Present during the misfire, Pilot Sarah Hawkins immediately calmed the situation—claiming the misfire was simply a drill—and containing what could have been an all-out firefight between the two delegations.

Several hours later, a sense of relief settled over the crew as *Starship Blunder* accelerated into its top inter-planet cruising speed. Exhausted and facing a seven-day travel time back to Neptune, most of the starship's leadership team retreated to their pods to sleep. Per their operational orders, only a skeleton group remained on duty to support the ship's functions. Sheriff Kojak took the first watch for the executive team.

☆ ☆ ☆

Two days into their return to Neptune, Chef Bluebottle walked out of the kitchen into the dining hall, seeking praise for his latest creation. "How do you like my fish dish?" he asked the navigation officers, who were busy munching on their dinners.

Most were kind enough not to reply, but the youngest asked, "You want the truth?"

Showing that he did not, Chef Bluebottle shuffled over to the next table where Xylo, the ship's engineer from Zentara, sat and repeated his question. Xylo asked, "Cook, why do you keep asking when you never get an answer you like?"

Bluebottle narrowed his already small eyes. "Xylo, I am a chef, not merely a cook. I am tired of your insults." He then approached the final table and repeated his plea for affirmation.

Four of the five crewmembers seated before him wore matching tight red shirts with laser pistols on their belts. The fifth sported a large white cowboy hat with a holster that contained a bulky old-school revolver.

Sheriff Kojak answered for the group: "Bluebottle, why the heck did you serve it with the four eyes still in it?"

The Chef had clearly expected this negative reply from the Sheriff. "Kojak, you have no taste for the finer foods in our galaxy. This dish is considered a delicacy on Hydra. I obtained these rare fish from Hydra's head chef during our visit."

"That explains it, then," Kojak said, pushing his plate away. "The Hydra chef pranked you because of the *Blunder's embarrassing* miscalculation during our landing. This fish is probably toxic."

"There you go with another one of your poison theories. Can't you think of any other conspiracy?" When Bluebottle did not get a reply, he turned and walked back into the kitchen.

☆ ☆ ☆

The next day, while patrolling the starship while the others slept, the sheriff craved a snack. Stepping off his black-and-white transporter, he entered the dining hall so intently focused on finding a Twinkie that he casually stepped over the two legs protruding out from underneath one of the tables. After locating the sweet golden treat, he turned and noticed the pair of size-twenty boots attached to the unique long grey overalls worn by the ship's mechanic.

Xylo was on his back, head tilted slightly to his right with a greenish-yellowish liquid puddling on the floor near his open mouth. Kojak noted that the crew member, a native of planet Zentara, was not breathing, and his slender body felt frozen. The sheriff called Xylo's name but received no response.

"1 Adam 12 to control, wake up all the security team and have them report to me in the dining hall right now."

The control operator seemed to sense a nervousness in the Sheriff's voice and asked, "Is everything okay, 1 Adam 12?"

"The situation is under control. Just send my team."

"Electronic requests are being sent out now, Sheriff."

☆ ☆ ☆

As his team arrived, Kojak refused to permit them inside the Dining Hall. He needed to show them that he took maintaining the crime scene seriously. He did not want his men to botch this scene like they did on the last one... and the one before that. Due to those previous errors, Kojak decided he would serve as the lead CSI investigator.

Although he had not received any formal crime-scene training, he had viewed several seasons of CSI Miami.

Addressing his redshirts, Kojak said, "I have examined the body of Xylo and determined that he died of food poisoning. I don't know yet if it was intentional, but I want three of you to take Chef Bluebottle into custody. If he offers any resistance, you are authorized a level-two stun."

As three redshirts left for Bluebottle's living quarters, Kojak assigned his second in command to awaken Pilot Hawkins and bring her to the crime scene.

The pilot arrived at the entrance to the dining hall five minutes later. "Sheriff Kojak, what's this I hear about a murder?"

"Come with me, ma'am," he said, leading her into the room. "Be careful where you step. I believe I collected all the evidence, but I haven't pronounced the area clear yet." He sucked hard on his lollipop.

Standing over the body, Sheriff Kojak assured Pilot Sarah Hawkins he had the case solved. "I've ordered Chef Bluebottle arrested for the murder. My men tell me he resisted, so they had to stun him a few times. He is currently in the medical unit under guard."

"How do you know Bluebottle is the murderer?" She asked.

"The entire crew knew the two argued almost every day. I believe he poisoned Xylo, and the poisoning was intentional, not simply one of Chef Bluebottle's recipes gone wrong."

"When did this happen? How long has Xylo been dead?" the Pilot asked.

"I don't know exactly. But the body is cold," answered Kojak.

"Cold? Aliens from Zentara have a normal body temperature of 21.3 degrees Celsius. Is he colder than that?"

Kojak widened his eyes and felt his forehead wrinkled. "I don't know, ma'am. I never took his temperature. He was cold to the touch, so I figured he'd been dead for a few hours. I didn't know Xylo's species had such a low body temperature."

Sarah's tone didn't disguise her frustration as she asked, "Sheriff Kojak... are you sure Xylo is dead?"

The sheriff straightened up and said, "Of course, Ma'am. He isn't breathing!"

Her face reddened, and she bent down and roughly shook the prone alien.

Xylo immediately opened his eyes and sat up. He began mumbling but was interrupted by a wide yawn. A strong odor of the cheap alcohol favored by the crew filled the area. Then he blinked twice and said, "What's goin' on? Can't a Zentaran down a few? Or maybe more than a few?"

"What are you doing on the floor?" demanded the angry sheriff.

"I don't know. Last I remember, I was drinking alone at that table. I guess I must have passed out."

"But you weren't breathing," an embarrassed Kojak barked as the lollipop broke in his mouth.

While Xylo chuckled, Pilot Hawkins said, "That's because when Zentaran bodies are in the resting stage, they completely shut down to conserve energy."

Eyes downcast, Kojak made out laughter coming from the hallway where his redshirts stood.

CRASH COURSE NEGOTIATIONS

By Beth Martin

Jordan Jackson adjusted his navy flight jacket as he looked around the career fair. Temporary tables with fabulous motion displays, eye-catching demonstrations, and enthusiastic recruiters crowded the Neptune University Student Center. With his graduation quickly approaching, Jordan desperately needed to find a job, especially considering his new responsibility of providing for his little sister.

"Hello, young man," a tall, beastly alien covered in brown fur greeted him with a much-too-firm handshake. "Have you ever considered a career with the Sovereign Stellar Federation?"

Jordan's sister ducked behind him, grasping his jacket with her fists. "It's alright, Candace," he said, guiding his sister to stand beside him while mussing her head. Little beads adorning her braids rattled against each other as they swung from his gesture. They both had thick, textured black hair, but he kept his cut short. "No one is here to hurt you," he added.

He directed his attention back at the hairy alien and responded, "Not really. Do they have openings for diplomats? I'm getting my bachelor's in interstellar affairs next week."

"Congratulations on your upcoming graduation!" The alien gave Jordan another palm-crushing handshake before continuing, "The Sovereign Stellar Federation hires several analysts every year, and after a few years of experience, you certainly could move up the ranks and eventually become a diplomat."

Jordan deflated. His aunt had warned him that his degree would only lead to a tedious analyst job, but he'd held out hope that something more exciting would become available. He wanted to travel through space and explore new worlds, not warm a desk chair in an office building.

An incredibly tall woman with a bulky frame, pale skin, and limp, blond, shoulder-length hair wearing a generic black flight suit elbowed her way into the conversation. "Pardon me," she declared in a deep baritone voice, "My name is Greta Eriksson-Byström and I'm a starship commander representing the Conglomeracy. I couldn't help but overhear—you're interested in a job as a diplomat?"

Jordan immediately perked up, and Candace grasped his hand and began jumping in place. "Yes, I'm Jordan Jackson. I'm getting my degree—"

"Come with me," the woman said, leading him through the throng of people to a less-crowded area of the student center. In the back corner sat a table with no tablecloth or adornments. A cardboard display similar to the type children used for school projects stood in the center.

"Hiring funny diplomat," Jordan said, reading the handwritten heading from the board.

"It's... uh... Funjy," the woman corrected. "I need a diplomat to negotiate with the Funjy alien tribe on my starship's next mission to Tokinokin. The Conglomeracy plans to initiate a trade alliance."

Jordan recalled what he'd learned about the various alien peoples in his coursework. The Funjy were a group of aliens who lived on the nearby planet Tokinokin, although they also had a secondary planet they used, which had a secret location. Both planets contained a rich supply of rare metals, which they used to make tall ceremonial structures. These structures could statically boost multi-frequency communication waves and were sought after by all the space factions.

"Wow, that's a huge deal," Jordan said. "The Funjy are notoriously difficult to negotiate with. They haven't signed a trading alliance for well over 100 years."

"You are correct," the woman agreed, nodding her head vigorously. "Most people just skip Tokinokin when making trade deals. But we're thinking a face-to-face meeting might prove successful. And we could really use someone young and enthusiastic like yourself. Now, this is a one-time gig and not full-time employment, but the mission will look *great* on your resumé. What do you say? Are you in?"

He looked down at Candace, who was shaking his hand while nodding and chanting, "Do it! Do it! Do it!"

"I'd have to take my sister along," he replied hesitantly.

"My ship is outfitted with a wonderful, functional day-care facility."

"Do it," Candace pleaded.

"Okay," he confirmed, nodding first at Candace and then at the enormous ship commander. She flashed a wide smile, and he couldn't help but smile back. "I'll be your Funjy diplomat."

"Great!" She gave him a tight, fast handshake. "Welcome to the *Starship Blunder* crew!"

He hesitated for a second—he was unfamiliar with that starship—then took a deep breath and smiled again, sure everything would be fine.

✧ ✧ ✧

Jordan was pleasantly surprised by how seamlessly the pieces fell into place for his first real job. However, he should have researched the *Starship Blunder* ahead of time and was sorely disappointed the first time he saw the ship.

Instead of hovering next to the gangway like the other interstellar vessels, the *Starship Blunder* was perched slightly askew on rickety legs. The exterior of the ship consisted of patches of differently textured and colored metal sheets that had been haphazardly riveted together, giving the impression of an old, worn patchwork quilt—nothing like the smooth, shiny hulls of the other starships awaiting their next missions. Considering its size, it likely housed a skeleton crew. Jordan guessed the *Blunder* held a hundred people, max.

"Does it fly?" Candace asked as she dropped her backpack onto the ground.

"Gosh, I hope so," Jordan replied, eyeing the rusty amalgamation of parts. "You need help with that?" he added, pointing to her bag.

"Yeah," she said, kicking the pink backpack toward him.

He shifted his duffle bag to one arm and grabbed his sister's pack with the other. Although his missions would likely take several weeks, Jordan and his sister didn't own much clothing, so their possessions fit in two bags.

A strange-looking blue-and-gray alien wearing coveralls greeted them as they boarded the ship. The compact hull required Jordan to both step high over the raised threshold and duck at the same time to pass through. He made sure Candace entered before navigating through the narrow hallways. The interior of the ship reminded him of a construction site where the primary structure had been erected and none of the finishing work had taken place. Exposed pipes and loose wires decorated the hallways. In some areas, the plastic slabs that made the surface of the walls sat loose on the floor, leaning against where they should have been fixed.

The two siblings found the tight room they would share among the crew quarters. A cot and dresser sat on the right side of the room, and the left contained a wardrobe next to a desk with a thin mattress bunked above it.

"Home sweet home!" Candace declared before plopping down on the cot. "This is my bed."

Jordan dropped the bags on the floor. "Guess I get the top bunk," he muttered. "Why don't we check out the daycare where you'll spend most of your time while I'm negotiating with the Funjy."

"Okay!" Candace said as she hopped up.

There were so many turns through the hallways that they got lost trying to find their way out of the crew quarters. Eventually, they found the school and daycare center.

The starship daycare resembled his university's, except everything was older. Tired toys and banged-up picture books lined bowing wooden shelves. A few human children and two small aliens were already playing with blocks on the colorful-but-stained carpet.

A young woman with pale skin and dark hair dressed in all black approached Jordan. He found her black lipstick and dark eye makeup off-putting and had to try his best not to stare. "This, uh, is my sister, Candace," he stammered.

"Hello, Candace," the woman responded, her tone surprisingly warm. "It's a pleasure to meet you. My name is Miss Luna, and I'll be your teacher while you're on this ship. I like your pink shirt. Is pink your favorite color?

"Yes!" Candace declared proudly, pulling on her shirt to show off the graphic on the front. "I like unicorns too!"

"I have a book about unicorns and dragons. Can you help me find it? It's on one of these shelves."

"Sure!" Candace skipped to the bookshelf and searched for the aforementioned mythical-creature book.

Luna directed her attention to Jordan and recited the daycare rules in a monotone voice: "School starts promptly at eight AM every morning, and pickup is from five-thirty to seven in the evening. You must check Candace in and out by signing this sheet." She picked up a clipboard hanging on a hook on the wall.

"The university daycare used a retina scanner. That would be much more secure—" Jordan began explaining.

"That's awfully presumptuous of you, assuming all care-givers have eyes."

"Oh! They don't? I... uh..."

"They do. That was a joke." However, she didn't laugh or smile, making Jordan even more uncomfortable. He was growing less at ease with the thought of leaving his sister here under this strange woman's care.

"I found the book," Candace said, bounding back to the pair while holding up a book with a large picture of a dragon, unicorn, and mermaid on the cover. "Isn't she pretty?" she asked, looking back at the cover. Jordan found the mermaid terrifying, with gills on her neck and large, sharp teeth.

"Very pretty and fierce!" Luna responded. "Mermaids are strong creatures. They can make entire boats sink."

"Uh, we should go," Jordan stammered.

"But I want to stay," Candace said with a pout.

"Everyone will need to sit down and strap in for take-off," Miss Luna explained. "I also need to go somewhere else, but I'll see you here again in a few days when your brother has to work."

"Okay, bye!" Candace said as Jordan grasped her hand and led her away from the school and residences. "I like her," she added.

"You don't think she looks a little scary?" he asked.

"No. *You* look scary." She giggled before skipping ahead.

☆ ☆ ☆

Having never experienced a lift-off before, Jordan and Candace found the starship's departure from Neptune quite thrilling. The pilot, Sarah Hawkins, even offered the pair prime seating on the bridge during the launch, so Jordan got to see the cloudy skies part to reveal multitudes of stars as they thrust away from the small planet.

The voyage to Tokinokin would take several days. Jordan didn't mind hanging out with his kid sister, but Candace adored Miss Luna and insisted on spending as much time at the daycare as possible. Feeling lonely studying the history of trade negotiations with the Funjy by himself in his cabin, Jordan loaded his references onto a computer tablet and brought it with him to the dining hall. Even though it was between mealtimes, the strange alien mechanic Xylo and a handful of other crewmates were already there.

They all sat around one of the tables, playing cards, reading, and fiddling around with technology Jordan didn't recognize. "What are you making?" Jordan asked the silver-blue alien, gesturing at the electronic gizmo in the mechanic's hands. He had tools and electronic components strewn on the table in front of him, including an LCD display the size of a dinner plate and a few lightbulbs.

"It's a multi-frequency communications-wave detector," Xylo explained. He grabbed his screwdriver and began stabbing at a bolt, realized he had the wrong tool, and switched to a wrench.

Jordan took a seat next to a man with blond hair flipping through a beat-up novel, who interjected, "Xylo can't fix anything, let alone invent tech that can do something useful. He's just making a glorified night light."

"It will light up, yes," Xylo admitted, "but if I do this right, the color should change depending on whether or not the detector is within close range of one of those Funjy statues."

A woman wearing tan medical scrubs snickered before addressing the lead mechanic. "Will it be the same color change as the last indicator you 'invented'?" she asked, using her fingers for air quotes. "Changing from amber to yellow-orange?"

"How was I supposed to know those were basically the same color!" the alien retorted defensively as everyone laughed. Even Jordan couldn't help but chuckle along with the crew.

"I gotta get back to work," the woman added, giving the group a casual salute before departing.

The silver-blue alien grabbed the soldering iron from among the tools on the table and started melting wires together. Suddenly, a lightbulb on the device flashed briefly before exploding with a sharp *pop*.

Jordan let out a yell and quickly jumped back in his seat, but the rest of the crew seemed unfazed by the loud interruption.

"Don't worry, kid," the blond man next to him said, turning a page in his book. "You get used to random explosions after a while on this ship."

★ ★ ★

How did this happen? Jordan thought to himself. He had only been on the starship for a few days, and Candace had already befriended most of the crew and had also orchestrated a date between him and Luna. How, he wasn't sure, since he got the distinct impression the daycare teacher could barely tolerate him.

Candace brought her pink backpack, which held a few borrowed toys from the daycare center. She skipped through the halls from the crew quarters to the dining hall, Jordan close behind.

"You seem excited," he pointed out.

"You should be excited too!" Candace said gleefully, swinging her arms into the air as she bounded forward. "Miss Luna is great! I wish I could come with you!"

He wished she could, too.

When they arrived at the dining hall, the room was packed with crewmates grabbing dinner. He easily spotted the pilot, who wore a bright purple flight suit, and a few other staff at a nearby table. Pilot Sarah Hawkins called out, "Hey, girlfriend!" to Candace.

"Hi!" the little girl squealed as she raced to join the purple-clad pilot and give her a big hug.

Jordan hadn't even noticed Luna was already there, but suddenly she was right next to him, holding up a large wicker picnic basket. "Greetings, Jordan Jackson."

He almost jumped back but gathered himself. "Oh! Hello, Miss Luna. I didn't see you there." Indeed, she blended in with the shadows with her dark dress and black leggings. She dressed similarly to how she did for teaching but still looked nice. Jordan had attempted to spiff up his appearance for the occasion, wearing his navy flight jacket over his regular clothes and gelling his black hair.

"Where would you like to sit?" he asked, gesturing at the various tables of the dining hall.

"Oh, we're not staying here. I've reserved the hologram hall so we can isolate ourselves from the others."

"I, uh..." he started to reply, concerned that maybe she wanted the privacy to murder him. "I shouldn't leave Candace behind."

"Pilot Sarah Hawkins can attend to your sister," Luna insisted. She glanced at the pilot, who flashed a winning smile and gave the couple a thumbs-up. "Come," Luna instructed before turning on her heels and walking at such a rapid pace Jordan needed to jog to catch up.

Jordan hadn't yet visited the hologram hall and was unfamiliar with this area of the ship. Although he had used similar technology before for many different things, his past experiences with holograms left him sorely disillusioned about the capabilities of the *Blunder*'s hologram hall.

Instead of lifelike projections to fully immerse him in an environment, the hall was a small rectangular room with four walls of flat displays depicting views of a graveyard at night. A small fog machine in the corner made sputtering noises as it pumped mist over a tattered brown rug—likely rolled out to simulate dirt since there didn't seem to be a display panel for the floor.

Luna let out a delighted sigh. "Lovely, isn't it?" She set down the basket and took a seat on the floor. Jordan cautiously lowered himself as well. The thin rug over the hard ground felt just as uncomfortable as it looked. "I find being surrounded by death incredibly peaceful," she added. "The quiet of final sleep with the calm of lying forever under the ground."

Jordan shuddered at her description, trying his best not to show his intense discomfort. He attempted to casually lean back and place his weight on his palms, but found the pose awkward, so he shifted to lean to one side. Although the hologram hall's depiction proved unimmersive, he appreciated the dated technology in this instance. He despised the idea of eating dinner in a realistic—or worse yet, real—graveyard.

"Tell me, are you ready to negotiate with the Funjy aliens?" Luna asked as she opened the picnic basket to reveal a slightly smooshed sandwich, a naked protein bar on a plate, and a transparent canteen filled with what appeared to be water.

"I hope so. From what I've read, the Funjys seem tough."

"You've never met one before?" she asked.

He shook his head in response.

"Oh, wow. I think they're terrifying." Her eyes widened for a moment before she returned her attention to the basket of food, removing items and placing them before Jordan. "Plus, the pressure of this entire mission being for the sole purpose of you doing this one job. I wouldn't be able to handle it."

He hadn't thought of it that way... but she was right. *Starship Blunder's* current voyage would take them straight to Tokinokin and back. If Jordan's assignment failed, the entire mission failed. *No pressure,* he thought.

"Please, help yourself," she added, gesturing at the food. "I asked Chef Bluebottle to prepare you a portable meal. It appears he's made you one of his famous bologna-and-cheese sandwiches."

He carefully unwrapped the sandwich from its plastic wrap cocoon and took a bite. It was the kind of thing he'd pack for Candace for a playdate, not what he would pick for a romantic dinner—not that he found anything about this evening even *slightly* romantic.

"You're not eating anything?" he asked when he realized the basket contained only a single meal.

"I find letting people watch me eat far too intimate," she admitted. "I usually consume my food alone in my quarters." She proceeded to stare at him as he took another bite. "Don't you find it oddly disconcerting, placing something in your mouth, tearing it apart with your teeth, and manipulating it with your tongue?"

He stopped mid-chew and swallowed hard. "I do now."

Then, the most miraculous thing happened—an interruption in their date. The whole ship seemed to jolt and shake for a moment, giving him the sickening feeling of falling. "What was that?" he exclaimed.

Red lights flashed from the ceiling while the song "I Will Survive" by Gloria Gaynor began to play. "That felt like *Starship Blunder* got violently directed off course," Luna answered. "We should brace ourselves for further disturbance." She curled up into a ball and held her hands behind her neck.

Jordan, who had no experience with turbulence, mimicked Luna's posture. "Does this happen often?" he asked, trying unsuccessfully to sound calm.

"All the time," she admitted. "Usually right before we crash—"

An enormous jolt interrupted her words, which sent the pair hurtling through the air. Luna kept her body in a tight ball, but Jordan flailed about, smacking against one of the display walls before landing with a *thunk* back onto the floor.

"Ow," he groaned.

Luna quickly got up and adjusted her dress. "We must have landed. Come quick, we need to check on Candace."

She had predicted Jordan's primary concern, and the pair rushed through the starship halls to the bridge in search of his sister.

Breathing hard, Jordan raced into the bridge to find a crowd of crewmates. He pushed through the people and aliens to the navigation and pilot seat. There, he saw Candace still grasping the yoke used to steer the starship as she turned to face him and yelled, "Jordan! Jordan! I got to fly the starship!"

"You *what*?!" he exclaimed between heaving breaths. He grasped his knees with his hands and leaned forward while waiting for his heart to stop hammering in his chest. As the adrenaline subsided, he asked, "What the hell happened?"

"Everything is fine!" Xylo proclaimed from his position next to Pilot Hawkins, who sat in the navigation seat. The blue circles on the alien's skin shone brightly, changing the coloring around him to a cool blue.

"Everything is *not* fine," Sarah Hawkins clarified. "Xylo's stupid invention interfered with the navigation systems!"

He meekly held up his lamp, which glowed green. "It works," he squeaked.

"You don't even know if it works," the pilot spat back. "It may or may not detect multi-frequency communication wave boosting, but it can *certainly* block the magnetic fields we use for navigation!"

While the pilot and mechanic bickered, Commander Greta Eriksson-Byström stared out the windows.

Luna turned her attention to Candace. "Are you okay?" the teacher asked.

"I'm great!" the little girl responded.

Jordan looked through the windows of the bridge to the landscape around them. They had landed on a rocky orange planet with a cloudy yellow sky. Deep purple vegetation sprouted among the cracks in the rock, and a paved road wove among the bushy plants and continued behind a tall rocky formation. "Where are we?" he asked.

Greta shook her head. "With the navigation dead, I have no idea."

A cold shiver worked down Jordan's spine. *How will we get home if we don't know where we are? Can the spaceship even fly after that crash?* He gritted his teeth, trying to figure something out. A thought came to him as he examined the view outside. "It appears there's intelligent life on this planet—that road didn't build itself. Maybe we could find someone and ask them for directions."

"You do it," Greta said as she turned to face the fighting crewmates. "Xylo, you go too, so you can inspect the outside of the ship—see if she needs any repairs," she added before walking away.

"Time to see if I'm any good at being a diplomat," Jordan mumbled to himself once she was out of earshot.

"Wait here," Xylo instructed. "I'm going to grab my tools, and then we'll head out together. Hold this." He handed Jordan the cursed lamp before dashing off.

Jordan examined the device in his hand. The immediate danger had passed, so although his body remained tense with anxiety, knowing the next few steps made him feel a little better. The rest of the crew had meandered out of the bridge and back to their posts elsewhere on the ship.

Candace jumped out of the pilot seat and grabbed Luna's hand. "I didn't actually get to fly the ship, but Miss Sarah let me sit in her chair," the young girl explained.

With a smile, Luna said, "Your brother has work to do. Let's go check the daycare room to make sure everything's safe for school tomorrow." Candace nodded, and the pair left the bridge together.

"I'm ready," Xylo called out as he returned with a tool-box in one hand a minute later. "I'll take that," he added as he grabbed the lamp from Jordan and plopped it in the box with various tools. The closest exit for the ship was just off the bridge, and Jordan followed the mechanic through the tight airlock.

Jordan hoped the planet's atmosphere was safe with plenty of oxygen since Xylo didn't grab a space suit or breathing gear. As soon as the inner door of the airlock closed, Xylo twisted the handle of the hatch, and the exterior door popped open. After a few kicks, the landing steps unfolded.

He walked briskly down the steps and onto the alien terrain. "Ah, smells like roses."

Jordan crinkled his nose. Instead of roses, the stench of rotting fish wafted through the air. Besides the smell, he found the planet pleasant with its cool temperature and constant gentle breezes.

"There appears to be some minor cosmetic damage here," Xylo mentioned, pointing to one of several dents on the front side of the ship. Jordan was surprised the beat-up vessel was able to look even more beat-up.

He continued to follow the alien around the starship's perimeter as the alien noted all the fresh damage. On the back side, a large metal tube at least a meter in diameter which had collapsed into a flat and crumpled mass protruded from the main engine. "Exhaust vent got crushed," Xylo remarked. "The ship won't be operational until that's dealt with. I could fabricate a temporary one that'll get us back to Nepture if this planet has some metal somewhere, but right now there's no way we're making it all the way to Tokinokin."

Jordan let his shoulders sag. *We're stuck here.* Just as he began wallowing in self-pity, something caught his eye. "What's that?" he asked before dashing away from Xylo and the ship.

"Hey," the alien called after him. "We're supposed to stick together." Yet, despite his protest, Xylo jogged to catch up with Jordan and examine what had grabbed the young man's attention.

In front of the rock formation stood a roughly humanoid figure. Constructed of the same rocky material as the landscape, it blended into its surroundings.

"It's a sacred Funjy statue," Jordan explained, not waiting for Xylo to inquire about the curiosity in front of them. "Thought it's smaller than I expected." The piece came up to the man's chest. He had never seen one in person before; his only experience with the communication-wave boosters was from images in textbooks and research articles. He wondered if he could lift the statue and move it onto the starship. "Does that mean we made it to Tokinokin?"

"No, definitely not," Xylo assured. "That planet has green soil and is almost completely covered in cities."

Jordan gasped. "Then this must be the sacred Funji planet! I bet the Funjy construct their statues here."

"So my detector *does* work," Xylo added before running back to grab the device out of his toolbox. When he returned with the electronic gadget in hand, the green light turned blue.

Jordan looking around. "I bet that road leads to a settlement or something. We should follow it!" Before Xylo could object, Jordan took off running up the road.

He didn't need to go far to find a clearing surrounded by six squat buildings made of violet-colored timber with blue-thatched roofs. "Hello," he called out. "We come in peace."

After a few seconds, several aliens emerged from the buildings, and soon, dozens of creatures surrounded Xylo and Jordan. Jordan immediately identified the aliens as Funjys: they each had rough orange skin, small mouths, two beady black eyes, and two antennae resembling fox ears. Each one carried a large, pointy stick. Robe-like garments in various shades of red and purple obscured their bodies.

"Maybe we should call for backup," Jordan whispered to Xylo.

"I left my comm in my toolbox next to the ship," Xylo whispered back. Jordan gave him a wide-eyed stare. "What? You ran ahead, and that toolbox is heavy. You're a diplomat, right? Just negotiate or whatever you learned to do in school. We'll be fine!"

As a single alien stepped forward from the crowd and into the sunny clearing, Jordan wished he shared Xylo's confidence.

"Trespassers!" the orange alien screeched in a high-pitched voice. "Why are you here?"

"Uh, I'm so-sorry," Jordan said, stumbling over his words. "My name is Jordan Jackson, and I'm a diplomat representing the Conglomeracy aboard the *Starship Blunder*. This is Xylo, the starship's head mechanic."

"Leave," the Funjy alien bellowed. "You are not welcome in New Tokinokin!"

"New Tokinokin," Jordan repeated, grabbing Xylo by the arm. "This must be the secret Funji planet."

The entire group of natives shrieked with laughter, an unnerving cacophony that made the *Blunder* crewmates stumble back.

"New Tokinokin is no secret!" the head Funji alien explained. "We have always been forthcoming about our location. The plentiful transmitium deposits in the terrain interfere with starship navigation systems, and you star-fleet lot clearly can't read a map!"

"That means my multi-frequency communication wave detector didn't make us crash!" Xylo proclaimed.

Jordan glared at Xylo, hoping his stern look would inspire the mechanic to shut up. "We would like to be on our way, but our landing on your planet was a bit rough, and our starship requires repairs. We need a new..." He turned back to Xylo.

"Exhaust vent," Xylo specified. "H size, if you have it."

"If you help us, we'll leave right away," Jordan added.

The orange alien paused for a long moment, making Jordan increasingly uncomfortable. The other aliens shuffled around, and a few of them aimed their sticks at the intruders. After what felt like forever, the lead alien replied, "Perhaps a trade."

"Of course," Jordan agreed. He had already given up hope of negotiating for the sacred statues, but he would call it a success if he could at least arbitrate their departure from this hostile planet. "Take this multi-frequency communication-wave detector." He grabbed the device from Xylo's hands and offered it to the orange alien.

The alien turned away, clearly skeptical.

"It doubles as a night light," Xylo added.

Finally, the Funjy alien walked right up to Jordan and snatched away the lamp. "My tribe needs time to see if we can help you fix your ship. I will seek you out once we make our decision." With that, the small orange army lowered their sticks, turned away, and shuffled back into the purple timber buildings.

"I can't believe you gave away my detector," Xylo said, letting his head and shoulders droop.

"Sorry," Jordan apologized as the pair walked back to the *Blunder*. "I wasn't sure what else to do. I guess now we just wait."

☆ ☆ ☆

Evening came fast on New Tokinokin, but Jordan didn't mind since the stress of the day had left him exhausted. He found Candace and Luna in the daycare classroom, drawing pictures of Funji statues. He collected his sister and brought her back to their quarters, where he carefully hung his flight jacket in the wardrobe before crawling into bed to get some sleep.

The following morning, the pair got sandwiches from the dining hall for breakfast before Jordan dropped Candace off at the daycare.

Candace ran up to her teacher and gave her a big hug. "Hi, Miss Luna!"

"Hello, Miss Pilot-in-training. How are you this morning?"

Jordan signed his sister in on the clipboard as he explained, "Xylo wants me to accompany him outside while he attempts repairs on the exhaust vent, so I might be out there most of the day."

Luna took the clipboard from him and hung it back on the wall. "I plan to bring the children out to join you at some point. They could use the fresh air, and the atmosphere seems tolerable."

"I'm not so sure about that," Jordan said. He didn't want a bunch of kids running around underfoot while he tried to work. "The locals don't seem particularly friendly."

"I've found most aliens to be more accommodating of youths," Luna replied with a shrug before turning her attention back to her students.

Jordan left the daycare center and met up with Xylo at the bridge. The two were the first ones outside, and Jordan watched with mild amusement as Xylo tried to bang some dents out of the side panels using a wrench. To his relief, none of the Funji aliens were around to observe them.

"Don't you have a mallet?" Jordan asked.

"Probably," Xylo responded. "But this works just fine."

Jordan shook his head, disagreeing.

As they kept working, other crew members came outside to enjoy the pleasant weather. The sun for the planetary system appeared quite large and glowed a pinkish hue through the yellow sky. A few orange clouds provided a little shade, but sunlight bathed most of the landscape in a warm glow.

By mid-day, Xylo had made little progress, so Jordan joined a group of young men and women throwing a disk to each other. To make sure that none of them hit the nearby statue with the disk, Jordan placed a couple of folding chairs from the dining hall in front of it.

"This way, class," Luna directed her six young pupils, who were filing out of the hatch and down the ladder. "Let's all play a game of follow-the-leader. I'll be our first leader." The kids kept close to their teacher as they did funny walks, balanced on small rocks, and leaped around the area close to their starship. When they skipped past Jordan and his disk game, Candace stopped and waved before jogging to catch back up with Luna.

With all the crewmates outside enjoying the pleasant weather, Jordan could easily ignore the dire situation they were in. If the Funji refused to cooperate, no one on the *Starship Blunder* would leave New Tokinokin. So far, his negotiations hadn't garnered any concrete results, and he was wary of his ability to convince them to cooperate. He kept an eye out, unsure what to do if Xylo couldn't fix the exhaust vent.

Over the next several minutes, a trickle of orange aliens in purple robes walked one-by-one down the road toward the starship, stopping about thirty meters away to observe the visitors to their planet. Jordan knew he shouldn't ignore them. However, he did exactly that until one brave Funjy ventured closer.

Jordan cautiously excused himself from his game and approached the closest orange alien. He gave the Funji a quick bow and said, "Hello! What a pleasure to speak with the Funjy once again."

The alien did not return the gesture and instead shouted back, "What is the meaning of all of this?"

"My apologies. The *Blunder* crew wished to take advantage of the wonderful weather on your planet."

"Why are there chairs?" The alien reached a small hand through their robes to gesture at the chairs blocking the statue.

"I can move them if you wish," he offered. "Some crew were playing a game where we throw a disk to each other, and I didn't want anyone to run into the statue or hit it with the disk."

Candace came running up the road to Jordan and interrupted their conversation before he could continue.

"What are you doing here?" he asked in a stern whisper. "Where's Miss Luna and the rest of the daycare group?" He looked down the road toward the starship and picked out the teacher dressed in all black among the crowd. "Miss Luna!" he called out, trying to get her attention.

"Is she one of the Funjy aliens you told me about?" Candace asked, her eyes wide.

"I'm so sorry," Jordan apologized to the orange alien. "This is my little sister, Candace. She's supposed to be with her daycare class right now." He turned and yelled, "MISS LUNA!" again, this time getting the teacher's attention. He waved for her to come over.

The orange alien lowered to Candace's height and addressed the child, saying, "Yes, I am a Funjy alien."

"*Wow*," the little girl gushed. "You look just as amazing as my brother described! I made something for you."

Jordan gritted his teeth, sure his sister was about to single-handedly ruin their already tense relations. Candace pulled a paper from her pocket and unfolded it to reveal the image she had drawn inside. "See, this here is your orange statue," she said, pointing to part of the picture, "this is me and my brother, and this is Miss Luna, my teacher. Here, take it." She held out the picture.

The alien took the picture and asked, "You like our statues?"

"Oh, absolutely!" Candace said, bouncing up and down. "They look just as cool as you do!"

The alien glanced from the little girl to the picture to the barricade of folding chairs protecting the statue. "Your people actually hold the art of my kind in high esteem?"

Luna finally reached the group along with the rest of the daycare kids. "Come, Candace. It's Kyle's turn to be the leader." An instant later, the daycare group had gone.

"Yes, we really do," Jordan said, answering the Funjy alien's question.

The orange alien nodded and seemed to think for a moment. "Previous negotiations with space federations have proved that your kind was only interested in the transmitium available in our mines. When we traded over a century ago, the statues we gave out were dismantled and gutted for their raw materials. We thought all space federations were ruthless like that. But seeing a child's family drawing with a Funjy statue incorporated..." The alien paused, doing what Jordan guessed was the Funjy equivalent of tearing up. Procuring a tissue with their hand, the alien used it to dab at their antennae.

After a moment, the alien continued, "This picture is exceptional. Thank your sister for me. I came over here to let you know that we have enough metal to fabricate a size-H exhaust vent for your starship. But perhaps we could also negotiate an ongoing trade agreement sometime soon. Once your ship is operational, do you believe you could find your way back to New Tokinokin?"

Jordan's body loosened with relief, and he almost laughed at the absurdity of *Starship Blunder* crash landing on the same hard-to-find planet twice. "Absolutely. I'll make sure that the crew knows how to read a map."

"Take this statue," the alien recommended, pointing to the nearby statue blocked by chairs. "It will boost the multi-frequency communication signals enough for you to find us again. I will have a few of my tribe deliver the metal for a new vent. Can your crew handle moving the statue?"

"Yes! Yes, we can. Thank you so much!" Jordan rushed back to the *Blunder* to recruit a few extra hands to help transport the statue onto the starship. It weighed significantly more than he'd expected, requiring six helpers to hoist it from its base and lug it to the ship. Getting the heavy artwork up the ladder and through the hatch took even more hands. Once they'd situated it in the center of the bridge, Jordan stepped back to admire the figure.

"Is that what I think it is?" Commander Eriksson-Byström asked as she approached the new centerpiece.

"Yep!" he exclaimed. "The Funjy gifted it to us so we can navigate back to New Tokinokin—this is their second planet."

"I can't believe it," she said, leaning closer to examine the Funjy likeness. "The Conglomeracy gave the *Blunder* this mission to negotiate with the Funjy since negotiations with them always fail. It looks like you're quite the diplomat, Jordan Jackson."

"Thanks," he replied, pride swelling in his chest.

☆ ☆ ☆

Aided by some of the Funji, the *Blunder* crew replaced their broken exhaust vent with a temporary vent, enabling them to return home. Although Jordan and Candace enjoyed their adventures on a real starship, they happily embraced the banality of being back on Neptune a few days later.

Jordan found a comfortable apartment for him and Candace to move into, and Candace started kindergarten at Watt Elementary School. She loved her new classmates but admitted missing Miss Luna. Jordan, on the other hand, was relieved he would never need to speak with that scary woman again.

As much as Jordan wanted to continue working as a diplomat, the Conglomeracy selected someone with more qualifications to continue negotiations with the peculiar orange alien race. Instead, Jordan took a boring but stable job as a junior analyst for the Sovereign Stellar Federation. And as promised, he was able to add the successful mission aboard the *Blunder* to his resumé.

HOPSCOTCH

Jason Abofsky

The Captain

Captain Parva Nemo took in the view of planet Tarpima from the bridge of *Starship Blunder*. The sickly-green hue of the atmosphere stretched across the landscape like a world composed of nothing but bogs and swamps. The inhabitants did not belong to the Conglomeracy, and their technology lagged behind most other cultures. The Tarpimas made up for their primitive society the way a chihuahua compensated for its tiny stature—by barking as much as possible until people considered them a threat.

Six months spent as captain of the *Blunder*, and she'd already begun dreaming of a transfer. Someone had cobbled together a hodgepodge of outdated technology into a semi-functioning ship worthy only of a washed-out drunk waiting to die in retirement, not the first command of a mid-thirties officer with only-a-little-less-than-stellar record. But what the job lacked in style and prestige, it more than made up for with obtrusive bureaucracy and running exciting errands like cargo delivery.

Judging by the stack of regulations required to land the ship on this world, she realized why no other captains in the Conglomeracy had volunteered for this assignment. The Tarpimas had fined the *Blunder* twice already since arriving in the system—once for not arriving precisely at the expected arrival time, and again for failing to announce themselves as non-combatant traders within the first three minutes of contact. The Tarpimas weren't even at war with anyone. Their excessive bureaucracy and militant posturing made the captain grate her teeth.

When the ship landed at the assigned docking port two hours later, Parva slunk down in her chair, ready to finish the assignment and get back to Neptune.

"The Magistrate's representative is calling again, Captain," the young and excitable Will Sanders called out from his station.

"Tarpimas," the captain muttered under her breath. "They're a real pain in my ass." She sighed and nodded to the cadet. "Put him on."

"Aye, aye, Captain," the cadet replied, far too eager to please as always.

Was I ever that young? she wondered.

Once more, the Tarpima Magistrate's highly punchable face appeared on the screen, with a grin showing all his teeth. He looked primarily human, apart from his eyes, which more closely resembled a cat's.

"Good day, Captain. I've registered your successful landing with the docking crew. Please be advised that while visitors are allowed into the city, you will be required to depart in precisely five hours."

Parva mentally noted their expected departure time to ensure they didn't accidentally leave even a minute too soon or late. "Of course. Thank you for clarifying."

"I also wanted to inform you that, regrettably, your ship landed over the line for your designated landing zone. Therefore, you will be fined five hundred cretins."

Parva hid her fist behind her back, clenching it so tight that her nails pierced her skin. "You have our deepest apologies."

"See you again in five hours, Captain." The link closed.

She turned to the cadet. "Let me know the absolute second we can leave."

"Will do, Captain!"

"I need a drink," Parva muttered under her breath.

The Stowaway

Five hours later, the cargo had been delivered, the crew returned to the starship, and the litany of Tarpima lift-off protocols had been followed to the letter. Captain Nemo released her stress in one long sigh of relief.

"Hawkins, get us the hell out of here."

"Yes, Captain," the pilot replied.

The ship rose into the air smoothly and headed into orbit.

"Um, Captain," the cadet started to say, then hesitated. "The Magistrate's representative is calling again."

"Of course he is. He'll probably fine us for a loose tail-pipe or something." She rose from her seat and nodded to the cadet. "Put him on." As soon as the Tarpima's face came into view, Parva wasted no time on pleasantries. "We have followed all your procedures. We have concluded our business, Magistrate."

"Magistrate's *representative*," he corrected. "The Magistrate's time is far too important to deal with such trivial matters. And this isn't about protocols. I order you to turn the ship around and land immediately."

Captain Nemo glared at the man, whose name she couldn't even remember. "Excuse me?"

"You are harboring an enemy alien. Land and allow our security to inspect your ship and detain the enemy—after which you will be free to leave."

"What enemy alien?"

"He's from a species called Handimen. They are the Tarpima's sworn enemy. You must comply."

"With all due respect, *representative,* this is a Conglomerate ship, and Tarpima is not a member of the Conglomeracy. We do not need to listen to you."

"You will comply. Or there will be consequences."

Parva brought up her console and checked the ship's manifest. "We don't even have a Handimen in the crew or as a passenger."

"We saw one delivering cargo from your ship." He nodded to someone off the screen, and a blurry image of a reddish figure carrying a box off the ship appeared. "You will turn this creature over immediately."

The captain pinched the bridge of her nose. "Fine. You've made a claim, and per Conglomeracy policy, we must investigate. Our ship will remain in orbit for now. If we find a Handimen, we'll turn them over."

The representative's lip curled and clicked his tongue, then glanced at something offscreen. "We shall give you two hours to comply. If you don't, we will fire on your ship." The link closed.

Parva turned to Security Director Kojak. "Find out if this Handimen did somehow sneak aboard."

Kojak stared at her, frowning. Finally, he said, "I'll see to it."

The Security Director

Captain Nemo waited on the bridge for the security director to complete his search. With each passing minute, the temptation to say, "Screw it," and flee grew. The ship would survive an impromtu departure. Her career would not.

"I've completed the inspection, Captain," Director Kojak said as he stepped onto the bridge. "No stowaways have been found."

Parva glanced at the shipboard time. "You've completed searching the entire ship in forty-five minutes?" She raised her eyebrow at him.

Kojak removed his white cowboy hat. "Yes. Reports from all sections found no sightings, and we examined all unoccupied areas."

The captain studied the man. Usually, he voiced his opinion with pride and wouldn't settle for anything less than finding and capturing a criminal. Now, he'd given up after less than an hour and refused to look her in the eye.

Something didn't add up. She glanced at the rest of the bridge crew, trying to figure out what to do next.

"The Tarpimas won't take our word on this, but if we let them board, their inspection will take forever," she replied. "And if they do find a Handimen, we'll be in a lot of trouble. So, I'll ask again: Are you sure you searched *everywhere?*"

Kojak's expression looked less confident.

"Captain," Cadet Sanders chimed in. "What about the BRI scanners?"

"What's that, Cadet?" Parva asked.

"Right before you started as captain, Neptune Techs integrated Bio-Resonance Imaging into the existing ship-board polaron scanners. The BRI can distinguish between organisms. It can't distinguish between species, but it should help us determine where to search next."

The captain glared at Kojak. "Why didn't you use the scanners earlier?"

Kojak looked away. "They are still experimental and undergoing testing. The results may not be accurate."

"Bring the scanners online, Cadet," she ordered.

Sanders beamed as he brought up the controls on his terminal. "The ship manifest says one hundred and fifty-three crew should be on board. The BRI is picking up one hundred fifty-four."

Parva wheeled on Kojak. "*No one else aboard*, huh?"

A bead of sweat dripped from Kojak's forehead. "I... may have been mistaken."

The captain glanced at the clock again. "We don't have time for this. I'll find the Handimen myself."

The Teacher

After confirming with the cadet, Parva headed for the classroom. Sanders' reading showed an extra non-human presence alongside the teacher and students. The captain pulled out her weapon and kept it ready.

If that creature harmed any of the children, I'll hand the Magistrate back a corpse.

She burst into the room, gun aimed high for safety. Kojak followed behind. She'd expected a hostage situation. She never could have anticipated the scene before her.

"Good afternoon, Captain Nemo," the roughly dozen students said in an eerie unison.

Parva hid her gun behind her back to avoid scaring them. "Um, good afternoon, students."

"Can I help you with something, Captain?" Miss Luna asked. Despite the sweetness of her voice, she wore a dark expression matching her typical gothic attire.

Parva hesitated. "Have you seen anyone else in here today? Someone who's not supposed to be here?"

The teacher tilted her head. "We haven't seen anyone else until you and Kojak came in. Right, class?"

"Yes, Miss Luna," the class sang in unison.

The last time Parva had visited the class, these kids hadn't been able to sit for more than a minute without pandemonium breaking out. She walked the perimeter of the room, peering behind art projects and cabinets, opening closed cubby doors and the supply closet. The teacher and class watched her the entire time.

This is getting creepy, she thought. "We should leave," she told Kojak, backing out of the room.

"Goodbye, Captain Nemo," they sang again.

What the hell was that? she wondered while putting greater distance between her and the classroom. She shook off the feeling and contacted the bridge.

"Sanders, I thought you said the Handimen was in the classroom?"

"I've been trying to reach you. The Handimen left the classroom just before you arrived and headed to the mess hall."

"I'm on my way," she said.

The Chef

Captain Nemo burst into the mess hall. The place was empty, save for Chef Bluebottle in the back kitchen, wearing his signature grumpy expression.

"You're too early for dinner," he grumped, pointing a knife in her direction before resuming chopping what Parva hoped was a vegetable. The smell did little to convince her. To the chef's credit, his cooking had improved significantly over the last few months. She'd reserve judgment until after he served the finished meal.

"A stowaway just ran in here. An alien called a Handimen."

"Nobody's here but me."

"I *know* he's here," the captain argued.

"What's he look like?"

"Average height, red skin, hooved feet," she recited from the description in the database.

Chef stabbed a nearby potato, leaving the knife hanging where it was, and rubbed his chin. "Let me think... Nope."

Maybe the cadet's tech isn't all that accurate, she wondered.

The captain glanced under the tables before entering the kitchen. She flipped open cabinets and storage rooms, then continued into the walk-in freezer.

"What do you think you're doing to my kitchen?" Bluebottle demanded.

"You're lying, though I don't know why."

For once, the man did not offer a comeback or sarcastic quip. He folded his arms and replied with a *harrumph*.

Parva wondered why she hadn't heard from the cadet yet, and called the bridge. "Sanders!"

"Captain? Something appears to be wrong with the communication links. I've been trying to tell you the Handimen left the mess hall just before you arrived. He's in the engine room now. Also, the Tarpimas have launched fighter escort ships. They're taking offensive positions around the ship."

The captain swore under her breath. "How much time do we have?"

"About twenty-five minutes before the deadline."

She recalled that the engines had security protections. "Lock down the engine room. No one gets in or out until I arrive."

"Yes, Captain. Right away!"

He's trapped. It's time to end this.

The Mechanic

As soon as Parva reached the entrance to the engine room, she called into the bridge. "Well? Is he still in there?"

"Yes, Captain," the cadet said, excitement in his voice. "No one has left the room as ordered."

"Good. Unlock the primary entrance only."

A heavy *click* resounded as the locks unhooked. "Done."

The door slid open, and the captain pushed into the room with her weapon raised. Her eyes found Xylo.

"Hello, Captain," Xylo said. "Is there something you require?"

"Where is he?" Parva demanded. "Where is the Handimen?"

"A Handimen, you say? Slender, red skin, hooved feet. I think I've run into one or two in my time. But I don't believe I've seen any in the last few decades."

"I *know* they're in here." Despite the vast size of the room, the clutter of antiquated equipment filled out most of the available space. *Clangs* and *pops* echoed as the engine bucked against the rusted bolts holding it in place. She walked through narrow pathways, peering into crevices too small to reach without injury. With a vast array of clever hiding spots, she knew she could spend hours in this room alone trying to find him.

"I know you're here, Handimen," she yelled. "Come out now. I'm open to hearing you out if you have a valid reason for sneaking aboard, but you need to show yourself first."

Nothing.

With time running short, the captain reached her last nerve. "Show yourself!" She banged on a nearby pipe. A decade of dust and soot rained down on her. "Just perfect."

"Ahh-choo!"

Parva turned toward the source of the sound, climbed over a large duct, and pulled away a wheelable console. She stared down at the Handimen, wiping his nose.

"Gesundheit."

The Helper

Parva leveled her gun at the Handimen. "Let's go. Out."

He raised his arms over his head and crawled out from the pipes. Although he stood around the same height as the captain, their similarities ended there. His red skin, broad chest, and hooved feet matched the database description of a Handimen. Deep blue eyes opened wide, turning glassy as he studied her.

"Captain, please," Xylo started. He stepped between her and the Handimen. "Don't hand Chor'ta over to the Tarpimas. He's a valued crew member."

"You know his name?"

"He repaired the lateral Hawking Compactor before I knew it was leaking cosmic radiation! He's been a great mechanical assistant."

"Is that why the engines have been running so smoothly lately?" Parva asked.

Xylo nodded.

"He helped me upgrade the shipboard scanners," Kojak admitted. "Ironically, he's the reason Cadet Sanders could track him so well."

The captain wheeled on her security director. "You knew?"

Kojak hesitated. "Captain, I didn't—"

"Don't lie to me. I can see it all over your face. As Security Director, you must have known."

Kojak stared at the floor, clearly unable to come up with anything to say to defend himself.

Both Miss Luna and Chef Bluebottle raced into the room.

"Let me guess," Parva said. "You two also knew about this and want to argue against turning over this criminal who snuck aboard a military vessel?"

"He's been so great with the kids," the teacher said. "The students' behavior has improved immensely thanks to him."

"Yeah!" her students yelled from the hall.

Miss Luna smirked but waved them back. "I told everyone to stay out here and be quiet."

"Don't you take away my sous chef!" Bluebottle added. "I'm the one who caught him stealing food. That boy didn't just take the food; he sliced, diced, seasoned, and plated it first. Kid's a natural."

"That's why the food hasn't tasted like garbage for the last..." Parva thought back to the last time she complained about a meal. "He's been here for *two months*? How did he even get on board the ship?"

"Hid inside one of the food crates we took on back at Cyphron B," Bluebottle said.

"And nobody thought the captain should know about this?"

Everyone suddenly became too fascinated by the floor to look her in the eye.

"I don't believe this." Parva glared at the Handimen, who offered a meek smile back. "What do you have to say for yourself?"

"Chor'ta," the Handimen gurgled.

Parva glanced at the others.

"We don't have a translation yet for his language in our database, Captain," Miss Luna said, "but Chor'ta can get quite creative at communicating with us."

Chor'ta smiled and nodded.

Parva clenched her fist. "What does everyone expect me to do about this? We only have a few minutes before we either turn him over to the Tarpimas or allow them to board and find him anyway. And if we refuse, those fighter escorts will not likely let us go in peace."

"Wait a minute!" Miss Luna called out, raising her hand like one of her students. "I have an idea!"

The Magistrate's Representative

The Magistrate's representative's vessel passed through the airlock energy barrier into the docks—a large open area at the back of the ship for smaller visiting craft. The representative sauntered off his craft with his entourage in tow—heavily armed security forces with identical chiseled chins, muscular arms, and stern expressions, ready and eager to kill should the opportunity arise. The representative wore a robe over his shoulders like a cape and held his chin high in a show of pompousness—which came in handy as the top of his head only reached the captain's shoulder.

"Your time is up, yet you still deny harboring an enemy Handimen? Per Tarpima law, your ship will be searched, and the Magistrate will hear of your lack of compliance."

"We humbly apologize to the Magistrate for the inconvenience his representative endured on his behalf.

However, we searched the ship and concluded there is no Handimen aboard. Your intelligence must be faulty."

The representative's cheeks reddened, but he didn't look away. "It's here. We'll find the creature. Have your entire crew assemble here in your docking bay."

"I will have all non-essential crew assemble only," Parva explained.

"Not good enough. Bring everyone here now."

"Essential means essential. This is non-negotiable— unless you're willing for the ship to lose its orbit and accidentally burn up in the atmosphere while you're on board because no one was monitoring critical systems?"

He pursed his lips. "Fine."

"And my security team will escort you at all times while on this ship."

"Absolutely not."

"You're not getting unfettered access to restricted areas of this ship. If you've contrived this Handimen ploy to steal our technology"—*our outdated, aging, patchwork technology*, she thought—"I will personally kick you off this ship. You can fire on us, but I've already sent word to the Conglomeracy regarding this incident. If anything happens to this ship while cooperating with you, they will see it as an aggressive action by a rogue planet, and all trade with your world by anyone in the Conglomeracy will cease. Are you prepared to take that risk?"

The representatives's jaw tightened. His eyes never left the captain, who met his stare with even greater intensity. He blinked first. "We need access to all areas of the ship."

"And you'll have it—with the proper supervision. Are we clear?"

Parva enjoyed seeing the man's face turn a shade of purple.

"Let's get this over with," he finally replied.

"Finally, something we can agree on," she said with a smile.

The Imposter

Seven hours.

After giving Parva just two hours to find the Handimen, the Magistrate's representative spent seven peering around every corner and looking in cubby holes too small to fit a Handimen unless they were a toddler.

The Tarpimas ended their search in the docks. After waiting so long, most of the *Blunder* crew members found ways to entertain themselves. The kids ran around and took turns jumping off—*hopefully*—non-fragile boxes. Much of the crew and the families gathered around a makeshift volleyball court using what the captain guessed to be an overinflated polyglorine overflow tank sealed off to keep enough air inside to use for a ball.

Clever. The captain smirked.

"Everyone, get in formation!" the representative yelled. The crew stopped the game and stared blankly in reply.

"You don't give the orders on my ship," Parva reminded him before waving them all over. "Everyone, please line up so we can finally end this ridiculous inquisition and get rid of the little troll."

The representative's face reddened to the point that he looked like a Handimen himself. *In fact...*

The captain spun around to hide her grin. As the representative examined each crew member, she slipped over to Kojak and whispered instructions. He winked and got to work on his console.

Meanwhile, the representative scrutinized each crew member, looking for the Handimen in disguise. He inspected their arms and legs, pulled on their uniforms—anything he could to prove something was out of place.

"What in the Tri-Stars happened to you?" he demanded, stopping in front of what Parva estimated to be the worst disguise in the history of disguises.

Pink paste covered the Handimen's head and hands, leaving no skin exposed. His uniform fit in in all the worst possible ways. The oversized shirt sagged down the front while his pant legs came to rest above the ankle. A blonde wig covered the top of his head, and oversized shoes better suited on a historical circus clown hid his hooves.

There's no way this will work.

The representative reached out to examine the sticky pink face.

"I wouldn't do that," the ship's doctor said. "Ensign Boils here is suffering from a bad case of agglutinate epoxia, which is a highly contagious and *extremely* uncomfortable condition. He picked it up at the last starport we visited."

The representative snapped his hand back.

"We've been keeping him in quarantine, but you insisted everyone come here. Now if you're satisfied, I'd like to take him back to the med center now." He gestured for the crewman to follow him.

Behind them, Parva heard Kojak whisper to the leader of the Tarpima soldiers and handed him a display. The Tarpima's eyes narrowed. "We'll take care of it."

The representative might have called their bluff, but before he could get the chance, two Tarpima soldiers grabbed him from behind and yanked him back, then restrained his arms.

"What do you think you're doing?"

"According to protocol 732-129.7 of the Tarpima Articles of Bureaucracy, an accusation has been made, and evidence has been provided," the leader replied.

"What accusation? What evidence?"

"You will come with us until we're able to confirm your identity."

"You can't do this to me! I'm the Magistrate's representative!"

"Take him," the leader ordered. The two soldiers escorted the hollering representative back to their ship. "I'm sorry for the trouble he caused you and your ship, Captain. As far as I can see, the search has yielded no evidence of a Handimen on board. Once we've departed, you are free to leave the system."

"Thank you," Parva said.

Parva watched them board their ship and exit the docks. She didn't dare move until the ship left her sight. Then she opened the communications to the bridge. "Hawkins?"

"Yes, Captain?" the pilot replied.

"Get us out of here. Now!"

"Understood."

"What just happened?" Xylo asked.

Parva smiled. "I let the Tarpimas think the *Magistrate's representative* was secretly a Handimen in disguise."

"How?"

Kojak chimed in. "I gave one of the soldiers a display that showed the shipboard scanners detected the representative's DNA as a match for Handimen. And their protocols are so strict, I assumed they wouldn't be able to overlook the possibility."

"But our scanners can't distinguish the DNA of individuals," Xylo argued.

"We know that," said Kojak. His smile broadened, "But they don't."

Parva didn't hold back her smile. "Well then, I guess we'll need to hold a welcome party for our not-so-newish crew member." She nodded to Chor'ta, who grinned and bowed. She looked for the teacher. "By the way, Miss Luna, what is that pink goo he's covered in?"

"School glue," she replied, drawing another chorus of laughter and cheers.

Once Captain Nemo returned to the bridge, she wasted no time putting as much distance from the Tarpimas as possible before anyone changed their minds. She opened her jacket and slumped down in her chair, letting out a long-overdue sigh of relief.

"By the way, Sanders," she leaned her head in the direction of the cadet, "did we ever figure out the earlier communications issue? Or were you also a part of this scheme to keep me from finding the Handimen?"

The cadet turned beet red. "I may have broken my communicator when I left it on my uniform in the laundry."

Parva shook her head. *Never a normal day on the Blunder*, she thought.

HELLSPAWN IN THE SWAMP

Susan Eschbach

The door of *Starship Blunder* slid open and Sarah Hawkins surveyed the landscape spread out before her. High oxygen content and no toxic gases, so she didn't need a helmet, but a cold fog cast a heavy pall over the scene. Only dim light from the planet's small red star penetrated the atmosphere, though the sun was directly overhead at this hour. She wrinkled her nose as the scent of rotting vegetation reached her on an unpleasant breeze.

Maybe they could breathe safely, but it hardly seemed hospitable.

Swamp surrounded the *Blunder*, which, by some miracle of obscenely good piloting, she'd managed to crash onto a patch of solid ground barely larger than the ship itself. On all sides, reedy stalks with willowy fronds poked out of a greenish-brown muck. The ship's scanners indicated the marsh waters were only about two to three feet deep in most places, though the ground underneath surely wouldn't support much weight. Visions of disappearing into quick-mud ran through her mind—not a way she was willing to die. Didn't even make the top, or bottom, ten.

Siki slithered up behind her. He looked somewhat like a bloated, twenty-foot-long coiled blue python, except for his eight arms, which made him the fleet's most prized engineer. How she'd managed to hang on to him was a mystery.

"What's our damage report?"

"The piratesss really did a number on usss. We only have one operational engine and more blown circuitsss than I can count. It's a miracle you landed usss in one piece—more or lesss—with only a fourth of our thrusters operational."

"Thanks. But how long is it going to take to repair all that?"

"We won't be repairing it without sssupplies from sssomewhere, and you managed to pick an uninhabited planet."

She stretched her neck from side to side, trying to stave off the headache building behind her eyes. "I didn't *pick* it. We're damn lucky we could get to it after the pirates shot us up. And if we don't get airborne soon, they're likely to find us and finish what they started."

"We're not going anywhere in thisss condition."

She let out a deep, frustrated sigh. "Kind of what I figured. I've sent messages to Terminus Space Command as well as our destination, Argenta."

While she looked out over the landscape, the entire field of willowy fronds began lengthening and pointing in unison toward the ship, as though it posed some haven of heat and light.

"I don't really like the look of that." Siki retreated back through the hatch.

Sarah tapped the comm badge on her purple shirt. "Sam, get SASU and report to the exit ramp. May as well run some studies while we're here."

Minutes later, Sam, a tall, muscular Aborigine, appeared behind her with a three-foot-wide by six-foot-tall box. Twelve robotic appendages provided an assortment of drilling and sampling tools. The Scientific Assessment and Sampling Unit was mounted on a series of wheels that allowed it to move in any direction.

Sarah stepped out onto the ramp, but Sam took her elbow, halting her.

"Better let me take some samples before you go out there. Even though this little island looks solid, there could be toxic flora."

Nodding, she stayed in the doorway while he proceeded to the bottom and held out a scanner. "The grasses on this knoll seem to be okay," he assured. "I'll have SASU move out farther to check the flora in the swamp." He cocked his head. "Why are the plants all pointing at us?"

She shrugged. "I don't know—they've actually grown longer since I've been standing here. Maybe you can find an answer. I have to go back in and watch for messages from the Conglomeracy and Argenta."

☆ ☆ ☆

SASU moved down the ramp. As it rolled out into the water, it deployed flotation devices to avoid sinking into the soft bottom. The nearby leaves shifted direction, reaching toward the unit. Remaining safely on the ramp, Sam sent instructions to SASU to sample the air, water, underwater soil, and plants.

Appendages reached out from the box, one stretching straight up, three disappearing under the water's surface, and two reaching out to pluck nearby leaves and the stem of one plant.

A few seconds later, a shriek split the air, almost ultrasonic, and the nearest plants jerked back. In all directions, high-pitched whistles arced from one group of plants to another, and the fronds waved frantically.

Screaming plants?

A report from SASU appeared on Sam's control device.

```
Highly acidic leaves pose a possible danger to
personnel and equipment.
```

Sam tapped his controller, sending a query back.

```
Is there any danger to the ship from the grass on
the island where the ship is located?
```

```
No. The island flora is a different composition,
as is some flora on the swamp floor. The tall reed
plants are unique in composition.
```

Sam scratched his head through his thick, black hair.

```
Are the tall reeds flora or fauna?
```

```
Cell structure has unique components but is most
similar to flora.
```

A moment later, the reeds closest to SASU converged and engulfed the unit. Its steel sides sizzled like bacon and appendages waved wildly. "Danger, danger. Help. Help!" the unit called out.

"Sam to Captain. I need backup. Those plants have grabbed SASU. They're acidic, and they're *dissolving* him!"

Three crewmen appeared at the door with grappling hooks and cables. One launched a particularly adept throw and hooked the top appendage. He began trying to drag the unit toward the ship, but the plants had a death grip on it.

The other two crewmen managed to hook their cables onto other appendages, and the three waged a tug-of-war over SASU, which continued to scream for help.

The acid ate through one of the hooked appendages, and it dropped into the swamp, forcing the crewman to toss the cable onto another target. After several minutes of struggle, the crewmen managed to drag the poor, besieged sampler onto the ramp. Slashes of dissolved metal exposed parts of its interior.

Sam stared. The plant was not just acidic but highly corrosive. A high percentage of *Blunder's* hull was acid-resistant titanium, but not all of it—hasty older repairs made with whatever material was available had left vulnerable areas.

As if sensing his thoughts, the plants collectively turned their fronds toward the ship, growing longer and longer. They'd be within reach of the hull in a matter of minutes.

"Sam to Bridge. We've got a problem. The plant life here is extremely corrosive and apparently has some level of intelligence. It's aiming for the ship and already severely damaged SASU."

"Did you have a chance to figure out what will kill it?"

"I assume an herbicide would work—but only if we have a large quantity already on board. We don't have time to manufacture any."

"Let's try flamethrowers. I'll send a guard unit."

Sam retreated to the top of the ramp. By the time the assigned guards arrived, the fronds had begun eating the bottom of the ramp. Three of the guards stepped out, the damaged ramp sinking lower as its end disintegrated. Spreading their feet and bending their knees, they managed to keep their balance and each faced in a different direction, raised their weapon, and opened fire.

The green fronds didn't burn easily, but the reed stems did. Again, screams and whistles split the air as the plants within range succumbed to the flames. When the guards stopped firing, the plants beyond their range did not surge forward. Instead, they began matting together, forming a solid wall of green. The fronds in front whipped like windmills, stirring up the nearby water and creating a frothy curtain in front of them.

Then, they advanced. How, Sam couldn't fathom—he'd assumed they were rooted in the swamp bottom. Now, they moved as though they had legs.

The guards opened fire again. The fire turned the water in front of the plants to steam, creating an invisible wall—a wall that slowly advanced toward the ship.

From somewhere inside the ship, Siki appeared at Sam's shoulder. "How's the battle go—oh ssshit!"

Sam retreated toward him. "This isn't going to work indefinitely. Plus, we're only defending one side of the ship. We need a better solution. Fast."

Two of Siki's arms twined and untwined. "We need a bassse compound."

Sam ran his fingers through his hair. "What would we have a lot of already on the ship?"

Siki's arms wrapped and unwrapped at dizzying speed, like someone twiddling their thumbs. "I gotta get Bluebottle."

Siki slithered away while Sam stared after him. *What good could the ship's chef do?* Sam thought. *He was no chemist.*

Three more guards charged past Sam to replace the first three who'd run out of fuel. An announcement sounded over the all-ship speakers: "Guards to the port and stern with flamethrowers."

The plants were closing in. Sam ran after Siki. *Hope that crazy engineer has a plan.*

When he reached the galley, he saw Siki had Bluebottle by the throat. "Lisssten, you ignorant ssson-of-a-bitch, if this ssship gets eaten by those damned plantsss, you die with usss. Where's the ssstash?"

Face sickly white, Bluebottle pointed to a fifty-five-gallon drum in a corner of the kitchen. Siki dropped him, leaving the chef gasping on the floor, and slithered over to it. Using four of his limbs at once, he pried the lid off.

"Sssam, go down to engineering and round up some guys. Have them bring the sssspray units we use for cleaning the hull and cargo decksss, and as many empty drums as they can round up."

He wanted to ask what Siki had in mind, but time was of the essence, so an explanation would only waste what little they had. He raced for engineering. Siki must have radioed ahead, because when Sam got there, the crew was already assembling hoses, barrels, and sprayers. Sam and the crew carried the equipment back to the kitchen.

Siki and Bluebottle carefully ladled white powder from the drum into the barrels, filled each one with water, and then clamped a lid on tight. Strange hissing noises emanated from the barrels. Siki ordered transport bots to carry the filled containers.

"Get to the top of the ssship. We'll have to go out the upper docking hatch."

Once the reached the highest point above the vessel, the engineering crew attached the sprayers to the barrels. The plants had begun attacking the hull, and some areas already showed damage. Not wasting a single moment, the engineers unleashed their secret agent. It fizzed and fumed as it sprayed, and the plants screamed and retreated. They didn't die, but they gave the ship a wide berth.

Pilot Hawkins appeared out of the hatch. "Stand your ground, men. I just got word from Argenta. A rescue ship is on the way. Their battleships caught up with the pirates and finished them off, so rescue should be here in a couple of hours."

A couple of hours seemed like forever when the flame-throwers had only held the plants off for minutes.

Sam walked over to Siki. "I don't think we've got two hours. How much of that stuff do you have?"

"Not enough, but they definitely didn't like the taste of it. Asss long as we ssstand here and threaten them, I think they'll ssstay away."

Over the next half hour, the plants made two more attempts to advance and got sprayed each time. After that, they retreated far out of range of the sprayers and kept their distance.

When the rescue ship arrived in orbit as promised several hours later, the spray crew re-deployed around the perimeter of the *Blunder*, and the rescue ship attached a tow line to the top of the disabled vessel.

It would take days to get the *Blunder* repaired to the point it could travel on its own, and no one was interested in staying on this planet that long. The Argentans were familiar with it and had blacklisted it long ago. They called the plants Hellspawn.

They effected enough repairs to allow *Blunder* to power up and assist in being towed off the planet and onto Argenta. As payment, Argenta's engineers took the formula for the secret agent that had proven so effective against the Hellspawn.

Once on their way to the safety of Argenta, Sam hunted Siki down in a remote corner of engineering, where he was using several of his arms to replace a series of electrical panels burned out by the pirate attack.

"Siki, I gotta know—what *was* that stuff you sprayed on those plants?"

Siki's head rotated one hundred eighty degrees while his hands kept working.

"Sssuper sssimple. You humans call it Alka-Seltzer. Bluebottle would never admit his cooking is so bad he has to keep a barrel of it on board."

FEELING SLUGGISH

Chris Morton

Pulling on her dressing gown, Miss Luna Knight slowly navigated a path across the piles of clothes strewn around her cabin floor. The only light in the room was that of the digital time reading. "One-forty-five," she mumbled. She'd been having trouble sleeping, and this disturbance was *not* welcome. Whoever it was, they were about to pay most dearly for interrupting.

"Okay, okay!" Luna shouted as the walls bleeped again. Once at the door, she hit the unlocking mechanism.

In the corridor of *Starship Blunder* stood three Taranthians. Light blue in color, these creatures were short and blob-like in appearance, with stubby arms and legs, like beach balls with pudgy faces. In the case of the three before Luna, two were slightly larger than the third. The smallest of whom Luna recognized as her student Celia, a recent addition to the class.

"Good ... morning, Celia," Luna managed, shielding her eyes from the bright hallway. "And to what do I have the pleasure?" she added, ignoring the excited parents who, immediately on seeing Luna, let out a series of excited chatters.

Unfortunately, the translator device these species carried still had a slight delay, something Xylo had apparently been working on.

Luna leaned back against the door frame, waiting.

"Our daughter, CEL124B, has something to tell you," Miss Luna eventually heard.

Unsure as to which of the Taranthian blobs this particular sentence had come from, she gazed sleepily from one to the other. All three of them seemed to be talking at once.

Suddenly, the translator kicked in on overdrive: "She calls her Celia ... She calls her what? ... Celia ... Yes, Celia ... CEL24B is far too— ... And how would you know? ... And why wouldn't I? ... Ever since arriving on this poor excuse for a starship, all you can talk about— ... Mummy, Daddy, tell Miss Luna— ... Yes, tell her, go on ... Since you seem to be the one— ... I tell her? It was you who insisted—"

"Hold on, hold on," said Luna. "One at a time. Please!"

The three Taranthians gazed back at Luna, their small mouths no longer moving.

The translator, however, continued to work away. "Our daughter makes one mention of having to see her teacher, and you're up and— ... But it was I who said this can wait until— ... Oh, no, no, no. You said— ... Tell her, Daddy ... Yes, I'm getting to that, my sweetcake ... Well, go on, tell her, my responsible husband ... Your respon—"

The three Taranthians blinked.

"Now," Miss Luna stated, "before we say anything else, I think we need some order here." She sighed, tightening her dressing gown and attempting to exude authority. "Hands up—which one of you wants to tell me what's going on here?"

All three Taranthians raised their stubby arms.

"How about Celia," said Luna. "Your parents say that you have something important to say?"

A shy chatter came from the smallest of the blobs.

"Yes, Miss Luna."

"Well, go on," encouraged Luna as Celia's parents quietly watched.

"It's the ship, Miss Luna. We need to turn it around."

"Turn it around?"

"We need to go back to ... to ..."

Celia's parents had both raised their hands, but Luna shot them a look. "Go back to Neptune?" Luna said to Celia. "Is that what you're saying? You'd like to go back to Terminus?"

Celia did her best attempt at a nod, imitating human behavior, but since her head and body were one and the same, it was more like a curtsy.

"And why would you like to—?"

A series of chatters came from one of the other two. It was hard to tell which since they looked the same. "Our daughter is convinced that if you don't turn around immediately, the ship will explode."

She ran her fingers through her long black hair and yawned. "Why, exactly?"

Both parents burst out in a series of chatters this time: "She had a dream ... A nightmare ... Quite convincing, she tells us ... She thinks it was a message ... And we promised ... She won't sleep ... And she's not usually like this ..."

Luna sighed. "And you thought it best to tell me, her teacher?"

Celia looked up at Luna, widening her eyes. She made a short chattering, and then the device translated, saying, "You *have* to turn the ship around, Miss Luna. That's what the message said. Turn the ship around before it's too late."

☆ ☆ ☆

Sarah Hawkins was having trouble sleeping. It was almost two in the morning, and in her mind, the options were either to spend another hour hitting the pillow or to make use of the night. The trouble was, as with most of *Starship*

Blunder's missions, there wasn't all that much to do. They were on a delivery job, bringing food and medical supplies to the dwarf planet Ceres. They would check in on the team of scientists stationed there, a rowdy lot in Sarah's estimation. She'd have to keep the crew away from their fire whiskey. Only essential personnel should leave the starship, and the engineers would complain—she could be sure of that. Jenkins had already started a collection for purchasing some fire whiskey of their own.

Sarah sat on the edge of her bed, scrolling through her rota. They'd been two days en route, and in *Starship Blunder's* current state of disrepair, it would take two more. Any other starship in the fleet could have gotten there in half that time, but oh, no, missions with as little importance as this were reserved for *Starship Blunder* alone.

Sarah smiled, still not quite awake. "One day, I'll show them," she said quietly. "One day, I'll get to captain the finest of the fleet."

She began to giggle, then quickly, ashamedly, ran a hand across her face and resumed her ordinary serious demeanor. Standing up, she threw the pad on the bed and stretched. When she was a child, her mother had always given her a mug of warm milk when she'd had trouble sleeping. Maybe that was all she needed: hot milk and maybe a sandwich. Now that she thought about it, she was feeling rather peckish.

★ ☆ ☆

Luna had just gotten back under her silk duvet when the door and walls began bleeping again.

"Cursed..."

Luna threw away the sheet and took up her dressing gown. Tightening it, she went across once again to the door and hit the unlocking mechanism, this time a little harder.

A tired-looking father and his son stood before her, both human and both wearing a matching set of perfectly fetching violet pajamas.

"Hello, Billy," said Luna tiredly. "Come to tell me about your dream?" She looked up at the father, who held on to Billy's shoulder, stoically meeting her gaze.

"I'm very sorry to disturb you, Mrs. Knight—"

"*Miss* Knight," Luna corrected.

"Of course." The father gulped. "It's just that Billy here was most insistent. He just wouldn't let it go, and he's not usually ... he's generally such a well-behaved boy."

Billy smiled up at Luna innocently. The students called him "Billy the Bully" in class. The child was prone to tantrums if he didn't get his way, and he reserved all the best toys for himself.

"And as I said," continued the father, "at this time of night, it is most unprofessional for us to be disturbing you in your..." He took in her dressing gown, his eyes moving down to her bare feet and painted toenails. "In your... in your state of..."

"Okay, that's enough," huffed Luna, ushering them away. "Dreams, dreams, turn the ship around. I know all about it. You lot are the fourth visit I've had tonight. Your message has been received, loud and clear. Now back to bed, the both of you."

Watching the father and son amble back along the corridor, Luna gave up on returning to bed. This, unfortunately, was a minor crisis that could no longer wait until morning.

☆ ☆ ☆

Xylo had been working on the problem all day, and now it was looking as though he might have to keep at it all night too. His mind felt scrambled from lack of sleep, and his spots were shining so brightly he hardly needed the small torch beside him that was shining into the power couplings on C-deck—one of the many sets of patched-up connections linking the warp drive to the bridge controls. *Starship Blunder* was due for another full maintenance check once this transportation mission was over, but before that could happen, Xylo needed to finish the task at hand.

"Goddammit!" he yelped as his head hit into the roof of the cupboard-like space. "Why isn't it here?"

Huffing, he sat back against the paneling. This didn't make any sense; it didn't add up for there to be no visible clue.

"Unless," Xylo whispered to himself, "unless the disconnections are shifting from one output to another. But for that to happen..."

Xylo shook his head. It was almost as if something alive had gotten in there and was moving around, playing him for a sucker and toying with him.

His eyelids began to close. What he needed was sleep. Sleep, and then in the morning, with a clearer mind, he might just be able to start afresh.

"So comfortable," thought Xylo, sliding down into a horizontal position. Clutching at his toolkit, he began to marvel at how strange it was that when as sleep starved as this, the hardest of surfaces felt so wondrously cozy.

☆ ☆ ☆

At two in the morning, Sarah Hawkins expected to find the dining room hall empty. Even the night shift, for the most part, remained on the bridge during the dark hours. However, she spotted Bluebottle in his chef's hat, glumly sitting at one of the tables playing a solitary game of cards. She wasn't entirely surprised to see the ship's chef in the dining hall at such an odd hour.

"Bluebottle, you old goat," Sarah muttered. "Don't you ever sleep?"

The chef looked up lazily. "Hawkins," he croaked. "The only crew member on board who wears a full uniform for a midnight snack."

"Only crew member who wears a full uniform, period."

"So what will it be tonight? Bologna sandwich? We have plenty of—"

"Not this time," replied Sarah with a grimace. "Your bologna sandwiches are famous among the crew for a filling and most tasty ... power snack, but I was after something a little lighter if you could. A little less—"

"I get it, I get it. You'd like to go back to sleep. How about some sherry?"

Sarah waved away the offer, sitting down opposite the chef. "I was more in mind of some hot milk. My mother—"

"Your mother, your mother. Yours and everyone else's mother was a gourmet chef. Heard it all before." Turning over a queen of diamonds, Bluebottle sneered at the card, then stood up, kicking his chair back. "Pilot Hawkins, tonight is your lucky night, because tonight I'm going to make you my once-most-famous specialty."

He disappeared into the kitchen, whistling a tune with the sort of iconic twang that only Bluebottle could manage.

Sarah took out her pad, hoping she wasn't in for a treat she would later regret. Bluebottle's specialties were rather... hit or miss.

As she swiped through her itinerary for the next few days, a bleeping sound indicated a new message was coming through.

"Commander Sterling," Sarah mumbled. "What in the world is he doing up at this time of night?"

She pressed the receive button.

"Pilot Hawkins," said the immaculate-looking Rex Sterling. He seemed surprised at her answering, his perfectly plucked eyebrows furrowing in confusion, but he composed himself quickly. "I wasn't expecting you to be awake. On the night shift, I take it?"

"Something like that," replied Sarah.

"Well, very good," said Sterling in a condescending tone. "Good to show the minions that you can get your hands dirty too."

"Quite," said Sarah. "Was there something I could help you with?"

"No, no, no hurry. It can wait until morning if you like." The commander smiled, showing his perfectly white teeth. "I'm here on Terminus putting in some ground hours. Doing the rounds"—he yawned—"sending out personal messages to all the ships in the fleet. It's been quite a job, I can tell you. You see, here on Terminus Station, we're experiencing a minor infestation."

"A minor—"

"*Spatium limax*!" bellowed the commander. "Space slugs to you and I!" There was a hint of softheaded fatigue in his voice. Had he been up all night delivering these messages? He shifted in his chair. "They get in the power systems. Most annoying creatures, but easily dealt with, I'm sure you know." He looked around behind him. "So now that you have the information, I think I'll head off to—"

"Wait, wait, wait," said Sarah, sitting up to attention. "You're saying there's a chance that *Starship Blunder* may have a space-slug infestation?!"

"Almost definitely," replied the commander. "But as I said—"

"And how long since the discovery of the infestation on Terminus?"

"Oh, I think patrol detected them earlier this morning. Or rather, yesterday morning, since it is now very much time for bed," the commander said with a laugh, ruffling at his hair. "So if you don't mind ... I'm assuming you know how to deal with them, yes? Or should I transfer you to one of our—"

"And let me guess," interrupted Sarah. "*Starship Blunder* is the last ship you decided to contact?"

"As a matter of fact, you are correct," replied the commander, showing his toothy white grin once again. "You know how it is. Priorities and all that. *Starship Blunder* is—"

"The least-important ship in the fleet," huffed Sarah. "Tell me, Commander, are you aware of what space slugs could do to our engines if their food source gets depleted?! A ship of this size is not large enough to sustain... Commander, I'm no expert, but don't you think you should have contacted the smaller ships *first*? Or at least sent a priority-one cluster message to all the fleet at once?!"

"Well, funny you should mention that," beamed Rex, though his smile had turned rather forceful. "You see," he continued, "it's a new policy that the Conglomeracy is trying out. The more personal, friendly touch." He gritted his teeth. "Increased morale for the far-flung vessels. Though I must say, I didn't quite expect it to take this long to—"

"Gourmet, á la soufflé!" came the voice of Bluebottle.

The chef placed down before Sarah what could have easily passed for a Michelin-Star eggnog.

"Oooh, that looks good," said Rex from within Sarah's pad.

"Just a sprinkling of nutmeg and enough brandy to knock out a bat for twelve days."

"Yes, err, thank you, Bluebottle."

The chef sat back down to his card game, satisfied.

"So, Pilot Hawkins," said Rex. "I think I'll be off. Feeling a little hungry now."

"Commander. If the slugs get into the warp core, it could cause a breach."

"Right you are, Hawkins. Flush them out into space. The whole process will take less than an hour. That soufflé, I must say—"

"Pilot Hawkins!" came a voice from the doorway behind them. "If one more of my students' parents comes between me and my bed again, I swear I'll give them something to remember me by!"

"Everything okay there?" asked the commander.

"Couldn't be better," replied Sarah, turning to see a rather disheveled-looking daycare teacher. "Just another night aboard the *Starship Blunder*."

☆ ☆ ☆

They found Xylo fast asleep in a corridor on C-deck.

"I've heard of sleeping on the job, but this one's full-on consummated the marriage!"

"Yes, that's quite enough of that, Jenkins," said Sarah to the night shift's engineering officer. "I think we'd better wake him gently."

"Mr. Xylo!" shouted Jenkins to the slumbering technician, who was still very tightly clutching his toolkit. "Mr. Xylo! Wakey, wakey!"

Shifting in his sleep, Xylo murmured something.

"Mr Xylo!"

"Enough, Jenkins!" Sarah bent down to put a hand on Xylo's shoulder, shaking him awake.

"Pilot Hawkins?"

"That's right," Sarah said in a soothing tone.

"Where am I?"

"The engine room. There's a problem we need your help with."

As Sarah explained the situation, Jenkins cut in, saying, "You're telling me there are space slugs in the systems? Nasty little vermin."

"Space ... of course!" muttered Xylo, raising himself to a seating position. "That explains the ... but wait? How long have they been...?" He turned to Pilot Hawkins. "We must flush them out immediately! In a ship this size—"

"I know, I know," said Sarah, helping him to his feet. She kept close to the unsteady alien's side as they followed Jenkins out of the engine room and down the corridor. "I've declared it a priority one. Jenkins here says we can create a vacuum—"

"Yes, yes, that's right," murmured Xylo, clearly still only half awake. "And siphon them out through the..." Xylo paused to think. "I'd say the best opening would be out through sector F on D-deck. We only patched that up last week. It would simply be a matter of connecting—"

"Already on it," muttered Jenkins. "First, we need to visit the bridge, Mr Xylo. We're about to lock out all unnecessary power systems on D. Then we'll boot the little blighters. Give them a good send-off to hell!"

"That would be the best course of ... the right thing to do." Xylo scratched at one of the many luminous spots on his arm. "Tell me, Pilot Hawkins. Have you received any ... forgive me: I'm trying to remember exactly. It was a paper I read a few months ago on a recently discovered strain of *Spatium limax*. It seems that some of these, err, space slugs have been recorded as showing intelligence. Just confirm for me before we extinguish them all: have you received any reports of communication from the slugs?"

"Communication?" asked Sarah. "What kind of communication?"

"Communication, he says," mocked Jenkins. "*I'd* say, Mr. Xylo, that you've been putting in too many shifts. Messes with the head!" He tapped at his skull.

"I seem to remember," continued Xylo, ignoring his feisty colleague, "something about ... children. That's it! Their underdeveloped brains are more susceptible to picking up ... Pilot Hawkins, have any of the children on board reported receiving messages of any sort?"

☆ ☆ ☆

"Miss Luna Knight!" called Sarah once they'd finally found her in the dining hall. For some reason, she hadn't returned to her cabin quarters. Instead, she sat opposite Bluebottle, or more accurately, slumped opposite Bluebottle.

"Miss Knight!" joined in Xylo. "We need you to confirm what the students have been saying."

"Don't think you'll get much out of her," croaked Bluebottle, who was still hard at it with the solitaire. "Not for a few hours anyway. Could even be days. Depends on the individual."

"What did you do to her?" asked Sarah, rounding the table to take in a very-much-out-cold Luna Knight.

"Not me. The soufflé."

"She drank my soufflé?"

"You disappeared. Didn't want to waste it."

"Well, I have been busy," said Sarah, noticing the empty glass and a very-satisfied-looking Luna Knight who was snoring quietly under a mat of jet-black hair. "Jenkins. Xylo. I don't think we can wait any longer. The risks are too great."

"Maybe we could talk to the children themselves," suggested Xylo.

"So what is it this time?" asked Bluebottle. "Gremlins in the systems? Another crash landing on our horizon?" He laughed hard, hitting at the table. "Never a dull moment on board *Starship Fu—*"

"Bluebottle! Enough!" reprimanded Sarah. "This is serious! Space slugs have infested the ship, and they may well be intelligent. That puts us in quite a grave dilemma!"

"Just kill the little grubs," said Jenkins. "I'll do it myself. Take the blame. Job done."

"Jenkins, if they are intelligent, you could be up for court martial."

"Space slugs, you say," put in Bluebottle, observing Sarah's rather worried face. "*Spatium limax*. Rather partial to bologna, as I remember."

"Rather ... what?"

Sarah, Xylo, and Jenkins looked down at the chef, all perplexed. Was he making another kind of joke?

"Been around as long as I have, you get to know what all sorts of creatures enjoy stuffing themselves with. Those vermin have raided my kitchen more than once. And it's always the bologna they go for."

"Bluebottle, just how sure are you? Time is of the essence."

"You're telling me that a creature that feeds on deuterium traces is *also* partial to seasoned meat product?" scoffed Jenkins.

"Just speaking from experience," replied Bluebottle.

"Now that he mentions it," said Xylo. "I seem to remember reading ... something about the myrtle berries."

"Okay, enough chit-chat," said Sarah. "Wake up every biologist, malacologist, and goddamn nutritionist on board! We'll put it to the vote!"

"Right you are, Pilot Hawkins."

"But just out of curiosity," said Sarah, turning again to Bluebottle. "Exactly how much bologna do we have in your kitchen? Because I have a funny feeling we're going to need it."

☆ ☆ ☆

When Luna Knight finally roused to a sleepy, fuzzy wakefulness, the dining hall buzzed with several crew members—many more than she recalled seeing before she dozed off.

Rising to her feet unsteadily, Luna took in the scene. Crewmates wheeled glass tanks to and from the kitchen. There was a bustle in the air, and everyone seemed to be wearing all manner of nightdress.

A sleepy Gutarak glided past with an empty glass tank, his flattened tentacles sticking out from under his night-gown. From the kitchen came one of the Taranthians, wheeling out another tank, this one full of sliced bologna.

"Bologna?" she thought. "What in the blazes is going on?"

Noticing the Taranthian's stubby arms were struggling to push the tank along, Luna moved over to help.

"What's all this about?" she asked wearily.

A series of chatters came from the Taranthian when a Sesmipod came across to aid them with the tank.

"Miss Luna Knight, I see you've finally woken up," squeaked the Sesmipod, who she now recognized as one of her student's parents. Usually, this individual was far too scared to even wish her a good day.

"Miss Luna, you wouldn't believe the night we've been having," came the Taranthian's translator. "It started, of course, with my daughter's dream, and wouldn't you know, it turns out it was space slugs sending her a message! 'Turn the ship around! We told you, didn't we?' That's what they were saying! Intelligent slugs were talking to my own daughter! She and your good self saved the ship!"

"Saved the... what?" asked a confused Luna.

"We're catching slugs!" squeaked the Sesmipod, beaming at Luna with all five of his cloudy gray eyes, as if this short statement made things perfectly clear.

Pushing the tank out of the hall, they emerged into a packed starship corridor. Nighttime lighting glowed around what had to be at least thirty crew in this section alone.

"They've opened up power hatches all over the decks. And there's a reward for the crew member who catches the most slugs!"

"I see," said Luna, even though she very much didn't. She looked to the Taranthian. "Slugs were communicating with your daughter?"

The Taranthian let out a series of chatters as they moved over to an open power hatch.

"Just hold it here, underneath," squeaked the Sesmipod. "The smell attracts them, you see. A little like, what is the correct word, like your human activity of fishing."

"Fishing?"

"The bologna is bait. And the slugs will—"

"The message the slugs were sending was to turn the ship around," cut in the Taranthian's translator, whirling into action. "They're clever little things and knew this small ship out here in the middle of space would not sustain them for long. They didn't want to go for the warp core, you see. So, they sent my daughter a message. And I told my wife. I told her. But she didn't listen—she never listens. But our Pilot Hawkins, bless her heart, came up with this plan. It seems bologna will do just as well. And Chef Bluebottle has promised a gourmet breakfast to all those who help. Actually, Pilot Hawkins indicated that Bluebottle should make something to thank the volunteers. It's like a slumber party, really. We're working together. Mind you, I'd say it's refreshing to have something productive to do for once. It's been weeks since anything interesting happened on this ship. Not that I'm a fan of crash landings and near-death experiences, but I'm just saying. Oh look, here comes one now!"

Luna watched as a tiny, silvery slug emerged from inside the power hatch. Slowly, it slid its way into the tank, where it dropped onto the pile of bologna.

"Who'd have known?" Xylo said as he came up behind them and placed a hand on Luna's shoulder. "A creature this small capable of telepathic communication!"

"Who'd have thought they'd like bologna so much?" said Sarah as she joined them too. "Well done, Miss Knight!" she said, raising her voice over the party-like atmosphere. "If you hadn't passed on the message when you did, we'd have been killing these innocent creatures!"

"Sure," answered Luna. "Don't mention it."

"Cute, don't you think?" commented Xylo, watching as another silvery slug slithered its way into the tank.

"Cute? You must be joking! They *stink*!" said Sarah.

"I think that's the bologna. There's quite a lot of it."

"Xylo, remind me to never eat bologna again."

Luna turned her nose up in agreement while Xylo simply smiled. "Cheer up, Pilot Hawkins. The scientists on Ceres will have a field day with this lot. Bound to make a mention of us in their paper."

"Ceres..." murmured Sarah with a faraway look in her eye. "Twenty-eight hours until we land. You know, Xylo, after the night we've had, I may well have to try some of their fire whiskey after all."

"Yes, well, if nobody minds," said Luna with a huge yawn, "I think it's about time I got back to bed."

"Not staying for Chef Bluebottle's specialty breakfast?" asked the Sesmipod, his already squeaky voice rising an octave in surprise.

Rather than reply, Luna waved away the offer. Tightening her dressing gown, she moved through the crowd of newly appointed slug-catchers. They watched her dark figure weaving about, intermittently holding on to a passing crew member for support.

"The daycare teacher who saved the slugs," marveled Xylo. "You think she's okay?"

Sarah narrowed her eyes. "I'm proud of her for coming to me when she did. If she'd waited till morning, then these creatures would not have lived. But as far as rewards go..." She smiled. "I'd say Miss Luna Knight over there has had quite enough of Bluebottle's specialties, don't you think?"

"I'd have to agree with that," said Xylo, watching Luna stumble through the far exit. "Although the next time I have trouble sleeping, I may well have to try some of that soufflé myself."

OUT OF THE DUSTY PLANET

Edward Cooke

Incense burned. Nose tickling, Sarah swallowed down a sneeze. At this point in the ritual, if she exhibited the slightest sign of levity, the P'arrish priest would hold her in contempt of the Temple and very likely call down a holy war on her unrighteous ass ... in which there was no longer any sensation at all, not after three hours of sitting still on the hard, wooden floor.

Beside Sarah, Rear Admiral Caide looked calm and collected. But then, Sarah would probably view her own discomfort more philosophically had she been in Caide's pilot seat during the War of the P'arrish Outing. Compared with the Battle of Creemt'e, it must be a picnic for him to sit here and listen to the Hierarch of P'arr recite his interminable psalms, each one punctuated by twelve ritual interludes during which he would play the sacred nose flute. Diplomacy: Better Than War™. On this occasion, just barely.

From Sarah's other side, Xylo whispered, "Do you think he'd let me have a toot on that flute? It looks kind of fun."

"Shush," Sarah urged. The Hierarch glowered at her. "Do you want to start another war with P'arr?"

"Sure. Nothing like a war to increase funding for R&D. Maybe the *Blunder* would get a refit—perhaps even some of those fancy torpedoes."

Sarah shook her head in disbelief, which throbbed in response.

The previous night, Chef Bluebottle had persuaded her to try his latest batch of homebrew. Sarah's tongue lay heavy, and her head still wouldn't stop spinning. She swayed backward and forward on the floor, but she reckoned that if the worst happened and she fell asleep, it would look to the priest as if she were bowing really deeply and with great reverence, humbling herself in the presence of the Most High.

However high P'arr's god was, he couldn't have been as high as Sarah the previous night. For all that she was regretting them now, Bluebottle's brewskis had made her feel better than she had in a long, *long* time. There was just something about piloting the *Blunder* that got her down every once in a while. Despite her technical skill, there was only so much she could achieve with subpar equipment.

She couldn't quite remember what she'd done under the influence, but that scarcely mattered when she'd had a good time. Hopefully, her drinking companions also had fun. She strained to recall what exactly had happened, and that took her focus away from keeping down the roiling tempest brewing in her stomach.

☆ ☆ ☆

Only minutes later in a tense meeting in a closed-door conference room at the Conglomeracy Base on P'arr, Admiral Caide stopped scowling long enough to speak. "For a moment there, I thought I was back holding the line at Creemt'e. I've never seen anything like that broadside you gave His Holiness."

"I really am *dreadfully* sorry," Sarah said for perhaps the fortieth time. She and Xylo were growing tired of standing at attention. Commander Rex Sterling stood at ease, though he had long been the Admiral's pet.

"Oh, I know you are. But don't tell me. Try telling the people of P'arr. You do realize P'arr is a theocracy, and the Hierarchy is not only the head of the Temple but also the de facto dictator and Fleet Admiral of the P'arrish Celestial Command? And, of course, you know perfectly well that the PCC has flourished since the war and presently outnumbers our fleet ten to one."

Sarah opened her mouth to say she was sorry. Again. But she felt a pang in her stomach and turned her head away from the Admiral, just in case.

"Such a personage demands respect," the Admiral said. "We would be well advised to treat him with kid gloves—a whole kid EVA suit if need be. What is *not* a good idea is projectile-vomiting at him so hard that he does a backflip off his stool and burns half his beard off on his own joss sticks."

Sterling spoke for the first time. "Forgive me for saying so, sir, but isn't there an easy way we can remedy our... diplomatic mishap?"

Caide crossed his arms. "Amaze me."

"You've heard of the Eye of the New Sun, the most sacred relic in P'arrish theology?"

"What about it?"

"I was talking to some of the acolytes over a drink last night, and they told me what an embarrassment it is to their Hierarchy that the Eye is presently in the hands of the Dustkings."

"Rex, you idiot. Dustkings are giant worms that live on the waste planet Kippax. Instead of hands, they have all those creepy cilia."

"Well yes, sir, but my point is, surely the Hierarchy would forgive us if the *Blunder* were to go to Kippax and recover the Eye. It's worth a try, don't you think?"

"What's the worst that could happen?" Admiral Caide wondered aloud.

"We all get eaten by giant worms," Sarah said.

"Sounds like the Conglomeracy has got nothing to lose," Caide replied. "I'll have you cleared for launch, and I'll try to keep the Hierarchy calm until you get back. I'd almost sooner come with you than listen to him sing and play his entire psalter. Dismissed."

On her way to the *Blunder*, Sarah felt weighed down by three things: her stomach, inside which burned a red-hot slinky that might leap into her throat again at any moment; her fear of being eaten alive by giant worms, which reminded her of Chef Bluebottle's version of ramen; and her curiosity over why Rex was so keen to help out in her time of need.

☆ ☆ ☆

"Thank you for having me on board," Reverend Doctor S'ock said formally. "God bless you."

"Don't mention it," Sarah said through clenched teeth as she ran through her preflight checks. His Holiness the Hierarchy hadn't been much impressed with Admiral Caide's offer of an Eye-retrieval mission. In fact he'd been so skeptical that he had insisted on sending one of his own inner circle along, supposedly as an observer. Sarah thought the Hierarchy ought to have more faith.

Dr. S'ock was almost indistinguishable from the Hierarchy, all flowing robes and looming hat, except he still had his full and bushy beard. When he had come aboard, Sarah had caught Chef Bluebottle staring at it, no doubt hoping it concealed some small mammal that he could cook on a rotisserie.

At the moment, the bridge was quiet, and the lights were low. The crew of the *Blunder* were in their usual pre-flight positions of queuing for the toilet in the final minutes before takeoff.

Over the comm, the tower AI said, 'You are cleared for takeoff. And on a personal note, give my regards to the Dustkings. It was nice knowing you.'

I'll show you, Sarah thought before sending the *Blunder* hurtling into space. It wasn't quite the majestic parabola she had envisaged. More a sort of lurch followed by a limp.

All right, then. If I can't show you, I'll show those stupid worms when we get where we're going. More will be at stake if the ship is about to be swallowed, and that will coax a better performance out of us all.

She suddenly understood the need for deep, unwavering faith when faced with situations of unlikely personal survival. No wonder men like the Hierarchy dove into the arms of organized religion.

☆ ☆ ☆

They were barely underway before trouble started. First, Xylo accused Dr. S'ock of being an alien spy.

"He keeps asking me how everything works," Xylo complained. "The drives, the communication device, the lot. Unless you order me to tell him, I am not going to give away the slightest information to a potential enemy." His blue spots flickered.

"The more I know about the ship," Dr S'ock explained, "the more accurately I can pray for her. You'll forgive me for saying so, but she looks to me like she could use all the help she can get."

Sarah was already fed up. Admiral Caide had impressed on her the need to maintain protocol with the P'arrish at all times, as well as the importance of avoiding any further faux pas. At the same time, it was abundantly clear that Dr. S'ock's presence was part of Sarah's punishment.

Feeling terrible, she decided to take S'ock's side. "Think of it this way, Xylo. You can make friends with Dr. S'ock, or you can make friends with the worms. Choose one."

Xylo's spots flushed.

"Besides," Sarah added, "the bright side of this ship's absence of anything remotely state-of-the-art is that we don't have any secrets to let slip."

"If we're such a museum, we should have charged this guy an entry fee," Xylo complained.

Unfortunately, Dr. S'ock wouldn't be the only individual Sarah needed to appease. Chef Bluebottle raised Sarah on the comm to vent about their guest's dietary requirements.

"In principle, Dr. S'ock could eat anything," Bluebottle grumbled. "But no! He has all these fiddly little rules about what he will and won't touch. Doesn't he realize how lucky he is? Most of the crew are allergic to this and intolerant of that. What right has any religion to go around imposing its will on otherwise-healthy people?"

Sarah felt she ought to trot out some formulaic response, but she hadn't forgotten her own unexpected reaction to Chef's beer. Nor did she want to get herself into any more trouble with the Admiral. If Dr. S'ock levied a single complaint once they got back to Neptune, Sarah could very well be out of a job.

Dr. S'ock intuited the gist of their conversation—not hard when the chef was yelling loud enough to burst Sarah's handset speaker—and replied on his own behalf. "Religion isn't a system of rules; it's a personal relationship with our Creator."

"A dysfunctional one at that," Chef hollered.

Dr. S'ock smiled tightly. "I suggest you cook whatever you feel capable of cooking, and I'll simply fast in reverence to God's greatness. I'm afraid I've lost trust in your ability to honor His Holiness with a compliantly clean meal."

Sarah hung up the comm in the midst of Chef's screamed retort.

Miss Luna Knight called almost immediately after that, letting Sarah know that Dr. S'ock wasn't permitted near her classroom until he submitted to the appropriate criminal records check and someone verified he wasn't on any untoward registry.

Dr. S'ock smoothly handed Sarah a holographic projector containing a recording of himself giving a short and simple talk about his religious beliefs. "Invite Miss Knight to play it to the kids, or not, as she feels led. What harm can it do?"

Sarah fought the urge to ask sweetly whether the recording included a nose-flute soundtrack. Instead, she passed Dr. S'ock's projector to Xylo. "Please give this device a thorough counter-espionage check."

Xylo ran off eagerly to his workshop, spots glowing.

Sarah grinned at Dr. S'ock. If his gadget still worked after Xylo had taken it apart, it would count as a miracle.

☆ ☆ ☆

The *Blunder* somehow navigated to orbit around Kippax. Dr. S'ock seemed positively gleeful.

"What did I tell you? Thanks to the power of my answered prayers, we made it against all odds."

"I like to think my piloting had something to do with it," Sarah said.

"Not to mention my maintenance," Xylo added. "I advise you not to rely on your god to guide every last one of your literal footsteps. If I hadn't replaced that loose floor panel, you would have had to finish your prayers in the heating ducts."

"By divine grace and mercy, we're here now," Dr S'ock said. "How are we going to get down to the surface?"

"I've been thinking about that," Sarah answered, "and I've reached the conclusion it's far too dangerous. We'll send down a drone that will search for the Eye based on your description, grab it, and run. That way none of us will have to go anywhere near a Dustking."

"Impossible." Dr. S'ock folded his arms, then seemed to realize he'd done so while looking down to check for dodgy floor panels, pinning his beard against his solar plexus. He couldn't raise his head without unfolding his arms and admitting his mistake.

He compromised by closing his eyes as though in prayer. "It would be an unforgivable insult to everything we believe if the Eye of the New Sun were to be touched by artificial hands."

Xylo smirked. "Isn't it already enough of an affront that even as we speak, your Eye has got slimy worms slithering all over it?"

Dr. S'ock ignored him. "I must go down to the surface personally and regain the Eye for the eternal glory of the Hierarchy."

Xylo gave a little wave. "Good luck with that, fella. It was nice knowing you."

"But since I am unskilled in the driving of your ground vehicle, you will have to come with me."

"You have *got* to be kidding." Xylo folded his arms and shook his head.

Sarah spent one whole second thinking about what Dr. S'ock would tell the Admiral when they returned home empty-handed. "Xylo, let's take our old Mobile Unit Shadow out for a spin. It's been so long, I can't remember the last time we used it. Keeping it running will be an excellent test of your ingenuity."

"I'm not fooled by your flattery," he replied. "I'll go with you, but only under protest. And, I'm going to sit at the back so I'll be the last one down a Dustking's throat."

☆ ☆ ☆

The cabin of Mobile Unit Shadow smelled musty. It had taken Xylo an age to remember where he had put the keys, and for a while, he had been threatening to break in using a stray bit of wire.

Sarah wiped dust off the dash and unhooked the furry dice from the rear-view mirror before Dr. S'ock spotted them and condemned them as Satanic or worse.

She put the key in the ignition, thought about praying, and turned it anyway. Xylo had assured her the diesel engine was still viable, though she had no idea where he had found any fuel. Come to think of it, she would have preferred to be informed if the *Blunder* was carrying combustibles. *Too late now.*

The engine wheezed and sputtered. Sarah tried again. This time, the engine caught and the whole cabin began juddering. Unluckily, it started up just as Dr. S'ock gestured in what turned out to have been a traditional blessing among the P'arr, so for the first ten or so miles, Sarah and Xylo had to listen to their unwelcome guest extol the virtues of his god.

There was nothing in the landscape to serve as a distraction. It was grey and barren, and, as promised, there was an awful lot of dust. They neared an outcrop that looked like it might be a rock, but when they drew closer, Sarah saw it was simply a dust dune blowing debris into the wind.

The only entertainment on offer other than Dr. S'ock's ongoing homily was Sarah's rusty driving. She couldn't remember the last time she'd had to handle a stick shift. She stalled a couple of times, flushing with embarrassment each time.

Sarah was on the verge of asking why an all-powerful god would ever allow his favorite trinket to get stolen by worms when the ground in front of them caved in and a Dustking reared up out of the pit.

Xylo screamed and put his hands over his eyes. Dr. S'ock made a gesture no doubt intended to ward off evil—to no effect—and began to chant.

Sarah crashed into reverse and slammed her foot down. Mobile Shadow withdrew in a cloud of diesel. All three of its crew felt the rubbery tang of the burning clutch in the back of their throats.

The windscreen filled with the dust-worm's maw, each long tooth flanked by two shorter ones. The creature's breath flooded the cabin like an exhalation from a vacuum cleaner.

Sarah got Shadow turned around and sped back toward the *Blunder*.

"What are you thinking?" Xylo cried. "You're leading it straight to our ship for its main course."

Sarah flipped the radio switch to instruct the *Blunder* to prepare for takeoff. Over the dash speaker, they heard Miss Luna inviting her class to draw the oncoming worm—and to please share the pencils. The daycare teacher sounded unsure, and Sarah didn't think it was a shortage of grey pencils bothering her.

Xylo began pressing buttons on the dash. Shadow's foglights and indicators went on and off, and the windscreen wipers flapped back and forth. Dr. S'ock leaned over to help and got squirted with lukewarm chocolate. Xylo was delighted. "How did you do that? I could never get it to dispense."

I am a good pilot. I can handle this, Sarah told herself. At some point on the voyage, her body had finally triumphed over Chef's homebrew. She felt alive and wanted to stay that way.

She released her seatbelt, braked hard enough to lock the wheels, and swung the wheel. Mobile Shadow ended up side-on to the oncoming worm. The force of the skid threw Sarah out through the driver's door, Xylo tumbling after her. The two of them rolled through the dust toward the *Blunder*.

The Dustking's head came down, blotting out the stars.

☆ ☆ ☆

Sarah and Xylo watched from the relative safety of the lowered cargo ramp as the worm burrowed back into the dust and vanished, taking the entire Mobile Unit Shadow down with it.

Sarah noticed Xylo was crying as well as coughing. She put an arm around him. When her throat was clear enough to speak, she said, "I know, it really gets to you, doesn't it?

As mad bearded priests go, he was an almost-decent one after all."

"I couldn't care less about him. It's Shadow I'm sorry for. The hours I spent polishing those spark plugs."

"Show a little respect, will you?"

Xylo coughed again. "You mean for the dead? Oh... I'm sorry."

"No, for the engine. A diesel doesn't need spark plugs."

Sarah pressed the button to raise the cargo ramp. Before it had closed completely, several figures in hooded cloaks rolled ninja-style through the narrowing gap. They landed on their feet and brandished blades.

"Who do you think you are?" Sarah demanded.

"We're the Dustmen," one of the lithe little figures said. "And don't ask us to take out your trash. We've heard all those gags before!"

"Don't tell me, your garbage or your life, right?" Xylo said.

"Quiet!" another Dustman ordered.

"I hope, for your sake, there are some Dustwomen hanging around on this wretched planet."

"Silence!" the third figure said while threatening Xylo with his sai. Sarah could see he had made it out of a triad of dust-worm teeth, one long between two short. She preferred not to ask how he had come by such a weapon.

She tried to keep her voice level as she asked, "What do you want from us?"

The Dustmen exchanged puzzled glances. Finally, one said, "We thought you wanted something from us."

Now it was Sarah's turn to look blankly at Xylo and see him equally baffled. "Like what?" Sarah asked.

"What a stupid question! It was your ship that signaled us from orbit and told us to meet you here so we could trade a large quantity of our finest product."

From beneath their cloaks the Dustmen produced black polythene sacks. Xylo started laughing. The Dustman with the biggest sai waved it at him but ended up slashing his own refuse sack, causing dazzling white powder to run out onto the deck.

"In our language, it is called fnar. We harvest it from the worms and use it to pass the time. We are surprised anyone else wants to buy it, especially dwellers on planets where there is view-on-demand television. Do you have such a wonder on board? We are desperate to know what happens in the second season of Our Friends from Frolix 8."

☆ ☆ ☆

"You've made my solar cycle," Admiral Caide told Sarah. "Feel free to watch the holographic footage of the moment I handed His Holiness over to Interstellarpol to answer all those tricky questions about P'arr's fnar-dealing operation.

If I'd had to listen to another psalm, I would have gone nuts. I knew he must have been using some sort of stimulant, the way he kept on singing and playing those tedious ditties for hours at a stretch. Great job, Hawkins."

Rex Sterling looked sulky. He clearly wasn't used to hearing the Admiral praise officers on other starships.

"It so happens I had a different favor to ask," Sarah said.

"Go ahead. Neptune is your oyster."

"I wondered if I might have a private word with Commander Sterling. Alone and without surveillance."

"In view of what you've accomplished, that sounds like the bare minimum. My office is at your disposal. So is this landlubber." Admiral Caide saluted Sarah, glared at Rex, and then marched out.

As soon as the door was closed, Sarah asked, "Why were you so keen to help me out of a tight spot?"

Rex wouldn't meet her eyes. "We're comrades in arms, aren't we? I'm certain you'd do the same for me."

"You told the Admiral you heard those fibs about the Eye of the New Sun from the P'arrish acolytes. While you were having a drink with them."

Rex said nothing.

"It's the drinking that interests me," Sarah persisted. "We were all at the same party, weren't we? Drinking Bluebottle's special brew."

"It was quite a party. Take my word for it."

"I don't take anybody's word for anything. I want to know what happened. Did you or I do something regrettable? Or were we both to blame?"

"You mean you don't remember?"

"Rex, I'm lucky to have escaped with my liver. Total recall would be too much to ask."

"Well, you'll just have to wrack your brains, because while you were in flight, I erased all the footage. What happens at a Bluebottle-brew party *stays* at the party. All I will say is, that if you really don't remember, then you've insulted me far more than His Drug-Dealerness.'

Try as she might, Sarah couldn't get him to say another word.

AS NATURAL AS FALLING

H. Hackman

Thank the cosmos that vacation is over.

It was nothing personal. Neptune was just as magical as Jay's childhood memories had promised.

She threw back the covers and sat up in bed. Her personal quarters were a mess, something she hoped to rectify soon. The leftover crumbs from a late-night snack made her sigh. She brushed them into a trash duct, which would expel all waste into the vacuum of space, then adjusted the photographs on her desk.

Recognizing her unique fingerprints, the photographs projected animated holograms into the air. The portrait of her brother winking, her parents smiling formally, Neptune's ocean glistening.

Jay had always bolted to her favorite window on stormy days. Clear weather permitted an enormous view as the expanses of sky and sea stretched out to meet the horizon, but on days when storms reigned supreme, any visibility swam behind a shimmering curtain of rainfall. She would curl up by the rain-washed window with her favorite textbook and read, soothed by the soft rumble of thunder and pattering raindrops.

No, Neptune was not the problem with its floating cities and glittering spires. But it had an unavoidable disadvantage: location—specifically, the proximity of Jay's family.

With the *Blunder* regularly returning to Neptune for fuel and supplies, there was no excuse for Jay to avoid family visits. And when she visited, the interrogations would begin. Was she the head nurse yet? Could she transfer to the *Prime*, the starship under her uncle's command? Or at least transfer to a *real* ship?

She always gave the same reply in a level voice, albeit through gritted teeth at times: it was an honor to serve, no matter which ship she was stationed on or which crew she worked with.

Her nurse uniform lay crumpled on the floor, its traditional green color faded from use. New uniforms weren't a high priority on the *Blunder*—not that many of the crew wore uniforms anyway.

Jay could imagine her uncle wincing if he found out about that. Rex was sympathetic about the family's judgment she endured, but she knew he shared some of their concerns.

Jaw set, she slipped into the uniform and smoothed it straight. *It's an honor to serve,* she reminded herself fiercely. Nursing was a noble calling in itself. It didn't matter what laughingstock ship she was stationed on. It also didn't matter how many of the crew wore uniforms. Reputations and dress codes didn't define ships. As long as the crew performed admirably...

The mirror began to levitate.

(Well. Her fault for setting the bar so high.)

"Gravity disengaged," an automated voice warned flatly.

Jay lunged forward to grab the mirror but stumbled off balance. Her bare feet swung through empty air as she rose off the floor. Other objects in the room were rising too: photographs, textbooks, the copy of her nursing degree. The gravity device must've malfunctioned. Or switched off.

If gravity came back, she didn't want to fall from too big of a height. Jay grabbed a railing where her clothes hung— at least, when she had time to hang them. She pulled herself closer using the railing like the rung of a ladder, her legs trailing in midair as if buoyed in water. Strands of her hair fanned out like the tentacles of an Orgoth squid.

Judging by the shouts of panic and exasperation outside, the gravity problem wasn't limited to her room. At least that meant the issue would get Xylo's full attention. Oh, she couldn't *wait* to hear what had happened this time. Maybe someone had forgotten which lever to pull or had spilled coffee on the control panels. It wouldn't be the first time.

"Gravity engaged."

Jay gasped as she dropped from midair. Her fingers clenched around the rail as her full weight yanked on her shoulders. She swung toward the floor and landed feet first among the clutter of her falling possessions.

Half of her expected gravity to fail again, so she held onto the rail despite her awkward position. But nothing happened. She released the rail and took a ragged breath. Both of her shoulders ached, but otherwise, she was fine.

That was fast. Xylo had a good reaction time. But accidents were unavoidable after an incident like this, and not everyone would have been as lucky as her. She yanked her shoes on, snatched up her bag of supplies, and rushed out the door.

Sure enough, Jay hadn't even reached the med bay before the comms transmitted instructions for her to check on the daycare. Her gut tightened at the thought of what might've happened to the children during the gravity failure.

However, she burst into the daycare to find a calm scene. Most of the children, occupied with reading or drawing, were sitting on blankets and carpet that must've softened their falls. Little faces jerked up at her sudden entrance. She froze.

"Over here," a voice called from the corner. It belonged to a young woman who looked about Jay's age.

No uniform, of course. Instead, the woman wore a jet-black dress with lacy black tights and tiny black boots. A spiked hairband secured the upper half of her hair in a long, dark ponytail. Tattoos covered her pale forearms with bright splashes of color. "Hi. I'm Luna Knight, the daycare teacher."

"Nurse Sterling. The gravity failed in here too, right? What happened?"

"Luckily, we were in the middle of nap time." Luna quirked a smile, her lips gleaming with black lipstick. "I told the kids that we were doing naptime on the ceiling today. Like bats."

"Right. And then?"

"That kept them calm for a while. Then, the gravity suddenly came back. Most of them landed on something soft, but this little guy fell on a table." She gestured to a little boy sitting on a cushion.

Drying tears shone on the boy's cheeks, and he had one leg propped up on a pillow. "It hurts, Miss Knight."

"I know, kiddo. But the nurse is going to take care of you."

Jay sure hoped so. Joining the *Blunder* hadn't been very eventful in terms of injuries and illness. Usually, she was occupied with stomachaches and indigestion, largely caused by Chef Bluebottle's cooking. And... she had never worked with children before.

Crouching on the floor, she pulled out her scanner and began to lean forward.

The boy instantly flinched away, the effort twisting his expression with pain. "What... what's that? What does it do?"

"It's a scanner. It's going to scan your leg and show me what it looks like inside." Jay wasn't sure what else to say. She just needed him to hold still. "Look, it isn't scary. Okay?"

"Will it *hurt*?"

"Yes," Jay blurted, then quickly amended, "a little. Only a little."

Fresh tears welled up in the boy's eyes.

Luna shot Jay a sharp look, then knelt at his other side. "Would you like me to hold your hand while she works?"

The kid nodded and grabbed her hand without hesitation, fingers squeezing tight. To her credit, Luna didn't even wince.

While Jay pressed the scanner against the wounded leg as gently as she could, she glanced to the side. Luna was pointing to one of the many tattoos on her arms, where a purple circle surrounded by rays had been inked on her forearm. "You see this, Lucas?"

He nodded again. He was rigid as if determined not to acknowledge Jay's presence.

Luna continued, her voice soft in the tones of a storyteller: "This tattoo was inspired by the Zelros. When humans first made contact with them on their planet, the Zelros showed them an image just like it. They said it was their sun. The humans were confused at first, because the only visible sun from that planet was yellow. But later, we learned that it wasn't yellow. Or it was only yellow to *us*."

"What does that mean?" Lucas breathed.

"The Zelros can see colors that humans can't, like ultraviolet. Their sun radiates ultraviolet rays, so to them, that's what color it is." Luna smiled. "It's hard to describe a color to someone who's never seen it, but they say that ultraviolet looks like a bright pinkish purple."

"That's so cool."

"It *is* cool, isn't it? That's why I got the tattoo. I want to remember that everyone has their own unique perspective. Sometimes, there isn't a right or wrong answer. People just perceive things differently. And that's why we need to listen to each other. Who knows? Maybe someone sees colors that you can't."

Jay's attention kept flitting sideways as if drawn by a magnetic force. There was no mistaking Luna's sincerity with her bright smile as she talked.

Then the scanner beeped. Jay quickly looked down to read the results, a faint flush warming her neck at how easily she had been distracted. "You've got a sprained ankle. It'll take a week to heal, and you won't want to move much during that time. Putting weight on the leg will only prolong your need for rest."

"No daycare?" the child asked.

Jay shook her head.

Crestfallen, Lucas glanced at Luna as if hoping she would object.

Luna sighed. "If that's what Nurse Sterling recommends, I can't argue. I'm sure your parents will agree. But don't worry, I'll stop by your room to see you."

"Miss Knight, if you could spare a minute, I need your help carrying Lucas to the medical bay. Once there, I can apply a cream to reduce swelling and wrap up the ankle." Jay stood up and slipped the scanner away before grabbing her heavy medical bag.

"Sure... I'll need to find someone to watch over the other children."

With perfect timing, Pilot Sarah Hawkins strode up to the daycare entrance and remarked, "I see Nurse Sterling found her patient. Do you two need any assistance?"

"Actually, yes," Luna remarked. "I need to escort Lucas to the medical bay. Could you keep an eye on the rest of the children until I'm back?"

Sarah came into the daycare and said, "Of course."

"I've never been to the medical bay before," Luna added.

Jay turned to Luna and said, "Then I'll show you where to go." Every nerve in Jay prickled with discomfort, but she didn't want to waste time—she had a patient to take care of.

They walked through a corridor in silence, then another and another. Lucas sagged in Luna's arms, tired from the shock and pain of the day.

"Your bedside manner could use improvement," Luna said quietly, likely not wanting to disturb the child in her arms.

Jay winced. "I wasn't trying to scare him. I just... it's my first time working with a kid."

"Really? Well, it's not that different from an adult. Kids are just little people with less experience."

"It's that easy, huh?"

Luna shrugged. "It is for me."

"I can tell." Jay couldn't deny that. She had found a weakness in her role, but at least she knew someone who could show her how to do better. "You're good. Really good. And if you don't mind, I hope to learn a lot from you."

"Oh." Luna blinked, and then a smile bloomed on her dark lips. "Yeah. I mean, thanks."

☆ ☆ ☆

Jay continued performing check-ups on Lucas until she was satisfied. Each day, Luna would join her to offer encouragement and fill Lucas in on what he was missing in class: story time, arts and crafts, and studying star maps. He always eagerly asked about the lessons. Even Jay felt lighter after spending time with Luna.

Slowly, she became more aware of... things. Odd details. How many steps apart her quarters were from Luna's. How often she could catch the pounding rhythm of a darkly defiant song as she passed by that door.

Then, one day, Jay's door wouldn't open. She *knew* she hadn't changed the password recently.

When she explained the situation to Xylo, he admitted that quite a few doors on the *Blunder* were having the same problem. "The good news is, the malfunction itself is a simple fix. Bad news is that it may take a while before I can repair *all* of the faulty doors."

"It's alright, Xylo." Jay could tell he was stressed, judging by the spots shimmering on his blue skin. Besides, what would taking out her frustration on him accomplish? "I'll... find a way to occupy myself."

He gave a tired nod and strode down the corridor.

Jay sighed. It wasn't a big deal. It *wasn't*. But she'd been so looking forward to just sinking into her bed. Unsure what to do next, she wandered around the halls until she came across another living being.

"What's up?" Luna asked. Twinkling silver earrings framed her face. Though her shirt had long sleeves, narrow slits ran from shoulder to wrist, so her tattoos were still visible. Jay could catch glimpses of pink, green, and purple.

"My door malfunctioned. Looks like it's part of a trend."

"Uh oh. I hope mine isn't broken too. Let's go check." Luna led the rest of the way to her room and tested her door, typing in the password. The door slid open. "Thank the cosmos. Maybe you could stay with me for now. We could hang out."

'Hang out.' Why did both "yes" and "no" bubble up from Jay's gut? "Oh. Well, I don't know exactly how long it's going to take for Xylo to fix it..."

"It's no big deal. I mean, did you have any *other* ideas?"

"Not exactly," Jay admitted as she followed Luna inside.

Luna's quarters were all black, of course. The floor was clean, which made Jay think of her own messy room with an internal wince. But the desk was cluttered: covered with scissors, glue, thread, rhinestones, and colorful socks.

Smirking, Jay plucked up one of the socks. It was fuzzy with orange-and-green stripes. "Have you decided to change up your style?"

Luna rolled her eyes and snatched the sock up. "Funny. No, this is for a puppet show for the kids. I'm using whatever fabric I can get. Socks and gloves I don't want to wear anymore."

"Don't you have puppets already?"

"Yeah, I do. But I wanted to get some new ones, and they're easier to personalize if I make them myself." Luna grinned. "Plus, making them is fun."

Jay smiled. "You'll have to stage a play for them too. I can't imagine what it'd be like." She paused, remembering. "I like that story you told."

"What?"

"The one about the violet sun."

Luna nodded. "Oh, yeah. Me too." She dropped the sock back on the desk. "Funny, before I joined the *Blunder*, people kept telling me to cover up my arms. They said the tattoos would scare the kids. But it seems like adults are the only ones who care."

Jay sighed. "That sounds just like my family. They're all about appearances. Whatever makes me, and by extension them, look the best." She folded her arms, bracing herself for an admission. "My uncle is the commander of the *Starship Prime*. It's not his fault, but sometimes it feels like I'll always be in his shadow."

Luna's eyes widened. "Commander...? Oh, right, your name's Sterling. I knew it sounded familiar."

"Yeah." Jay sighed. "They mean well, I think. But they're pretty good at making me feel like I'm wasting my time."

Eyes flashing, Luna drew herself up straight. She rested a hand on Jay's arm and fixed her with piercing brown eyes. "You're *not* wasting your time. Helping Lucas and the rest of the crew is just as important as commanding a ship."

A pleasant warmth spread through Jay. She ducked her head, unable to hold Luna's gaze. "Thank you."

☆ ☆ ☆

It took longer than Jay would've liked, but it was finally ready.

Luna opened the door, black hair hanging loose over her shoulders. A silver crescent moon dangled from the choker around her neck. Her features looked startlingly bare without makeup, her lips a vulnerable pink instead of black, but Jay didn't mind the new look.

Jay stood in front of the door, shifting on her feet. She held a basket full of old socks, gloves, and even jewelry.

Blinking, Luna peered into the basket. "What's all this?"

"It's for your puppet show." Jay swallowed. "I asked some of the crew if they had stuff to donate. Things they wouldn't miss."

"*What?*" Luna jerked a step back. "Jay, that's... so sweet. You didn't have to do that."

Jay's reply evaporated as she looked up. Luna's warm brown eyes, the color of gingerbread, searched hers. A knowing sparkle had begun to light up within them.

Jay drew a deep breath. "Do you... want to have coffee? Just the two of us?"

Grinning, Luna squeezed Jay's hand. "It's a date."

SALT IN THE WOUND

By Ariele Sieling

Jace glanced at the clock. One hour left. And then she would be on her way, and in no time, striding slowly into the warm, salty water with sand squishing between her toes and the hot sun on her back.

She smiled at the thought.

"What are you grinning at?" her boss, Grimes, grumped as he stomped by. "Focus!" He'd been her manager for over a year at AstEroiD Enterprises—Asteroid Engineering & Digging Enterprises—and he mostly kept to himself, other than acting annoyed at one of his subordinates for superficial reasons.

She rolled her eyes behind his back, and then leaned forward to peer at the numbers streaming across the obnoxiously small screen in front of her.

Jace was responsible for monitoring the drill. It hummed deep below them where it drove a narrow, cylindrical hole through the asteroid they sat on. Though she'd yet to see any sign of it, supposedly the asteroid was filled with quantumite, a rare element used to stabilize wormholes for galaxy hopping.

Quantumite was barely detectable by any technology currently available, but if they found even the slightest hint of it, an AstEroiD Enterprises demolition crew would turn this asteroid to rubble and sift out every ounce of the rare element.

She gazed numbly at the screen. The numbers all remained average. No spikes or dips, nor any flashing orange or green lights.

All was normal.

As usual.

Every minute, Jace glanced at the clock, only to find that barely a minute had passed. Time crawled. This had to be the slowest hour of her life. And that was saying something.

Her life was little more than exponential tedium. She'd thought taking this job would bring her life excitement and thrills, space travel and adventure! Instead, she'd been working a mostly corporate data job—she just happened to do so on an asteroid instead of a planet. And to make matters worse, she lived where she worked, so there was never any escape.

She needed this vacation, more than she'd needed anything in a very long time. Especially if she wanted to make it another two years to the end of her contract.

With only a half hour to go, she heard some commotion outside the door to the drill-monitoring room where she sat.

"They're here!" her boss hollered from the other side of the door.

A grin split Jace's face. She wasn't allowed to move from her seat just yet, but "they" were her ride out of here. Her ticket to the beach, vacation, and relaxation.

The *Starship Blunder*, on a mission from the city of Drayia, which floated on the surface of Neptune in the great Cerulean Ocean, had docked with the asteroid station. They were dropping off several new workers, and Jace was hitching a ride back to Neptune for her break from work.

She focused on the screen. She had to do her job. Her vacation was just around the corner. Doing her job shouldn't be this hard!

Yet she couldn't help but glance at the clock as it ticked, one second after another. Tick... tock... tick... tock...

Then something flashed on the screen. It was so brief Jace wasn't even sure she'd seen it. But almost immediately, a flashing red light appeared on the console, notifying her of the blip in the data.

Squinting, Jace scrolled backward, watching the measurement line carefully.

Sure enough, there it was. A spike. A *big* spike. It could be an error... or it could be exactly what they were looking for.

She groaned. This was going to delay her departure, no doubt. Hopefully, not so much that the ship would leave without her. With a sigh, she pressed the comm button.

"Boss," she stated. "Spike."

It was the first time anyone had seen a spike on this asteroid. There hadn't even been a false reading yet, at least not that she knew of. Her boss was going to be completely—

He burst into the room, interrupting her thoughts. "Show me!" he demanded, jogging toward the console, an intense expression in his eyes.

She pointed at the line and zoomed in so he could see the readings more clearly.

"A spike," he murmured, excitement palpable. He was practically vibrating beside her, bouncing up and down on the toes of his boots.

"Let me see," a voice commanded from the door. A tall woman with a strong, confident posture strode in. She'd pulled her hair back up in a curly ponytail and wore a crisply starched uniform. Her expression was serious.

"Pi... Pilot Hawkins," Jace's boss stuttered, scowling at her. "You're not supposed to be in here."

"Your security officer said the same thing," she said blandly.

"And she let you in anyway?" Grimes grumbled.

"Said something about it being above her paygrade." Hawkins shrugged. "Besides, you know this asteroid is owned by the Conglomeracy. They extended your company permission to mine here. Which means nothing you find is a secret." Pilot Hawkins leaned forward to scrutinize the data. "Hm." As she examined the output, the computer pinged again, indicating a second spike.

Another one? Jace stifled a groan. On one hand, this was very exciting. But on the other... all she wanted was to lie in the sand on the beach and forget about everything for a few days. Was that really too much to ask?

She scrolled forward to reveal the new data, and sure enough, there was not just one, but two more spikes. Three in a row. After months of nothing.

"I'll have to take word back to the Admiral," Pilot Hawkins said firmly. "This is important news. Grimes, please work on confirming these results. In the meantime, we will leave right away to reach comm range as soon as possible. Please alert any loading and unloading crews that we leave in fifteen. And tell anyone catching a ride with us too. If they're not on board in fifteen, they're stuck here."

Jace glanced at the clock. One minute left on her shift. Her gaze shifted toward her boss.

"Yes," he muttered, waving a hand at the door. "Go. Just go."

☆ ☆ ☆

Wearing a backpack stuffed so full the seams looked like they were about to pop and dragging a suitcase along the corridors behind her, Jace raced toward the docking area of the asteroid station. The *Starship Blunder* was the first ship to arrive on the asteroid in months, so the corridors were crowded with curious gawkers.

It didn't matter though. She would escape from this asteroid station if it was the last thing she did. She just hoped nothing got in between her and that ship, because she would run it right over.

Through the window, she could see where the unusual ship jutted out from the station. The hull looked like a patchwork quilt, with colorful panels and various technological components of all different varieties cobbled together in a haphazard way. The bulky, robust ship hosted multiple thrusters, and antennae extended from its body.

It was ugly and beautiful at the same time, but regardless, Jace couldn't wait to be gone from this godawful place.

"Jace Venitara," a voice called from the gate.

She dashed forward, barely avoiding an older man with a long beard and irritable expression. She skidded to a halt breathlessly before a steward. "I'm Jace."

"ID," the man intoned blandly. He wore a crisp uniform with a Conglomeracy patch on the shoulder, and his hands hovered over a keyboard.

She held out her wrist to be scanned and watched as her face and name popped up on the screen.

"You'll be staying in corridor L, room 16."

"Thank you, sir!" she exclaimed, then rushed past him before some act of fate—like another damn quantumite data spike—could get between her and her vacation.

Jace scurried through the corridors of the *Starship Blunder*, amused to see that while they were well-marked, some of the signs had been scribbled over with marker or scavenged from other ships to replace those that had broken or fallen from the walls. She found her quarters easily enough—a long, narrow room with a single bunk, a chair, and no window. A desk folded down over the bed and a vid screen hung on one wall. Under the bed, she found an empty locker with metal doors for her to store her stuff in.

That was it.

The shared facilities were just down the hall, and a sign that looked like it'd been pulled from some generic corporate building read, "Cafeteria," with an arrow pointing deeper into the vessel.

"All passengers and non-essential personnel," a robotic voice intoned over the speaker system. "Please secure yourself and your belongings in your designated takeoff area. We will de-dock at exactly seventeen hundred hours."

Five minutes? The pilot wasn't joking when she said they were leaving right away. Jace was amazed that a ship this large could make such a quick turnaround, but perhaps the crew and passengers hadn't been allowed off to explore.

Jace raced back to her designated room and shut the door. She'd already stuffed her bags under the bed and latched the cabinet. Now, she threw herself onto the bunk and felt around for the safety straps she knew would be fastened to the edges.

She lay down and buckled herself in, feeling excitement rush through her. It was finally happening! The beach was only a few days' journey from here. And then, at least for a few weeks, she could forget all about the asteroid, quantumite, and her miserable life in the darkness of space.

A short while later, Jace felt a slight tremor rumble through the ship as it detached from the station dock. The gentle hum of the engines grew more pronounced, sending a subtle vibration through the floor. A momentary sensation of weightlessness washed over her as the starship escaped the gravitational pull of the asteroid, and then she was pulled firmly back against the mattress as the artificial-gravity kicked in.

The lights flickered briefly, then steadied. Jace could hear the faint creaking of the ship's hull settling into its autonomous state, no longer connected to the station.

This was an old ship, there was no doubt about that. It had no luxuries as far as Jace could tell and had probably been repaired so many times that nothing of the original ship remained: a real-life Theseus' vessel.

But Jace didn't care—she was finally off that blasted asteroid.

☆ ☆ ☆

Jace spent the evening in her bunk, opting to spend her first night on board the starship eating the snacks she'd brought along and watching vids.

The asteroid station had been tiny and packed full of people. There, Jace had hardly had a moment alone to even go to the bathroom, let alone just have a snack in peace. She found the quiet of *Starship Blunder* uncomfortable at first, but as the evening grew on and the lights dimmed automatically, she found her time on the asteroid fading from her mind.

She didn't have to think about her boss, annoying coworkers, or mundane tasks. She could forget about the sun lamps and the deep, dark emptiness outside the metal structure affixed to a large gray rock hurtling through space.

Closing her eyes, she pictured yellow sand, lapping waves, blue sky, and the warm sun. Her life would be perfect. And in the meantime, she was traveling in space once more! No more boring, gloomy asteroid. *Freedom.* And to this thought, she drifted to sleep.

When she awoke, it was well past breakfast.

It was the first time she'd had the opportunity to sleep in since... well, she couldn't quite remember, honestly. Life on the asteroid was strictly regulated, and while she was allowed free time, her alarm still automatically blared at the same time every day.

She rose, dressed, and stopped by the head with her toiletry kit before wandering down the hall to the cafeteria. Not many people milled about this late in the morning. A few sat at tables in the sitting area. The food was laid out buffet style so anyone could eat at any time, no matter when their shift was.

"You must be the newb we picked up on that asteroid," said a voice from behind her.

She spun around and almost smacked face-first into a broad chest clad in green coveralls. His outfit lacked all the identifiers required for starship crewmembers, so she couldn't find a nametag.

"Um, hello," she said awkwardly, taking a step back so she could look up to see his face.

He was tall. Really tall. His eyes were wide open like an owl's, and he had what looked liked feathers in place of hair, that wrapped down around his eyes and across his nose.

He was beautiful.

"I'm Elivirianoit," he said.

Her eyes widened trying to imagine replicating his name. Not only was it long, he rolled his Rs and buzzed his V and—

"You can call me Eli," he added, cutting into her panicked thoughts with a grin. "I know you humans can't pronounce my name."

"Oh, uh... hi, Eli." She tried to smile back at him but was afraid the expression came across more as a grimace. "I'm Jace."

"Welcome aboard!" Eli gestured toward the food. "You hungry?"

"I... I am," she replied, almost stumbling over what should've been a simple enough statement. What was it about this—man?—or alien?—that made her tongue-tied? "What's good?"

"None of it!" Eli laughed but then launched into an explanation of what to avoid and what to try, and Jace was relieved because she only had to nod and laugh at his jokes while she worked on processing the fact that he a.) was not a coworker, b.) was not an employee of the AstEroiD

Enterprises in any capacity, and c.) had initiated a conversation with her. Also d.) he was drop-dead gorgeous.

"What do you do here?" she asked when there was a break in his monologue about the food.

He gave a wry grin. "Nothing that interesting, I'm afraid. I do maintenance on residential systems."

"So you're like... a spaceship plumber?" She grinned at him.

"That's about the gist of it," he replied, returning her grin.

"It must be exciting to travel." She heaped her plate full of foods she hadn't seen the likes of since her arrival on the asteroid—what, eleven months ago now? There were vegetables and biscuits, eggs and even dried fruit!

"I love it," he answered sincerely. "Whoa, didn't they feed you on that asteroid?" He eyed her heaping plate of food as she piled on more potatoes.

"Mash and gruel," she replied. "It keeps us alive, is cheap to transport, and has a long shelf life."

"Lovely." His tone was wry as he led her to a table on the far side of the room.

The cafeteria wasn't all that busy, so there were plenty of open seats. As soon as she sat down, she dug in, taking a huge bite of biscuit. The butter melted on her tongue, and she sighed happily. She was so glad to be off that stupid station, out from under the eye of her annoying boss and free for the first time in ages.

"What did you do on the asteroid?" Eli asked before slurping up a spoonful of hot soup with bugs in it that had been clearly labeled, "*NOT FOR HUMANS.*"

"Drill monitor," she said. "Nothing exciting. Just watched data streams all day."

"You find anything interesting while you were there?"

She shrugged. "I signed a nondisclosure, sorry."

He gave a half smile and moved the conversation along. "I always thought living on an asteroid sounded terrifying. You're basically strapped to a giant rock hurtling through space, with nothing more than some metal beams to protect you from the harsh vacuum outside."

"I mean, a spaceship isn't all that different, is it?" she asked before taking a swig of juice from the glass. She'd gone so long eating bland and uninteresting food, the juice was almost too sweet for her.

"But we have control of the spaceship," he countered. "You can't control the asteroid."

"I guess," she answered. "But even on a spaceship, you could lose control at any time. And what about living on a planet? Or a space station? We're *all* subject to the whims of physics."

A broad smile swept across his face. "A philosopher, I see."

"I... I mean—" she stuttered, a red flush warming her cheeks, but she was thankfully interrupted by a shadow falling over them.

"Ms. Venitara?"

She looked up to see a tall, slender alien standing over them. He had shimmering blue skin dotted with small, luminescent spots that emitted a soft glow. He gazed down at her with large, expressive eyes—which at the moment looked rather stern.

"Sir!" Eli sat up straighter and addressed his superior.

"Not you," the alien replied. He faced Jace once again. "Ms. Venitara, the pilot has requested an audience with you. Immediately."

"I... uh..." She glanced at Eli, whose eyes had widened a fraction. "I guess... sure? Why?"

"Are you questioning me?" The alien's expression grew angry. "The pilots's word is law on this ship."

"I think she's just curious," Eli offered hesitantly.

"Oh." The clouds brewing in the alien's eyes vanished, and an expression of polite neutrality returned to his face. "My apologies, miss. I do not always read human's non-verbal cues correctly."

"Ah, yes, er, I was just curious," she said. "Of course I'm willing to meet with Pilot Hawkins."

"I believe she wants to discuss something of a confidential nature with you," the alien replied. "Please, follow me."

Jace shot Eli a panicked glance, but he just gestured for her to follow the alien.

"I'll find you later," he mouthed silently. "You'll be fine!"

The tall blue alien strode swiftly through the corridors, never once hesitating, though to Jace the whole place seemed like a giant maze. It was much larger than the asteroid station, and so many parts had been replaced that there was no visual continuity between one area and the next—and equally, no clear difference. It was just... chaos.

She scurried to keep up and was so focused on not losing him that she nearly ran into his back when he stopped abruptly. She jerked to a halt only inches away and then quickly stepped backward to maintain an appropriate distance between them.

The alien pressed a button on the door, which slid open to reveal what looked like a conference room. The ship's pilot sat at the head of the table.

"Please, come in," she said. "Thank you for bringing her, Xylo. You may also stay."

Xylo, which was apparently the name of the shimmering blue alien, sat down at the conference table. Jace hesitantly followed suit, taking a chair across from him.

"I apologize that I must ask you to discuss something of a rather sensitive nature," the pilot said. "When you were on board the asteroid, just before we left, you saw a spike in the data. Multiple spikes, is my understanding."

"That's correct," Jace replied, wondering what exactly the pilot was getting at. She'd been there, looking right over Jace's shoulder at the screen.

"Could you please tell me the meaning of those spikes?"

Jace glanced at Xylo, who was gazing back at her with an empty expression. Telling someone would violate the terms of her nondisclosure. But sitting here, in this room, she didn't think she could say no. And if she did, they could toss her out an airlock. *Hawkins saw everything that happened. Why is she asking me?*

The pilot sensed her hesitation. "I already know what your company was searching for, and I already know what you found. I am simply trying to determine what your personal level of understanding is."

Jace's eyes flicked back to Xylo.

"I have already informed him as well," she added.

It would still technically violate the terms of Jace's nondisclosure... but what was she supposed to do?

"Uh, my understanding is that those spikes meant that our instruments detected traces of quantumite," she said. "More than one spike is quite significant."

"To your knowledge, have there been any other discoveries of quantumite on that asteroid?" the pilot asked.

"Not to my knowledge," Jace answered. "This was the first."

"And why are you leaving the asteroid?"

"Vacation," Jace replied.

"Thank you," Hawkins replied. She glanced at Xylo for a moment, then looked back at Jace and continued, saying, "And how much do you know about your boss?"

"Grimes?" Jace raised her eyebrows and then shrugged. "Not much, I guess. He's a hardass. A micromanager. Don't know when he sleeps. Wouldn't trust him with my cat."

Pilot Hawkins gave a short laugh.

"But he's never done anything... you know. Blatantly unethical. Not that I've noticed, at least."

"And are you planning to return to the asteroid after your trip?" the pilot asked.

"I was," Jace answered. "But now that they found quantumite, they might rubble it and send me somewhere else." She sighed. "That would be a nice change."

Jace couldn't quite understand just what the pilot was trying to figure out. Jace wasn't exactly important on the asteroid station. She was one of a dozen drill monitors. She did her job, hung around the common areas, and slept. That was about it. She got paid decently because she was willing to work on an asteroid, but the job was far from glamorous. What exactly Pilot Hawkins expected her to know, she couldn't even begin to guess.

Before the pilot had a chance to ask another question, the door burst open.

"Hawkins!" A tall white man with a chiseled jawline and perfectly styled hair stood in the open doorway. His stature and posture screamed undeniable confidence, and Jace felt that when he was in a room, all eyes were on him.

"Yes, Commander?" the pilot asked.

"Unidentified ships have been detected in the area. They are not responding to our attempts to communicate."

Pilot Hawkins stood abruptly. "How many attempts?"

"Three, Pilot."

The pilot strode through the room and paused at the door, glancing back at Jace. "You, come with me."

Jace's eyes widened as she hurried into the corridor behind the pilot, the commander, and Xylo. A hush seemed to have come over the corridors, and an ominous yellow light glowed at every corner.

After a short walk, the pilot pushed her way onto the bridge. A large screen took up part of the room, and several humans sat in front of various instruments, reading streams of data that were illegible to Jace.

The pilot seemed to have forgotten about Jace the moment she laid her eyes on the data streaming across the screen.

"Sixteen starships?" the pilot hissed under her breath. "What are *they* doing here? Have you mapped their trajectory?"

"They seem to be flying toward the asteroid, as far as we can tell," the commander replied. "If they continue to fly in a straight line, that is."

"Have you picked up any signals?"

"Working on it!" called a woman with braids from the other side of the room. She had on a large pair of headphones and was surrounded by a variety of instruments, all feeding into a bay of screens. Jace sidled a little closer, watching the little lines flutter and wondering what it all meant.

"Life signs?" Hawkins pressed.

"Yes," the commander said, "but they seem to have a signal shield activated, so we can't determine much more than that."

"Sixteen," Pilot Hawkins muttered again. "You don't think—" She spun around to face the woman with braids. "Nima, skip to radio transmissions."

"Radio?" the woman exclaimed. "That's so rare—"

"Just do it," Hawkins ordered.

"Yes, ma'am." Nima flipped a few buttons and waited a moment, and then her eyes widened as she looked up to meet the pilot's gaze. "Space pirates," she whispered. "Not just any space pirates, either."

"Slugs," Pilot Hawkins groaned.

"You think they're here for—" Xylo glanced around the room and broke off without finishing his sentence.

"I do," Hawkins replied. She turned around, scanning those nearby as though she was looking for someone. Then, her eyes landed on Jace. "I'm going to need your help."

"Mine?" Jace squeaked.

"Tell me everything you know about your company, your boss, the asteroid, and the asteroid station. Immediately."

☆ ☆ ☆

Jace spent the next several hours sequestered in a small storage room with an ensign named Hayna, who reported directly to Nima.

Hayna asked question after question about Jace's life on board the asteroid, sometimes asking the same questions in multiple ways until Jace felt like she'd repeated herself several times. She imagined jumping out an airlock from the sheer boredom of it. All she wanted was the warm sand under her feet, the hot sun beating down from the blue sky above, and foamy water rushing over her skin. But until the *Starship Blunder* made it back to Neptune, Jace was at their mercy.

If they made it back.

And with sixteen pirate ships drawing steadily nearer, Jace had to admit she was happy to violate her nondisclosure agreement if it meant she made it back planetside alive.

After Hayna had finally asked her last question, she escorted Jace back to her quarters and then vanished. Jace collapsed back onto her bed and closed her eyes, letting the headache she'd held at bay for the past several hours wash over her. Whether it was from hunger, dehydration, or fatigue, she didn't know. She just hoped she'd given them whatever information they needed to survive the imminent encounter.

She hadn't lain there long when a soft knock sounded at her door.

Frowning, she swung her legs over the side of the bed, hopped down, and peered through the peephole. She was inexplicably pleased to see Eli standing in the corridor.

She pulled open the door and saw that he held a plate of food.

"Can I come in?" he whispered, glancing over his shoulder. "Just a little worried about you."

She nodded and stepped back. He hurried in and closed the door behind him.

"I'm not really supposed to do this," he said with a conspiratorial wink. "But they had you closeted away for so long, I thought you might be hungry."

He pulled open the tray table over her bed and set down the tray. She hopped up and dug in immediately, taking a bite out of a hot roll.

"Thank you," she said with her mouth full. "I'm *starving*."

"What is going on?" he asked. "Everyone is all hush-hush. The yellow alerts have been on all day, but no one will tell me what's happening!"

"I shouldn't say," Jace said.

"It has to do with you, though?" he asked.

"Sort of," she replied and then took another bite of the roll to give herself time to think. *Should I tell him? Or not?*

"Something to do with the asteroid, then." He grinned and waved a hand in the air. "I'll stop guessing."

"How was your day?" Jace took the reprieve from questions gratefully. She might not owe her company anything, but she *had* signed a contract.

"Asking about my day, huh?" A slow grin spread across his face. "We're getting familiar real fast."

She almost choked on her food, and Eli burst out laughing.

"I'm kidding!" He leaned back against the wall, his gaze resting on her as she gathered her composure. She wondered what he was thinking about. "My day was normal. A few clogged pipes. Some overly familiar critters. The usual. Except for the yellow alert." He frowned.

"What is a yellow alert?" Jace took a sip of the soup he'd brought. It was warm and savory.

"Just means to be prepared in case of an emergency. An orange alert means an emergency is imminent. Red means panic. Or rather, man the battle stations!" He raised an overdramatic fist into the air.

"Are battles the only emergencies?" Jace asked.

"No. Sometimes we experience unexpected asteroid fields or a breach in the hull. But stations are the same for all emergencies for most people. Really, all it means is hunker down and wait unless otherwise instructed."

"Got it."

At that moment, the intercom system blared, and a robotic voice intoned, "Please be advised that the *Starship Blunder* has been updated to an orange—"

The robotic voice was cut off as Pilot Hawkins' voice took over. "This is Starship Pilot Sarah Hawkins. We have sixteen pirate ships headed our way. We do not know if they will attack. Please report to your battle stations in case a red alert is called."

The message ended abruptly.

"Great," Eli grumbled, shoving himself away from the wall. "And here I was, having a nice chat with a beautiful woman, and I have to go prepare to plunge."

Jace laughed out loud at the joke, but her mind caught on the fact that he'd called her a beautiful woman. Was she really? She was pasty and pale from her time spent on the asteroid station. She never wore makeup, and her clothes were old and tattered. What did he see that she couldn't?

"Catch you on the flip side, Jace." Eli pulled open the door to her room just as the ship shuddered under their feet. "That's not good," he muttered and took off at a sprint down the hall.

At the same time, the lights in the corridor began to flash red.

The red alert was here.

And Jace had no idea what she was supposed to do.

☆ ☆ ☆

The ship shuddered and creaked so roughly that Jace was surprised it was holding together. She lay in her bed, straps fastened and tightened, her door shut and locked.

Battle stations for civilians, according to Eli, meant remaining in your quarters. And honestly, Jace really didn't know where else she would've gone.

So she waited, with no idea what was happening outside her door, on the bridge, or in the vast vacuum of space that surrounded them. And she didn't know who would inform her of what had happened. Would Pilot Hawkins come back over the system and tell everyone it was safe? But how *could* it be safe? With sixteen pirate ships? That was practically a whole fleet! And this old beater of a spaceship certainly wasn't fast enough to outrun a fleet of pirate ships.

At that moment, Jace fully expected to die.

So, she pulled up her mental image of the beach.

She imagined the blue sky dotted with fluffy white clouds. The hot sun beaming down on her skin. The sound of the waves crashing against the shore, and the ripples of sand left behind as the water cascaded back out to sea. The glittering shells abandoned on the shore. And the feeling of the wet sand beneath her toes.

If she was going to die, she didn't want the last image in her mind to be the asteroid. But if she couldn't have a real beach, her imagination would have to do.

And then her door crashed open so hard that the metal component toppled into her room.

"Found her!" a deep, wet-sounding voice slurped.

She looked up with wide eyes to see a short, squat, slug-like alien staring at her. Its face was slimy and grimy; its eyes were like marbles sucked into the greenish muddy goop that made up its cheeks; and its hands dripped slime on everything they touched.

So Jace did the only thing she could think of: she shrieked.

The sound startled the creature, and it leaped back. It appeared to be wearing some sort of armor over its chest. *Did it have three legs? Or maybe a tail?* Another creature glooped through the door.

"What's the noise about?" it asked.

"Human feeling scared," the first alien replied.

"Just how we like it. They do make the ugliest noises." The two began to make harsh guttural tones that Jace was pretty sure were laughter, but if someone had tried to persuade her otherwise, she wouldn't have argued.

"What do you know? Tell us!" the first one demanded once they'd settled down. It turned back to Jace, who was suddenly wishing she hadn't strapped herself in. She might have been able to make a run for it otherwise. Instead, she stared up at the ceiling, not daring to make another move lest it irritate the alien creatures.

"About what?" she whispered, holding as still as she could.

"The asteroid!" it replied.

"Oh," Jace said. "Well, it's a day or two behind us and..."

"Tell us about the asteroid!" the thing interrupted.

"I was trying," Jace replied, thinking back on all the information she'd given Pilot Hawkins' team members. "It's got a station on it—that's where I lived. I was a drill monitor."

The alien seemed to be listening now.

"There were eighty-seven people on board, and we each had a different job to do every day. Mine was particularly boring—basically serving as human-based accountability for the machines. But when the algorithm is programmed like it is, you know, the human element is basically useless."

She was babbling. She wondered if they could tell. Or if they thought she was making polite chitchat.

"What did you find?" the creature pressed.

Jace knew they were asking about the quantumite. But she couldn't tell them. She'd signed a nondisclosure! With a corporation! However, hadn't Pilot Hawkins said something to Grimes about the asteroid being leased from the government? Maybe her nondisclosure didn't count. Maybe she should just... let it all out. What did she have to lose?

There was no beach anywhere to be seen. No future job prospects other than working for this same company on asteroid after asteroid after asteroid—which was not even close to the romantic adventure she'd envisioned when she had signed up. Sitting at a computer all day. Staring at graphs with wiggly lines. Looking for elements that weren't there... until they were. Not to mention, she was currently standing on a piece-of-junk spaceship that looked like it'd been welded back together by a twelve-year-old, and it had just been boarded by slug pirates with sixteen ships at their disposal.

It was not a good day. And she didn't really have all that much to lose.

She unclipped her harnesses and sat up. The creature squelched backward but didn't lower the weapon.

"Nothing," she said with a shrug. "We found nothing." She slid her legs over the edge of the bed, trying to look like she was cooperating. "We thought there was something, but it turned out to be a malfunction in the equipment." She eyed their squishy leg tentacle, or whatever it was called. How fast could they really run? "A false reading, they call it."

"That's not what we heard," the slug glurped. "Give us the coordinates!"

"Coordinates?" Jace repeated. Was that what they were after? The asteroid coordinates? "You know asteroids move..."

"Coordinates!" the slug demanded again.

"This is ridiculous!" She flung her hands up in an over-exaggerated shrug. As she did, the slug asking the questions scooted back ever so slightly, its grip on the weapon wavering for a brief second. Jace took the opportunity and leaped from the bed, squeezed between the two slug creatures blocking the door, and dashed down the hallway.

"Get her!" the creature screeched in a very slurpy sort of way.

Jace raced through the corridors, noting the flickering lights and the complete absence of crew. She couldn't believe they'd been boarded by space pirates—space pirate *slugs*, at that! What a way to start a vacation. Though at this rate, it was probable her vacation would end before it even began.

At the same time, she could feel herself grinning just a bit. This was the kind of adventure she'd been hoping for when she'd left home all those years ago. The asteroid hadn't provided it, but this? This was almost fun.

She skidded around the corner, trying to get her bearings, and then saw the sign for the cafeteria. Excellent. She knew where she was.

Following the arrows, she raced faster and faster until the wide doors of the cafeteria appeared before her. She burst through and slid to a halt, looking around rapidly for a hiding space.

"Over here!" a voice hissed.

She followed the sound and ducked down behind the buffet.

"They're after me!" she whispered as she squinted through the dim light to see who else was hiding with her. There were four people, all huddled together. She didn't recognize three of them, but then her gaze landed on Eli. She was inordinately pleased to see him—though she did wonder if his "battle station" was the cafeteria, or if he'd just gotten stuck here for some reason.

"What for?" he asked, keeping his voice low.

"Information—" she began, but then the cafeteria door burst open.

"We know you're in here, human!" the slug's voice bubbled. The lights blazed on, and the squelching of its movements across the floor grew louder.

Eli met her eyes and then abruptly stood, facing the ugly creatures. "Take me instead!" he exclaimed.

"Where is she?" the slug gorgled.

"There's no one else here," Eli replied firmly. "Just me."

Jace hoped the slugs were too dumb to see through his lie.

"We know there are more humans here," the slug retorted. "We can sense them." It pointed to its antennae.

Apparently they weren't that dumb after all. Tough luck.

"Come out, human!" There were the sounds of a scuffle and a muffled *meep!* from Eli. Then the slug added, "Or we'll kill the tall creature!"

Kill?! Eli?

Jace jumped to her feet and peered at the pirates from behind the buffet. "No! Don't kill him!"

"There you are," the slug said. It had one slimy tentacle wrapped around Eli, and the other holding its zappy weapon against Eli's abdomen. Two other slug pirates slurched around, peering under nearby cafeteria tables with their weapons drawn.

"Don't kill him!" she repeated.

"We won't," the slug said, "if you answer our question."

"Fine!" she said. "I'll answer your question. Just... just let him go!"

"Answers first," the slug spit back.

"Don't tell them," Eli said. "It's not worth it!"

"It is definitely worth it if it means saving your life," Jace retorted. She pointed to the weapon. "Put it down. Or I'll give you nothing."

After hesitating for what seemed like an eternity, the space slug placed its weapon on the table beside it.

Jace immediately began to rattle off a series of numbers. Technically, they *were* the asteroid's coordinates—the day she'd arrived. They'd have to figure out where it had traversed on their own. Or find someone else who actually knew the asteroid's current location.

The slug tossed Eli to one side, and faster than Jace could've thought possible, snatched up its weapon. The creature lurched toward her, blaststick outstretched.

Jace jerked backward, almost tripping over a chair. She scrambled away from the slug, but the other two slugs were blocking her path out of the cafeteria.

"What do we do?" Eli cried. "We don't have weapons! I'm a plumber!"

The other people who'd been hiding behind the buffet had begun crawling away from the slugs, all three of whom had their attention fully fixed on Jace.

"I don't know!" Jace cried out, grasping at the first thought that popped into her mind. "Salt?"

To her shock, Eli didn't hesitate. He grabbed the nearest saltshaker, ripped off the lid, and tossed the white powder at the creature. It cascaded across the alien's goopy skin, and for a moment, everyone froze, waiting to see what would happen.

Then, the creature let out a terrible shriek, the sound making Jace clap her hands over her ears. It was a high-pitched, piercing noise that was somehow garbled and wet-sounding at the same time. Jace found it *extremely* distasteful.

But she didn't hesitate. She skipped toward the buffet, grabbed another saltshaker, tossed the lid, and dumped the contents onto one of the other slugs. Eli continued his efforts as well, and several of the others in the cafeteria grabbed salty foods and dressings in lieu of dry salt. Fortunately, it worked.

Once all three creatures were incapacitated, Jace and Eli filled their pockets with shakers from the tables and encouraged the other humans to do the same. Then they raced down the corridors, shouting, "Salt! Salt!"

Each time they saw a slug pirate, one of them would empty as much salt as they could onto its slimy carapace and watch as it curled up with a piercing shriek.

Whether or not the creatures were dead, Jace didn't know. But they couldn't do any further harm, and that was all that mattered as far as she was concerned.

By the time they made it to the bridge, they'd managed to salt about fifteen of the slugs. They found Pilot Hawkins, the commander, and Xylo wrapped in sticky, goopy strands of slime.

"Disgusting," Pilot Hawkins said as Eli freed her with his plumber's wrench.

"Salt!" Jace exclaimed. "It dries them out."

"Go!" Hawkins ordered the commander, and he raced out from the bridge, still dripping with the sticky stuff.

An hour later, the crew had rounded up all the incapacitated space slugs and trapped them in the brig. The salt hadn't killed them, it turned out, but it had rendered them nearly comatose.

"You should be there when I question them," Pilot Hawkins told Jace and Eli. "You deserve it."

Jace and Eli hung back as the pilot stood before the ugly creatures.

"Who are you?" she demanded.

"The Plunder Wyrms," the leader hissed. "And you'll pay for what you've done to us!"

"You and what army?" Hawkins retorted. "At last count, we've rounded up over forty of you. And our sensors indicate that hardly anyone is left on your own ships—you all came over here."

"Wyrms are known for being territorial," Xylo added. "We know you rarely travel more than two or three to a ship."

The slug gorgled angrily.

Two or three? That meant that even though there were sixteen ships, there were still far fewer slugs than crew. Jace was relieved. It also meant that they'd already caught or killed most of the creatures.

"We also know you don't travel for nothing," the commander added. "You're looking for something."

"Mercenaries, the lot of you" Hawkins added. "Who paid you? And to do what?" When the creature didn't answer, the pilot reached into a satchel she wore over her shoulder and withdrew a handful of white powder. "There's a lot more where this came from."

The slug let out a pitiful squeal.

"We've got all different varieties, too," the pilot added. "Table salt, black salt, flecked salt, Himalayan salt. We've got calcium chloride, magnesium chloride—"

"Fine!" the slug choked. "We were on a job to acquire an element from an asteroid. That's it."

"Then why were you on our ship?" the pilot pressed. She waved her hand threateningly, which was still covered in salt.

"To get the coordinates and then eliminate anyone who might know about the element!" the slug answered hastily. "But we didn't eliminate anyone. No harm, no foul? Right?"

Hawkins laughed uproariously, and the commander joined her.

Jace didn't feel like laughing. The slugs had been sent here to *kill* her! If they'd succeeded, she'd be dead! No beach vacation in sight! And certainly no more exciting adventures in space.

The pilot broke off laughing abruptly and glared at the slug. "Who. Hired. You?"

Somehow, she'd managed to fill both of her hands with salt, which she now waved quite close to the space slug.

"Just... a guy!" the slug cried. "He promised us a cut. That's it!"

"What guy?"

Hawkins really is relentless, Jace thought.

"A human named Grimes."

"Grimes?" Jace exclaimed, jolted from her train of thought. "My *boss*?"

"As I suspected." Pilot Hawkins returned her fistfuls of salt to the satchel. "Thank you, slug. I appreciate your willingness to talk."

She turned on her heel and strode toward Jace. "You. You're coming with me."

Jace hurried down the corridor until they reached the bridge. There, the pilot pushed forward and offered Jace a chair, which she gratefully accepted.

"So." The pilot leaned back against the main console, arms crossed. "You turned out to be weirdly important after all."

"I really have no idea what happened," Jace told the woman. "it's all a bit of a confusing blur. A lot of moving pieces."

Pilot Hawkins laughed. "I don't doubt it. It's quite a story." She glanced at the commander, who was issuing orders in hushed tones to the rest of the crew. "Here's the short version." She cleared her throat. "Your boss, Grimes, discovered quantumite probably quite a while ago. Instead of alerting his superiors, he reached out to space-slug mercenaries and hired them to 'steal' the metal. But since you discovered it last minute, he had them alter course and told them to kill you and me, in order to hide his crime. The Conglomeracy, of course, was already clued into the possibility this might happen, so they instructed us to look for clues while we were there to pick you up."

"That's... insane." Jace's eyes were wide.

"We've obviously dealt with the Plunder Slugs—I mean Wyrms, as they prefer to be called—so our next mission is to take you to your destination so you can put all of this behind you."

"Thank you so much."

"We will of course be alerting our superiors, and someone will be sent to arrest Grimes. Do you have any further questions?"

Before Jace could attempt to ask any, the pilot added, "Then you are dismissed."

Jace stood awkwardly for a moment and then exited the bridge as Pilot Hawkins returned to her duties. Jace had no idea how to get back to her room, but she thought maybe the signs would tell her how to find the cafeteria, and then she could locate her quarters from there.

She wandered around for a while, getting lost and then unlost and then lost again, until she heard someone call out from behind her, "Jace!" She turned to see Eli jogging toward her.

He grinned as he neared. "You seem a bit lost."

"I'm not lost," Jace protested, though it was likely obvious to anyone who saw her that she was at least a little... confused.

"You know you could just ask someone for directions, right?"

"I'm not lost," Jace insisted. She wasn't lost. She was learning! At least, that was what her father had always said.

"Only one day away from your vacation!" Eli gestured for her to follow him—in the opposite direction she'd been going, naturally.

"I can't wait." Jace grinned at the thought of the warm sun, foamy water, and cool breezes.

"You know," Eli said, "I get leave when we stop."

"What do you mean?" Jace eyed him.

"I'll be on vacation too," he clarified. His expression had become slightly awkward. "I just thought, you might, you know, like to meet up for... er, drinks. Or coffee. On your break." He took a deep breath. "Uh... no pressure though."

Jace felt a smile grow across her face. Drinks or coffee. That sounded nice. Really nice.

"I'm in," she said. "You name the place. I just have one request."

"What's that?" he asked. "Anything at all."

Jace grinned at him, feeling a rush of excitement that her beach vacation might be just a bit more than a vacation. It could be the beginning of something new.

"They have to serve salt."

MAROONED

Ross Baxter

P etty Officer Khan stood by the airlock, waiting patiently. Time passed slowly, but he continued to stand there, knowing the airlock would eventually open. After an hour had passed, a loud crash sounded on the other side of the thick door, followed by the tortured screeching of metal on metal. Khan sighed and continued to wait. Twenty minutes of tapping noises followed—Khan guessed the source was those on the outside struggling with the simple locking mechanism. Suddenly, the heavy door parted with a loud *hiss*, and a figure stood in the steamy opening, fully suited in a standard-issue Conglomeracy space exosuit.

"You're late," said Khan gruffly.

The figure carefully removed her helmet, frowning deeply at the sight in front of her. "You're naked."

Khan glanced down, raising his eyebrows at his oversight. "I am, yes. But don't change the subject. You're late, Ensign Darris. Eight *years* late!"

Ensign Darris held her hands up in admission of guilt. "Yes, I suppose we are. Sorry."

"Sorry?!" Kahn cried. "You were only supposed to be away for a couple of days, not eight bloody years!"

"We did try and come back, but we lost your position," she said with an apologetic shrug.

"How can you lose something as big as this?" Kahn challenged, throwing his hands up to convey the huge size of the space station in which they stood. "It's massive!"

"The navigation computer deleted it."

Khan shook his head and said under his breath, "Typical *Starship Blunder*."

"Well, we're here now," she offered.

"Yeah, I suppose you are," muttered Khan. "Are you still an ensign?"

Darris's face flushed. "I am. As you probably remember, promotion is not easy on the *Blunder*."

"Funny, that," Khan replied.

"You're still naked," she added, screwing up her face.

"Oh, forgive me!" he cried. "When you're marooned alone on an ancient abandoned alien space station for eight years, one's wardrobe stops being a concern!"

"Still, it... is a bit weird," she countered.

"Fine! My quarters are on level seven, about a fifteen-minute walk from here. I have clothes I can put on there."

"Shall I wait here?"

Khan frowned. "No, come with me. I can't take the risk that you wander off and get lost again."

"Okay. I was going to say lead on, but I'm not sure I want to follow you for fifteen minutes having to look at your hairy backside."

"What's wrong with my backside?" Khan demanded.

Darris screwed up her face again but said nothing.

"Well, then you walk ahead, and I'll tell you where to go."

Darris shook her head. "Why don't we walk side by side? That way, I can avoid seeing your hairy backside *and* your equally hairy front side."

"Now you're just being mean."

"Not really," she said. "We'll walk side by side, and you can tell me everything you've discovered about this station and the long-forgotten race who built it."

Khan turned away from the airlock and moved toward a large, unlit corridor that disappeared into darkness. Every surface was faced with smooth, grey, featureless metal. As they approached, narrow strip lights set in the floor illuminated, bathing the shiny and uniform surfaces with a soft glow.

"At least you had lighting," Darris offered, interrupting the silence.

"Everything in the station still has power," replied Khan. "There's a nuclear-fusion reactor on level twenty that still keeps churning out electricity."

"Nuclear fusion?" Darris uttered, clearly surprise. "How does that work?"

"Two light nuclei merge to form a single heavier nucleus, releasing energy," explained Khan, as if reciting from a school textbook.

Darris tutted. "I know the *principles* of nuclear fusion, but no one ever got it to work in practice!"

"Well, these lot did," he replied flatly.

"How?"

Kahn shrugged his hairy shoulders. "How should I know? I'm a simple security NCO, not a boffin! If you wanted answers to everything, you should have marooned a scientist, or maybe that Xylo dude."

"We didn't maroon you," argued Darris.

Khan stopped walking, turning to face her with eyebrows raised in question.

She quickly looked away, glancing around the corridor before finally setting her gaze on the top of his head. Her constant fidgeting indicated she must have been uncomfortable with the naked NCO within view. "Not intentionally."

Khan resumed walking, his bare feet stepping quickly across the smooth floor panels. "Anyway, what have I missed on the *Blunder* over the past eight years? Did you get that major refit?"

"Nope. But they did redecorate the children's crèche after a new daycare teacher joined the crew."

"Great," muttered Khan without any enthusiasm. "What about the accommodation deck? Surely the crew quarters received a much-needed remodel."

"Nope."

"I'm assuming I still have my cabin," said Khan.

"Err, it got reallocated to the new daycare teacher. She has painted it completely black inside, with black furniture and fittings. She's a bit scary, really. Makes me glad I don't have any kids."

"It just gets better and better," groaned Khan.

"They'll find you another cabin, I'm sure," she offered. She didn't sound too convinced, though.

They walked farther along the bland corridor, passing numerous closed doors made from the same shiny metal. After a few minutes, Khan stopped. "Oh! You have to see my farm."

"Farm?" she asked.

"Mushroom farm. What do you think I've been eating for the last eight years?"

Darris shrugged.

Khan thumbed a switch in the wall, and a large door slid silently upwards. He beckoned her inside, and she followed, but not too closely. She gazed in wonder at the cavernous space, easily as big as a baseball field and with a high vaulted roof. Instead of the cold, dark metallic of the corridor, the walls and ceiling were a warm cream. Paths led between large, square, raised areas, which gave the vast room a patchwork appearance. The place had a strange smell, which Darris could not quite place.

"Each square grows a different type of fungi. Some taste absolutely disgusting, but some are really nice," explained Khan, a hint of pride in his voice.

"What do they taste like?" Darris asked, wrinkling up her nose as she inspected a sickly orange patch of fungi in the nearest square.

"Chicken, mainly," he answered. "The patch of red fungi to the left taste like strawberry chicken, while the pinkie-purple ones ahead taste like sarsaparilla chicken. They're my favorite. Try one!"

"What do they grow in?" she asked, glancing at the brownish slime from which the foot-high fungi sprouted.

"I dunno," he shrugged. "But I never have to do anything except pick them. It's great. You have to try one of the red ones as well."

Darris shook her head. "You've just been eating fungus all this time?"

"Well, it's better than Bluebottle's cooking!" Khan smiled. "Speaking of, I'm assuming he's either long dead or retired?"

She shook her head again. "No, I'm afraid not. He refuses to retire, and the Conglomeracy can't seem to find a way to get rid of him."

"Surely they must be able to charge him with crimes against cuisine or breaking a million food-hygiene rules! I must have spent countless nights with my head down the toilet after his ghastly meals. Is he still the biggest know-it-all in the federation?"

"He is," she confirmed. "Last week he told me that I lace my boots up in the wrong gender!"

"He accused me of doing that too!" Khan snorted.

"Who knew that boot lacing is gender specific?" Darris mused.

"Well, I don't have that problem now," said Khan, looking down at his hairy feet and wiggling his hairy toes. "I can't tell you how good the freedom of nakedness feels."

"Please don't," she muttered disparagingly. "Hopefully our next stop is your quarters, where you can put some clothes on."

"Fine, follow me," he said, leading her back out to the corridor.

"It must have been tough living here on your own for the past eight years," she said, yet again trailing far behind

Khan's hairy backside as they went through the open doorway and back into the corridor.

"It's actually been nice and peaceful," he answered. "No noisy accommodation deck, no screaming kids running around everywhere, and no hassle from you and all the other bossy officers."

"You take that back!" she demanded. "I'm not bossy."

Khan raised his eyebrows.

She stopped and sighed, crossing her arms for a moment before prompting, "You were saying what it is like living on your own. And I really am not bossy."

Khan shrugged. "It was difficult at first, but I spent a lot of time exploring this space station, yet I still haven't managed to explore it all. It's fascinating, really."

"So, what were they like? The race who built and lived in this place."

Khan shrugged again. "There's not much evidence of them, to be honest. There are no pictures, images, or artwork anywhere on the station. I get the feeling they must have been really dull."

"Surely you must know more than that?"

He shrugged again. "Well, given the size of the furniture, they were slightly taller than us. Bipeds. Great engineers, in that everything still works perfectly after all the millennia. They had a fondness for functionality and dull, neutral colors. They were a bit like the Swedes in the old days, I suppose."

"After living here for eight years, with nothing to do but explore and eat mushrooms all day, the only thing you've been able to conclude is that they were a bit like the Swedes?"

"Well, I have made some drawings based on all my findings. That might help," he offered. "They're in my quarters, just up here on the right."

"Great, and you can finally put on some clothes on."

Khan did not reply, instead moving over to an unmarked door and thumbing a recessed switch to open it. He beckoned Darris inside.

"Wow," she murmured, looking around at the grandness of the place.

A large circular room greeted her, with a generous circular bed in the center. Directly above the bed, a huge transparent dome showed the infinity of space beyond. She glanced up, clearly marveling at the multitude of stars and galaxies that glittered in the absolute darkness.

"I do enjoy sleeping under the stars," Khan said with a grin.

"Wow," she repeated, transfixed by the view of space and the nearby horseshoe nebula. Off to starboard, the *Blunder* floated serenely, the light from the nearest star showing her in all her beat-up glory: mismatched panels, dented engine nacelles, and a snapped lateral communication mast.

"Just as I remember her," mused Khan sadly. "She does rather spoil the view."

"I always thought of the *Blunder* as an *it* rather than a *she*," Darris countered. "The ship is far too messy, disproportionate, and crass to be feminine."

"I can't argue with you there, although I'm sure Chef Bluebottle would."

"They fixed the dorsal arrays," said Darris, trying to sound upbeat. "And the plumbing is a little better now."

As Khan peered toward where Ensign Darris pointed, a large flap in *Blunder's* stern opened to jettison a cloud of swirling sewage. Instantly freezing in the void, the numerous brown lumps spun away into the darkness of space.

"Charming," sighed Khan with disgust.

"Maybe I can look at those drawings of the original inhabitants while you get dressed," suggested Darris.

Khan rummaged through a featureless beige cabinet by the bed before pulling out a large notepad. He handed it to her, having to place it in her hands since she refused to look in his direction. "I've spent many long hours on these pictures, drawing and redrawing until I got them perfect. See what you think while I find something to wear."

She peered down at the notebook, slowly flicking through the many pages covered with charcoal drawings.

She stared closely at each image to take in the lines and all the details.

"Well?" shouted Khan from the other side of the bed.

Darris guffawed loudly. "They're *rubbish*!"

"If you wanted high-end art, you should have marooned an artist rather than a security NCO! I tried my best!"

"For the last time, we didn't maroon you. It was just an unfortunate accident!" Darris yelled.

"Sure it was," Kahn replied sarcastically.

"And all you've drawn is a load of stick people," she continued, trying not to laugh so much at his artwork. "They could be humans, or monkeys, or a dozen other different alien races. What use are these?"

"You really are mean."

"Come on, Khan. The five-year-olds in Miss Luna's class could do better than this."

"That settles it," Khan fumed. "I'm *not* going back aboard the *Blunder*. I'm going to stay here. Now get off my space station!"

"Don't be such a big baby," Darris retorted. "Get dressed, and I'll take you back home."

"Home?!" Khan cried. "The *Blunder* is the same heap of junk it was when I left, some daycare teacher has stolen my cabin, and Chef Bluebottle is still poisoning the crew. No thank you, I'm staying here. And I'll escort you back off this vessel naked!"

Darris rolled her eyes. "I can see my own way out, thank you."

"No, I insist," said Khan.

They returned to the airlock in stony silence, Khan marching ahead of her to make the ensign as uncomfortable as possible.

"Well, thanks for ruining my appetite by making me look at your hairy backside all the way back here," said Darris.

"I'll have you know that there are many who appreciate a body like mine," Kahn replied defiantly.

"Keep telling yourself that."

"I don't need to."

"Anyway, I'll go, but I'm sure the *Blunder* will come back for you," said Darris. "And in the meantime, you should keep working on those drawings."

Khan said nothing, double-locking the airlock behind her. After a few moments, he heard the shuttle engines thrumming to life, followed by a couple of loud *bangs* and scrapes as the starship attempted to move away from the space station.

A door to Khan's right opened a few seconds later, and a dozen tall, pale, blue-eyed, skinny humanoids appeared, crowding around the stocky, hirsute ex-security NCO. Completely naked and devoid of any hair, they looked like highly evolved Scandinavians.

Khan's mind filled with their telepathic chatter.

"I know, I know—she's not as beautiful as me," he replied, trying to calm them. "There's no need to worry. It was a total fluke that they found us again. Given their skill at navigation and the reliability of their equipment, the *Starship Blunder* won't be back any time soon. I promise you, Space Station IKEA could not be safer."

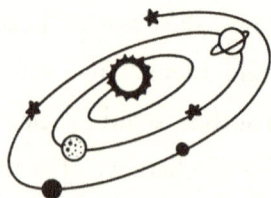

THE LAST VOYAGE

Beth Martin

Pilot Sarah Hawkins took a slow, deep breath to help steady her nerves. She looked pristine with her violently violet uniform freshly dry-cleaned and her hair slicked back in a smooth ponytail. Her previous performance review hadn't gone well, but she suspected that things would be different this time. The *Starship Blunder* had actually *made* it through another year, and she expected she would get commended for the achievement. Perhaps she'd even get a promotion to commander.

An alien with scaly yellow skin and large black eyes suddenly opened the door, yanking Sarah back to reality. "Admiral Vance is ready to see you, Pilot Hawkins," the alien announced. It used two of its four hands to hold the door and allow Sarah to enter the conference room.

"Thank you," she muttered as she strode into the room. She quickly glanced around to identify the familiar faces sitting on the other side of the long conference table. Admiral Vance was seated in the middle, and she spotted Commander Rex Sterling situated to the Admiral's right. In all, eight officials peered at her.

Like Xylo, Admiral Vance was from Zentara. While Xylo had brilliant blue spots, the Admiral's coloring was more of a dull green. "Pilot Sarah Hawkins," he greeted in a deep voice. "Thank you for joining us."

It's not like I had a choice. "Of course, Admiral," she said, forcing a smile. "It's a pleasure to be here."

"I wish I could say the same," Vance responded with a snort. "You seem to have a lousy track record as a pilot. It says here"—he consulted some papers in front of him before continuing—"that the starship you pilot has crash-landed on seventeen of the last twenty missions."

Sarah realized very quickly that she would *not* be getting a promotion. Instead, she would need to fight to keep her current job. "Well, the landing thrusters haven't been operational for quite some time."

"A flimsy excuse," Vance spat, pressing his hands against the conference table.

Sarah was not the only visibly uncomfortable person in the room. Rex glanced warily from Sarah to Vance before staring at his thumbs, which he twiddled in front of him.

"You know what they say," the Admiral continued, his spots now glowing a whitish-green. "Once is an accident, twice is a coincidence, and three times is a pattern. But *seventeen*?"

"If my starship got all the proper repairs—" Sarah began.

"*Your* starship?" Vance cut in, slamming a fist against the table. "You are not a commander! *Starship Blunder* is not your ship. But if she was, do you really want to take ownership of the follies of that vessel?" He shuffled the pages in front of him, looking for one in particular. Upon finding it, he continued: "Almost getting eaten by dust worms, attacked by plants—twice, multiple space-slug infestations, crash landing on the wrong planet *three times*. Clearly, the *Starship Blunder's* track record speaks for itself. In fact, I think the best course of action would be to decommission the *Blunder*. What do you say to that?"

The Admiral looked around at the other officers, who all seemed to be trying to avoid eye contact.

Sarah was surprised when, of all people, the commander of the *Starship Prime* spoke up on her behalf. "Perhaps if Pilot Hawkins did have the opportunity to command the *Blunder*, the starship could achieve a successful mission without the crash landing part."

She mouthed "Thank you" to Rex while the Admiral continued shuffling papers.

"You know what, why not?" Admiral Vance finally stated. "It's not like the Conglomeracy has anything to lose. Plus, I have the perfect mission you can sink your teeth into as the acting commander of the *Starship Blunder*. What do say, Pilot Hawkins?"

She bowed her head slightly. "Thank you, Admiral. Thank you so much." *Promotion secured.*

☆ ☆ ☆

Instead of spending the rest of the day preparing to be commander for a mission and running a pre-flight check on the *Blunder*, Sarah Hawkins went to Terminus's seediest dive bar for her last evening in the city.

As she nursed a galaxy cocktail in a dark corner by herself, she saw a handsome figure in a navy flight suit approach. Her initial excitement at a possible anonymous tryst was eclipsed by disappointment when she realized she knew the approaching man.

"Are we drinking to celebrate or to forget?" Rex Sterling asked as he settled into the seat next to her. He raised a hand to summon a bartender, and a furry, pink Soo-sacan alien wearing a black apron came over. "I need a terra-whiskey, neat, and another Argentan berry spritz for her."

Sarah didn't answer his question, but that was all right since Rex seemed more keen on listening to himself talk. "I don't know how you drink those things," he remarked, pointing at her beverage. "Argentan berries are way too sour for my tastes."

She raised an eyebrow along with her glass. "The leaves are acidic enough to eat through metal. You should have seen what they did to the *Blunder*..." She stopped, realizing she had just brought up the starship she was drinking to forget.

"Can I tell you a secret?" Rex confided.

"I doubt I can stop you," Sarah responded before chugging the remaining contents from her glass.

"It's not the capabilities of the starship that really matter—"

Says the man who commands a state-of-the-art starship, Sarah interjected in her thoughts.

"—it's the aptitude of the crew that really makes the job of commander rewarding. Just think about it. I bet you've got at least one or two gems on your crew. Hell, it'd take a pretty bang-up mechanic at the very least to keep the *Blunder* flying."

Sarah almost spat out her drink, laughing. "You mean Xylo? He created a night light that caused the *Blunder* to crash land. And his biggest achievement, a nano-particle bio-tracker, gave the entire crew food poisoning!"

Before she could list more of the lead mechanic's follies, they were interrupted by the pink snowman-shaped alien delivering their drinks. Sarah grabbed hers from the alien's tray and took a big gulp. "Not to mention all the time Chef Bluebottle's cooking made the crew sick."

"He makes a mean brew, though," Rex countered.

Sarah sighed. She *still* couldn't remember what happened the last time she'd drank Bluebottle's homemade beer. "Mean is definitely the right word."

Rex looked at her, his piercing stare glaring straight at her soul. "Look, Sarah, I know the *Blunder* is a hunk of junk, but as the acting commander, you're not just leading a piece of metal and technology. You're leading a team. I know you're a good pilot, but I also know you could be an amazing leader. Make this last mission memorable. Show the Conglomeracy what you're made of, and get assigned to something better than that pile of bolts you lot call a ship."

She'd almost felt inspired until Rex had called her beloved starship a pile of bolts. "Screw you," she declared as she slammed her drink on her table and stood. This was actually her fifth cocktail, so she wavered on her feet for a second. She was about to walk away but thought better of wasting the drink, chugged the rest, set the glass down again, and then stormed off. Of course, she couldn't exit gracefully and tripped on a chair leg, landing flat on her face. She refused any help as she got up and continued to amble away.

☆ ☆ ☆

Sarah took her seat in the pilot's chair of the *Blunder*, gripping the yoke so firmly her knuckles cracked under the strain.

Miss Luna Knight sat in the second chair, the one typically occupied by Xylo, and used the reflection from the glossy control panel to aid in applying a fresh coat of black lipstick. "So, what is this mission that's so important we have to leave right away?" she asked between pouts. Satisfied, she tucked the lipstick tube into a pocket of her black dress.

"There's an abandoned cruiser in the outer Eagle Nebula," Sarah explained. "Normally we'd ignore something like that, let it get sucked into a black hole or something, but the cruiser belonged to an important person, and by some accident, his pet was left on board."

Luna side-eyed Sarah and then shook her head. "That explains the skeleton crew. But why am I going? There are no children on this mission."

Sarah shifted uncomfortably. "You have experience with the pet's guardian. You volunteered for the mission when he went missing—"

"You all ready to rescue Boomerang Black's Proximarian Pomeranian pup?" Xylo asked as he strolled onto the bridge.

"You've *got* to be kidding me!" Luna exclaimed, glaring first at Xylo and then Sarah, who simply shrugged in response. "The flipping hack loses his dog in space, and we're the ones sent to rescue it? Bats in heaven! Surely Chef has some cyanide or something toxic in the kitchen to put me out of my misery." With that, she got up and stormed out of the bridge.

Sarah tried to yell after her, saying, "We're launching soon, so maybe buckle up *before* you chug any poison!"

Xylo took Luna's recently vacated seat and strapped himself in. "I'm ready, boss!"

☆ ☆ ☆

Thankfully, the Eagle Nebula wasn't too far from Neptune, so the *Starship Blunder* was almost at the cruiser's last-known coordinates by that afternoon. However, Sarah's indulgence from the night before caught up to her. There wasn't much she could do for the headache, but she knew Chef Bluebottle kept stomach medication in the kitchen.

"Hey, Xylo," she said. "Could you find Bluebottle and ask him for some antacids? I had a bologna sandwich for breakfast and it's not sitting right."

The blue alien looked up from the toy yo-yo he had been playing with—an artifact he'd picked up from the planet they visited on their previous mission. "Sure thing."

He took his time getting out of his chair and rewinding the string around the toy before walking away.

Finally alone, Sarah let out a long sigh. *Why am I trying so hard to save this Starship? What has* Blunder *ever done for me?* Glancing out the thick windshield, she saw the bending of starlight that indicated the Pickle Stick Black Hole must be nearby. Almost subconsciously, like a moth to the flame, she turned the starship toward the black hole and gently accelerated.

They say your life flashes before your eyes when you're about to die, and in that moment, Sarah found this phenomenon to be true. As she led the junky starship directly toward the abyss, scenes from her life flashed through her brain, almost like a slideshow.

Growing up on Neptune, wanting nothing more than to join the Conglomeracy as an Officer. The fateful test she'd failed miserably because she had slept through her alarm, giving her not enough time to finish and dooming her to pilot the hunk-of-junk Blunder. *Her first mission and Bluebottle telling her not to take crash landing a sophisticated starship so rough—*Blunder *wasn't that sophisticated, and every previous pilot had crash-landed her as well. Luna sharing her love of bats with little children and telling Sarah the stories and alien fairytales that had inspired her colorful tattoos. The numerous times things Chef Bluebottle's stores of inedible food had saved the day. The time the Sherriff Kojak had* *thought Xylo was dead. Discovering a secret orange planet and negotiating the first trade deal with a previously hostile alien race. Xylo's obnoxious disco tunes playing whenever the alarm went off.*

"What am I doing?" she questioned out loud, snapping her from her reverie. She quickly looked around, realizing that they would get sucked into the void if she didn't act decisively. She increased the thrusters to max and turned hard to the left, rotating the starship ninety degrees before pulling up hard on the steering yoke, forcing the *Blunder* to take the sharpest turn possible.

Red lights began to flash and the song "Staying Alive" blared over the emergency speaker system. Sarah grabbed the comm and announced through the whole starship, "Emergency maneuvers engaged to avoid the Pickle Stick Black Hole. Hold onto something bolted down—this is about to get rough!"

She let out the guttural cry of a fighter as she accelerated into the turn, increasing the g-forces that slammed her body into her seat. Meanwhile, the gravitational pull of the black hole grabbed at the starship, ripping pieces of shoddy repairs off the hull. As long as the warp drive stayed intact, they'd make it home okay.

Xylo stumbled into the bridge—an action that, in the current situation, more resembled climbing a jungle gym. A large bottle of antacids bulged from the top of the chest pocket of his coveralls. "What the heck are you doing?" he yelled as he clamored into his seat and strapped in.

"Avoiding us getting sucked into a black hole!" she yelled back.

"Use the dog!" Xylo shouted.

"What?"

"The dog!" he reached over and grabbed the comm.

Sarah was losing the tug of war between the *Blunder's* warp drive and the pull of the black hole. The ship began sinking slowly closer to the void.

Xylo began cooing into the comm, saying, "Hey, boy! Who's a good boy? We have a treat for you if you show us who's a good boy!"

"What the heck are you doing?" Sarah shouted, engaging even the landing thrusters, hoping that an extra little push would help them escape. As the landing thrusters sputtered, the warp drive made an obnoxious sound, something between a cough and an explosion. More warning lights flashed on, making Sarah aware that the warp engine just died, and the starship began accelerating toward the hole.

"I'm radio-ing the cruiser," Xylo explained. "Proximarian Pomeranians can create gravitational pulls. You can see the cruiser right over there." He pointed to a speck of flashing lights just safe from the vortex of the black hole. "If we can get the dog to help, he might pull us to safety."

"Considering the dog's name is 'Princess,' I'm pretty sure it's a girl. Gimme that." Sarah grabbed the comm and began pleading as well. "Princess, you're such a good doggy! Good girl! Pull us to you and we'll give you a special treat. We have lots of bologna!"

The mention of spiced ham product seemed to do the trick, because the starship suddenly lurched away from the black hole and began zipping through space toward the cruiser. "It worked!" Sarah gushed.

"Of course it worked," Xylo said in a mocking tone as he crossed his arms. "My ideas always work."

She ignored his slight, now in commander mode and ready to lead a successful mission. "Xylo, shoot the grappling line at the cruiser. We're going to tether to it so we don't lose track of vessel."

He uncovered the appropriate button and smashed it with a long finger. They could see the line shoot through space, the hook at the end swinging gracefully around the tail of the cruiser and hooking tightly.

"Perfect!" Sarah exclaimed, punctuating the word with a clap.

"Not perfect," Xylo corrected. "Our warp drive is dead. How are we going to get back?"

Sarah dismissed his concern, happy to be alive and full of adrenaline. "We'll use the cruiser! We can simply land on a nearby planet after we let Admiral Vance know we successfully completed the mission."

"What about the *Blunder*?"

She shrugged. "We'll tow it behind us." Not waiting for Xylo to further rain on her good mood, she used the comm to update the other two crew aboard the ship. "Luna, Chef Bluebottle, come to the bridge. And Bluebottle, bring a bologna sandwich with you."

Xylo removed his restraints, stood out of his chair, and stretched. "Seriously, you want a snack now? After all of that?"

Sarah shook her head. "It's for the dog. I promised, remember? Now come on."

★ ☆ ☆

Boomerang Black's cruiser had been a personal spacecraft, so fitting the four *Blunder* crew onto it would be a tight squeeze. They'd needed to don their space suits to navigate through the vacuum of space to get from *Blunder* to the cruiser, but now that they were all aboard, they removed their suits and crammed all of them into the tiny sleeping compartment.

"Here you go," Sarah said, putting the plate with the bologna sandwich on the floor in front of the alien-dog. The bright pink miniature pup wearing little bows and a diamond-studded leather collar immediately dug into her treat.

"That is exactly the type of dog I would expect Boom to own," Luna commented with a frown.

Bluebottle took a few quick sniffs and asked, "What is that smell?"

Xylo waved a finger through the air before licking it, and then answered, "I believe that is Mr. Black's newest fragrance, *Constant Drip*."

Sarah slipped into the only seat within the cruiser. Luna squeezed in next to her, sitting on the right armrest, while Xylo and Bluebottle stood shoulder to shoulder directly behind the driver's chair. It was tight, but they didn't need to go far.

"Where's the comm for this thing?" Sarah asked, looking around the smooth dash, which was devoid of any mechanical doohickeys or buttons.

Luna leaned forward a bit and announced, "Communications on."

The computer responded in a sexy, alto early-Hollywood-style voice. "Please state the recipient of the communication."

"Admiral Vance," Sarah announced.

"Connecting... Connection made. Begin communication." A hologram of Amiral Vance appeared in miniature above the dash.

Sarah launched into her report: "Admiral Vance, this is acting Commander for the *Starship Blunder* Sarah Hawkins, reporting from Boomerang Black's personal cruiser. We have secured the lost vessel and have Mr. Black's Proximarian Pomeranian, Princess, safely on board."

"What took you fools so long?" the Admiral's voice boomed over the cruiser's state-of-the-art sound system— clearly an aftermarket addition. Boom must have turned the bass setting to the max, because the Admiral's voice sounded more like the voice of god. "The journey should have only taken an hour, an hour and a half tops! You know what, I don't want to hear your excuses. Just get back to Terminus Base, pronto!"

"Actually, we'll need to meet you at Gallantria," Sarah responded, naming the closest planet.

"Don't tell me you broke the warp drive again." He covered his miniature hologram face with his miniature hologram hands and groaned.

Sarah glanced at Luna and then Xylo and Bluebottle behind her before replying, "Uh, it did break, yes."

"I'll send a small team and a warp mechanic to Gallantria to meet you. Over." The little Admiral hologram disappeared before Sarah could explain that Xylo was fully capable of fixing the drive himself.

"Thank goodness!" Xylo exclaimed.

Sarah turned to face him and gave him a puzzled look.

"I have no idea how to maintain a warp drive."

"*What?*" the other three crew shouted in unison.

Sarah shook her head. "Then how have you gotten it back online in the past?"

Xylo bowed his head a bit. "I've just tuned it off and then back on again. Usually that does the trick."

They all groaned for a moment, and then Sarah added, "Let's just focus on completing the mission at hand. Hold on tight for entry to Gallantria's atmosphere."

The personal cruiser was much more enjoyable to fly than the bulky and unresponsive *Blunder*. They made a smooth, graceful landing on the space strip. The *Blunder*, however, acted like a dead weight. The starship smashed into the space strip, destroying the pavement underneath it.

A small group of five individuals waited with their eyes wide and jaws slack at the end of the space strip. One of them, a man wearing garishly bright clothing with spikey black and silver hair, came running toward the cruiser. Sarah recognized Boomerang Black and the other four individuals as Admiral Vance, Commander Rex Sterling, EMT Jay Sterling, and an alien who she assumed was the warp mechanic.

The four *Blunder* crew members raced to get out of the cruiser, but they got stuck in the door. Bluebottle pushed the rest hard enough that they were able to squeeze out and stumbled onto the tarmac. Then, the chef turned back to scoop up the pooch and marched her straight to her owner.

"Princess!" Boom squealed as he grabbed his little alien-dog and gave her a tight hug. The pup excitedly greeted him by licking all over his face.

The other four of the welcoming committee walked up behind the famous musician as he began talking. "Admiral here didn't want to commend you guys for saving my precious Princess, but I couldn't leave such a thoughtful act unrecognized," Boom explained. He grabbed something from his pocket and handed it to Admiral Vance. "Here, you do the honors."

With a groan, the Admiral held up the sparkly medal of honor, which consisted of a gold medallion encrusted with hundreds of diamonds, hung on a glow-in-the-dark green ribbon. "Yes... honors..." the Admiral said.

However, before the Admiral could give the crew a rousing speech on their successful mission, a loud *bang* from the *Starship Blunder* stopped him. All nine of them and the alien-dog turned to observe the broken starship.

A fissure from the top of the starship slowly progressed down until it stretched to the bottom. Then, the whole ship fell into two disparate pieces, not dissimilar to a chicken egg cracking in half. Sarah audibly gasped.

A minute later, green goo began to ooze out of both pieces of starship and puddle onto the ground beneath it.

"Uh, might need something to take care of that glob before it spreads," Bluebottle warned.

They were too stunned to react, however, and instead continued to stare at the two pieces of the *Blunder*.

Without warning, a sudden blaze of violent flames erupted from both sides of the broken vessel. Luna shrieked and jumped back as thick black clouds began to fill the sky.

Xylo leaned toward the warp mechanic, a handymen alien with red skin, and asked, "You can still fix it, right?"

As a slew of silver-colored space slugs slithered out and away from the *Blunder* to save their sentient lives, the warp mechanic responded with a sad shake of his head.

Chef Bluebottle glanced at the EMT and then Luna before asking the daycare teacher, "Hey, didn't you used to date her?"

Rex answered for the gothic daycare teacher, stating, "I'm pretty sure that woman has dated every organism temporarily stationed on the *Blunder*."

Bluebottle chuckled. "Well, she can't anymore. Not much of a *Blunder* left."

As if taking the chef's words as a personal challenge, the *Blunder's* warp engine sprung to life, launching one of the halves of the *Blunder* high into the sky before turning sharply and propelling the flaming metal hunk into the starport like a missile.

The Gallantria Starport building crumbled under the impact as Sarah whispered under her breath, "Oh, shit." She decided that she needed to get out of there before the Conglomeracy could blame her for her starship's destruction. She yanked the gaudy medal from Admiral Vance while declaring, "I believe this is mine," and running away. "Come on, *Blunder* crew!" she yelled as she continued sprinting as quickly as she could.

Luna, Xylo, and Chef Bluebottle raced after her. The *Starship Blunder* crew ran toward the sunset, which currently resembled a post-apocalyptic hellscape filled with toxic smoke.

ABOUT THE AUTHORS

Beth Martin

Beth Martin writes science fiction novels and escape room style puzzle books. She has her degree in mathematics, enjoys all things numbers, and is always up for a board game. Other hobbies include playing the piano and making quilts. Although she's terrible at video games, she loves watching her husband play. When not writing, she can be found petting her two fluffy cats and chasing her two kids.

Jason Abofsky

Jason Abofsky is an author of Science Fiction and Fantasy stories, including his novel Celoven, Stormchaser. He holds a B.S. in Computer Science. His hobbies include reading, video games, and board games, and he participates in different conventions and festivals each year. Software Engineer by day, writer by night, Jason has blended his technical experiences and love of Science Fiction and Fantasy to craft a unique and imaginative universe influenced by some of his favorite authors and the lessons they've imparted.

Sill Bahagia

Sill Bihagia is a suburban chicken farmer with a M.S. in evolutionary neuroscience, despite learning to read on homeschool books featuring dinosaur saddles. Sill's primary writing project is a science fantasy series called the Oria universe, which feature action-packed stories of resilience, found family, and redemption.

Ross Baxter

After thirty years of naval service, Ross Baxter now concentrates on writing short stories. He has won a number of awards and had a story included on the 2017 HWA Bram Stoker reading list. Married to a Norwegian and with two Anglo-Viking kids, he now lives in Derby, England.

Edward Cooke

Edward Cooke trained as a technical writer in Flensburg, Germany. He has written songs, stage musicals, and other extended fibs.

Susan Eschbach

Susan Eschbach is convinced she's an alien accidentally born on Earth and forced to live in a small town in Southwest Missouri. She writes science fiction in the hopes her real people will find her. Eschbach has two published novels, *A Trial By Error* and *Man On The Fringe*, short stories published by Crowder Quill and Cloaked Press, and has won numerous contests.

H. Hackman

H. Hackman has always loved reading stories. In early childhood, she began writing her own and hasn't stopped since. Her favorite genres to read and write are fantasy and science fiction.

Mac King

Mac King is a retired police officer and a member of the MWA and the Howard County Writer's Group.

Melisa Peterson Lewis

Melisa Peterson Lewis is a science fiction writer residing on the outskirts of Baltimore, Maryland. She's published the Lazarus City series and several short stories. Most days, you can find her writing, gardening, hanging out with friends, or jamming to live music.

Chris Morton

Chris Morton's stories have been described as being in the genres of slacker lit, sci-fi lit, sci-fi psyche, magical realism, and avant-garde. He is the author of the novels, *English Slacker* and *Hard-Boiled Wonderland*. His science fiction stories have been published by Cannon Press, The Colored Lens, State of Matter, Longshot Island, and the Untold Tales Podcasts. An English teacher for over twenty years, Morton is also the author of the teaching guide: *TEFL Flashcard Games for Young Learners*.

Ariele Sieling

Ariele Sieling is a prolific science fiction and fantasy writer with over fifty published novels, novellas, short stories, and essays. She lives in NH with her spouse and zoo—two dogs, five cats, two goats, and quite a few chickens.

Edward Swing

Edward Swing is a writer of stories, software developer, avid gamer, and otaku. Books he's written include the New Pantheon series (Young Adult modern fantasy, 3 books), the Gozen Saga (military mecha sci-fi, 2 books), and the Adventures of Gavin Greene (Middle-grade fantasy/sci-fi, 2 books). He has been a member of the Society for Creative Anachronism, learned taekwondo, traveled both within the United States and internationally, and studied diverse topics including astronomy, mythology, and mathematics. The father of three young adults, he lives with several pampered cats.

SHAREVERSE ANTHOLOGY

One world. Several voices. Infinite possibilities.

Welcome to a Shareverse Anthology book. Shareverse Anthologies strive to be more than simple collections of stories. They are communities of writers working together to make new and exciting fictional universes come to life.

In each volume, you'll discover engaging characters, unique settings, and exciting events, all interwoven through a series of interconnected tales. While one writer takes the role of editor and builds the framework and a few characters for the universe, it's up to the contributors to fill the universe with creative settings, complex new characters, and heartfelt stories that align with the universe's themes. The resulting collection of stories comes together to weave a complex world with consistent rules and shared lore.

While not every collection bearing the Shareverse Anthology name will follow the same editorial process or structure, they all share a singular purpose: to bring writers together and provide them the opportunity to contribute to a larger work, fostering a sense of community and collaboration.

Made in the USA
Middletown, DE
06 October 2024

61738010R00191